Esha Patel is a contemporary
diverse romances and empow
college student in the Midwest
so greatly that the resulting y.
eleven-man soccer teams. When she's not writing, you can find her drowning in papers, spending time with family and friends, dancing, or watching Real Madrid matches. You can follow Esha on social media @eshapatelauthor or visit her website at eshapatelauthor.com to learn more.

Also by Esha Patel:

*Offtrack*
*Overdrive*

# Cross My Heart

## ESHA PATEL

avon.

Published by AVON
A division of HarperCollins*Publishers* Ltd
1 London Bridge Street
London SE1 9GF

www.harpercollins.co.uk

HarperCollins*Publishers*
Macken House,
39/40 Mayor Street Upper,
Dublin 1
D01 C9W8
Ireland

A Paperback Original 2025
1
First published in Great Britain by HarperCollins*Publishers* 2025

Copyright © Esha Patel 2025

Esha Patel asserts the moral right to
be identified as the author of this work.

A catalogue record for this book is available from the British Library.

ISBN: 978-0-00-874906-4

This novel is entirely a work of fiction.
The names, characters and incidents portrayed in it are
the work of the author's imagination. Any resemblance to
actual persons, living or dead, events or localities is
entirely coincidental.

Typeset in Birka by Palimpsest Book Production Limited, Falkirk, Stirlingshire

Printed and bound in the UK using 100% Renewable
Electricity at CPI Group (UK) Ltd

All rights reserved. No part of this publication may be
reproduced, stored in a retrieval system, or transmitted,
in any form or by any means, electronic, mechanical,
photocopying, recording or otherwise, without the prior
permission of the publishers.

Without limiting the author's and publisher's exclusive rights, any unauthorised use of this
publication to train generative artificial intelligence (AI) technologies is expressly prohibited.
HarperCollins also exercise their rights under Article 4(3) of the Digital Single Market Directive
2019/790 and expressly reserve this publication from the text and data mining exception.

This book contains FSC™ certified paper and other controlled sources
to ensure responsible forest management.

For more information visit: www.harpercollins.co.uk/green

*To anyone who has ever waited
for someone who never came back for them.
You deserve to find someone who will.*

# *Prologue*

### **Colt**

*Seven Years Ago*

May was supposed to be in the barn, where her *quinceañera* was still in full swing. The drinking and dancing were turned up to a hundred-and-ten, but the birthday girl was nowhere to be found.

I was unfortunately too self-absorbed to notice. I was busy being a dramatic fifteen-year-old guy and moping because May hadn't chosen me to be a *chambelan* in her court of honour. She'd chosen Dylan Wright as one of them, though. I guess it made sense. Dylan was starting quarterback on the football team and worshipped the ground May walked on. Great guy.

To be fair, even if she had chosen me, I was self-aware enough to know I wasn't the party-planning type. But I'd have got my shit together for May Velasco.

At the end of the day, I didn't care if Dylan was a better waltzer than me. It was the sentiment that mattered. Dylan Wright 1. CJ Bradley 0.

I had just left the barn and hit the dirt path, kicking rocks with my dress shoes, all angsty teenage main character. I'd headed out of the party through the back of the ranch after Ma and Pop announced they'd bring the car around because my kid sister, Savannah, was getting cranky. I was alone in the field.

Or at least I thought so, until I realized that May was out there, too.

I guess she hadn't let anyone know, just dipped out on a whim from her own party. She had escaped to the lacrosse field her dad made her a couple years back in the fields behind the Velasco family ranch, lines spray-painted in the trimmed grass, goals on either end. She still wore her surprise dance outfit, a tight white blouse with frilly straps and bootcut jeans, paired with her shiny gold county barrel-race champion belt-buckle. She hadn't bothered to change out of her boots, brown ones with butterflies across the front. Her black hair was perched precariously on her head in a very curly half-up, her crown and makeup and fake eyelashes still in place. The lacrosse stick in her hands, completely ignoring the long bedazzled acrylic nails she must have had done not too long ago, May swung. The ball went flying from the head of her crosse with a swoosh, and then the satisfying whack when it hit the back of the net. She turned to me slowly, cognac-coloured eyes probing, crossing her arms as if to say, 'Well?'

'Wanna join?' she asked.

'Sure.'

Hesitantly, I stepped forward on Oxford wingtip-covered feet that were not nearly as agile as hers, adjusting my tie awkwardly. She tossed her stick my way, and I grabbed it as she rifled through her bag for another. My hands were literally clammy with nerves, and the slick metal of the stick threatened to launch itself right out of my slippery grip. Yeah, I feared this girl. We'd been at each other's throats since we started playing in the same town. But fear was definitely not the explanation for my state at the moment.

'I'll probably go in there again in a minute. Just needed to . . . clear my head, I guess.' She nodded, a nervous little head-bob, fidgeting with the brand-new gold pendant she'd just got earlier that day at the start of the party: an elaborate cursive M in a heart with scalloped filigree edges. 'I've never been much of a dancer.' And then she did something entirely weird, and she said, 'Do you think I binned that *zapateado*? My *baile sorpresa*?'

For my part, I tried and failed to do my darnedest to hide my shock, and I replied totally honestly. 'You care what I think?'

May looked about as shocked as I was. 'That's a question?'

'What's that mean?'

'Whatever,' she said with a scrunch of her nose. 'Guys never get it.'

I opened my mouth to say something – anything, at that point – but then immediately closed it again. Instead of some witty comeback, I answered her question.

'Even if you binned the dance,' I said, 'you looked really good doing it.'

Her response was a ball thrown at me. I moved my stick to catch it.

'You suck.'

'Thanks.'

I could've sworn she smiled, a spark of light dancing across her glossy lips, even if it was just a little. 'I appreciate it. But I think I'm better at this.'

'Good thing I can agree.'

'Oh, for sure. Because I'm glad I got out here before your parents made *you* join the open dancefloor.'

'Come on, that's mean.'

'Best of five. Winner gets to shit on the other one's dance skills.'

'God, clear your head, May.'

'Shut up!' She threw another ball at me, and I caught that one in hand, an eyebrow raised.

'*You* suck,' I retorted. 'Stop chucking those at me, I have two now.'

'Or what?' She mirrored my expression, planting her stick in the grass, a hand on her hip. At that time, at least, we were literally eye to eye. Her stare bored right into my head, and I realized we'd moved much closer to one another. I could smell her expensive perfume, make out the little lacelike edges of her pendant. 'What'll you do about it, Colt?'

Man. I look back and think that things would be so different if I'd put my fear aside and done exactly what we should've about it. But I was a dumb teenage boy. So I did the only thing I knew, instead.

I reached around May blind, my eyes still on her, flicked my stick towards the goal, and sent one of the two balls she'd launched at me flying straight into the net. The sound echoed in the night, the kind you could hear even over the party raging on in the barn.

'I'll have you play that best of five, probably.' I cleared my throat, holding the second ball out to her.

Something in her face flickered for a moment. It could've been the terrible floodlights going out for a millisecond, or May trying to blink a hair out of her face. But I swear, I saw *something*.

'Let's do it.'

## *Chapter One*

Heard Round the World

**Colt**

*Major League Lacrosse Playoffs, October 2024*

'WE GET IT DONE, YOU HEAR ME? WE GET THIS DONE, IT'S FINALS, BABY!'

Arms linked to form a huddle, my teammates reply by way of whoops and shouts. I feel a hand clutch my stick and give it a good shake, and another tap the back of my helmet. The energy is electric, and we're all at the point of the night where we're just itching to hit the turf. Heavy bass pours through the speakers mounted all around Mill River Stadium, but I hear nothing but the guys' roars.

'WE GET THIS DONE, WE INVADE NATE'S!' adds Drew, earning excited yelps at the mention of the New Haven Woodchucks' unofficial team bar.

'WE GET THIS DONE, I MOVE OUT OF MOM'S!'

I'd groan and grumble at that one from Connor, but we're too hyped up on adrenaline to make a joke about Connor's home in his mother's basement. We're also too broke to make a joke about it, for the record. No one ever warns you that all pro athletes are made very, very unequal.

'GOOD FOR YOUR MOM!' JJ beats me to the punch.

Chaotic laughter and jersey-tugging ensue, at least till I get the boys back on track.

'Listen, guys.'

Their voices fall, the huddle tightening when they hear the dead serious undertone. We've never been a serious team. In fact, we're the most unserious in the league. We're also the youngest, on average. But when it comes to it, as captain, I refuse to drop the ball if our season depends on it. We'll switch up when we need to.

'We've had *shit* seasons before.' Nods and grumbles of acknowledgement all around. 'Maybe I only saw one of 'em. But I saw enough *this* year to know that no matter what people have to say, no matter how many times they tell us we're too young, too hopeful, this team has proven them wrong. This team was *made* for the championship.'

Team dad Rodney 'Rod' Wilson is the stern voice that joins mine in encouragement; nothing new from my best friend on the East Coast. 'Picture us with that trophy. Out there under the lights with the hardware. Top of the league. Top of the damn *sport*.'

Rod gives me a nudge. *Keep it going*. I nod, picking up his energy. 'We are *four games away*, boys. Four. Three, after this, and we'll be on top of the world. Does "national champion" sound fuckin' good enough?'

Gloved hands slap padded shoulders, as every single one of us howls in agreement. We've always been close – you have to, to play a sport that involves so much trust – but we're never closer than we are right before a match. Especially the most important one we've played to date.

'ALRIGHT, BRING IT ON! ONE, TWO, THREE, BREAK!'

We scatter and jog onto the field on autopilot as we take positions, cleats crunching in the grass. I can't help looking up at the stands. It's a bigger crowd than we're used to pulling in, the usual New Haven Woodchucks lacrosse fanatics sitting front row, but new faces packing the upper bleachers in anticipation of tonight's underdog event. I tug at the strap of my helmet, relish the bit of peace we get before the game starts and all hell breaks loose for four quarters of chaos and stress.

Way more so than usual, Mill River Stadium is all Woodchucks today, fans toting banners and posters for our first playoff ever as a Major League Lacrosse team. Granted, we're as young as the league – only about ten years old – but history is history. If we can break this playoff game, we can prove we've got a good shot at it all: the championship title.

JJ smacks me in the back with the butt of his stick as I start my trek towards the centre of the field, wrinkling my crisp blue jersey. Technically, I can't see him, because he's behind me the entire time, but the insufferable snicker that follows the blow tells me everything I need to know about my attacker.

'Chucks've never gotten this far. Get it done,' he hums, quoting my words and wagging his stick off to my left.

'Yeah, yeah.' With a roll of my eyes and a chuckle, I take my midfield position just behind the site of the face-off, marked by a midline and a circle at its direct centre. The ball is placed on an X in the middle of the circle, at which the face-off specialist from Boulder and our specialist, Andy, are each crouched in what's best described as a lopsided squat, crosses parallel to the ground. Andy's like me, never been the biggest player on the roster – medium height; doesn't carry some crazy quantity of muscle. The Boulder guy is the picture of his team's home city, about the size of a small lighthouse. Dull eyes the colour of steel glare past Andy and shoot lasers at me from behind his helmet grille. If this man stick checked me, he might take my entire arm off while he's at it. I pray he's a FOGO – face-off, get off, meaning he'll be subbed off once he's done his thing – because if he isn't, and he stays on to play, I'd consider it a miracle if all my appendages were still attached to my body by the end of this game.

The whistle blows, and Boulder and Andy are arm to arm. He pushes, Andy skirts around, knees scrabbling against the turf, trying his best to counter the massive opponent in the bid for the ball that sits between the both of them. Andy, thankfully, is just barely able to flick upward and get the ball in the air. I pluck it right up, look hard for an attacker, and then I hear a reliable, 'BALL!' I don't give it a second thought before launching the ball his way.

Hot Rod Wilson zooms away with the goods, cradling it to keep it from falling out of the net on his way up to the goal. His stick moves in an arc of silver and pink owing to the Peppa Pig stickers his kid's put all over the crosse. As much as we give him shit about it, he's fast – he whips the ball straight towards the goal mere seconds into the game. Unfortunately, it's just short of the goal by maybe an inch.

One of Boulder's attackers makes his way towards our crease

in the tenth minute, but our defender JJ is fast to sneak in a stick slap, causing the ball to fly out towards Drew. He snaps it out of the air and feeds it to Connor on midfield.

'OPEN!' I yell.

Swinging his stick around to avoid an opposing attacker, Connor thrusts the ball at me, and from there, it's muscle memory. As a midfielder, it's not my primary job to score, but when my team slides me the ball, it's clear they're placing trust in my judgement. I bolt down the field, all the while deciding my next move. I can pass this ball, or I take it all the way. At least two attackers are covered. The final Boulder defender is heading my way.

*SHIT.* He darts left, I go right, he mimics me, I spin the other way, and with a whip of my stick, it's in the air, and then . . .

The lights go out like they always do when New Haven scores, crowd whooping as strobes streak across the field and my teammates rejoice. But when they turn back on, a distraught 'ooh' ripples through the first couple of rows, yelps of shock from the guys.

Turf pricks at my bare arms. The Boulder defenceman nearest to me – the one who'd covered me – mutters a shaky expletive. I immediately wonder why I'm not in more agony, and as the adrenaline wears off, it hits me like a ton of bricks to the face.

'*FUCK!*' I nearly scream. Tears well up in my eyes, sweat beading on my brow. I claw at the ground. My teeth saw at the mouthguard as they try in vain to bite away the pain.

A whistle blows in the distance, and the red fabric of the first-aid bag appears in the corner of my blurry field of vision. 'Okay, okay. Take a deep breath,' the team medic tries to calm me. 'Take—'

'My knee, my fucking knee.' The energy trickles right out of my body like something's sucked it all from me. I whimper as I try to clutch my right knee, but it won't move, I can't move, and it's my worst nightmare. I run. I hustle. I'm a midfielder, it's what I do, and now I can't move.

'Colt! Colt, bro . . . bro, hang in there.' JJ's voice joins our medic. He tosses his stick off to the side and kneels beside me. Even through the grille, I can see the fear in his eyes.

'What happened? How does it look?'

It's a dumb question. When you play lacrosse, you know exactly what different kinds of injuries feel like. We've been taking knocks to the head since we were ten. We grow up thinking we're indestructible. Usually, I get back up right away. My mom used to call it one of my best qualities. This time around, I can't manage it.

'You gotta shut up, man.' JJ, usually loud and boisterous, is mumbling, stringing his words together. 'You gotta shut up so they can help you. Don't look.'

I couldn't if I tried; my eyes can barely stay open. It feels like someone's wrenched my ligaments apart fibre by fibre, and while that pain should be all I'm able to concentrate on, I cling to desperate pleas instead, stuff that I pretend will be able to erase the injury as quickly as it happened.

'Call my parents, man,' I croak out, clutching JJ's arm. 'My mom.'

'Yeah. Yeah, yeah, yeah, we'll call 'em. Colt, they're far, dude, you know they're far. Won't be here till tomorrow—'

'Shut up.' I grit my teeth against the now free-flowing tears streaking my cheeks. I just want my mom. I *really* just want my mom.

And as I grip my knee for dear life, the pleas of a desperate man weave their way through the tears. *I want May.* 'May,' I manage through waves of pain that send dark spots into my vision.

'Who?' Rod's voice now, the thump of his knees against the grass as he presses a hand to my shoulder. One of the medics protests, and he says something I don't catch in reply. 'Who – Colt, I'll call your mom,' he assures me, voice wavering.

I blink away the floaters in my vision, and one more time, I barely manage to move my lips to form her name. No sound comes out.

Despite feeling like I'm going to pass out, I vividly recall every second when they load me onto a backboard to take me off the field and to the ambulance. The humiliation of not even being able to walk off the field on my own is almost as painful as the injury itself. Because it's all crowds see now.

The paramedics buzz around me, asking me dozens of questions about scales from one to ten. Somewhere between it all, the realization dawns on me that it's not just now. This is all anyone will see for the rest of my career.

'You're more than your injury,' the doctors and therapists will tell me for weeks afterwards. I heard it enough times when Rod had his ACL injury the season I joined the team, and I'd love to believe it all.

I'd love to believe I'm still unbreakable, but I know that couldn't be further from the truth.

# Chapter Two

Southern Hospitality

**May**

*Three Months Later*

I pull at the laces of my cleats, shifting on the turf to get the optimal angle to free my feet from the snug shoes. Somehow, even after a practice straight from hell, the knots I made at the beginning of the afternoon haven't budged a bit. I bob my head in tune with the Mt. Joy song thrumming from someone's portable speaker as the first lace slides loose.

Jordan is already packing her stuff up, having a wrestling match with her duffel bag to get the overflowing thing to close. 'Chores?' she grunts between shoves, a simple one-word question.

'Yep,' I reply. I pop my right cleat off my foot and toss it to the side, getting to work on the left. 'Cattle.'

'Same.' She finally manages to get the zipper all the way

around her bag and turns to me. 'How are you feeling about this season?'

I make a dismissive *psshh* sound, to which my best friend raises an inquisitive eyebrow. 'May. Be nice. I'm asking as a concerned citizen.'

I stop in my tracks and give her a look. 'You sure about that?'

'Asking as a concerned citizen who's going to be playing alongside you this year and doesn't want to be tanked for senior season,' she adds with a snort.

'Jordan!'

'You asked!'

I got to know a lot of the girls through lacrosse, and I know all of them well now, but it's different with Jordan. She's the only one I'd allow to talk shit about my terrible junior year. We've been joined at the hip since we started playing in elementary, when Jordan Gutierrez-Hawkins walked up to me one day, tapped her stick against mine, gave me a partial-toothed grin, and told me we were going to be friends. We were the only two girls of colour on the team – we still are – but our connection went way deeper from the first game we played together. People confuse us not only because we look the same from the back (wavy black hair, exactly five foot six), but also because we're more often found side by side than we are apart. They're partially right, considering one word, sometimes even one look, is all we need to get our points across.

We grew up together in Eagle Rock, just outside Prosperity, bought our first crosses together, broke our first bones in the same game. When it came time to join the local branch of 4-H, affectionately 'farm kid club', meant to teach us the importance of agriculture and rearing animals, Jordan and I did every single cattle show right beside one another in the line-up. We match hairstyles every game, our braids so identical it looks like someone has copied and pasted them. In our freshman year of high school, when Tuck Decker called Jordan a disgusting slur in the middle of the hallway, we were totally ready to pummel his face in – together.

'Fine,' I give in with a hard roll of my eyes. 'I feel . . . better. I was drilling alright today. It's not gonna be like last year. I promise. I guess now we just have to see how far we go this time.'

'Oh, we'll go far. You know we'll do whatever it takes,' promises Jordan. She grins menacingly as ever at unassuming Maddie, who's still trying to get her cleats off. Jordan's hazel eyes glisten with a burgeoning joke. 'Not more than you will, though, Mad Dog. Did you have to kiss a frog today?'

Festival queen Miss Bellmare herself sticks up a middle finger Jordan's way. 'That was *once*.'

'One more time than I'd have put up with,' I snort, chucking my shoes into my duffel bag and slipping my feet into a pair of Birkenstock sandals.

Maddie waves my quip away with a French-tip-nailed hand. It's common for the girls to balance plates the way we do on this team. Sure, the school's paying some of us good money to play for them, but we don't get the kind of scholarships that the men's team does – even at the Division One level we compete. Putting 'Lady' before 'Riders' diminishes our monetary value just like it does our spectator count, but we still play. A lot of us do whatever it takes: classes, study, lax, and then work, whether that's waitressing at Moonie's, nabbing extra hours in research, or playing Queen on the weekends, if you're Maddie.

Pageantry gets you good sponsorships, and Magdalena 'Mad Dog' Marrone is bringing in a stipend, too. Her new crosse, metallic silver with orange and white netting, does all the talking for her.

She releases her blonde hair from its bun atop her head and slings her bag over her shoulder. 'Peace, ladies. See you tomorrow.'

Maddie, first to leave, announces her departure as any good festival queen would, and Lexi is next, executing a flawless Irish exit. Most of us don't mess around with Lexi outside of lax – she is *terrifying* – but in here, we have a grudging respect for the chick. She's been the most reliable goalie in the conference since we were freshmen. She gets it done. Jordan and I head out soon after, scoping out our respective vehicles in the parking lot riddled with cracks and potholes.

Jordan nods thoughtfully as she saunters easily towards her sedan. 'Seriously? I think this one's the year.'

I have to hide my laugh, and even then, it still creeps out. 'Girl, you said that last year. And the year before. And—'

Jordan pulls a lacrosse ball from her bag and chucks it at me over my truck. I narrowly duck a shiner to the forehead. 'It's called *optimism*, Miss Gloom and Doom. You should try it. What's your mom been saying?'

As a result of us being inseparable for years, Jordan and my mom have grown so close that Mumma considers her another daughter. I'm pretty close with Mrs Gutierrez-Hawkins, but nothing like Jordan and Mumma. It was one of those cases where you make a friend that your parents love so much that they adopt said friend. Jordan is now a regular at family gatherings, church, and gurdwara road trips alike.

'My mom,' I grumble, 'thinks I've been given a "second

chance". Says this is "the family I chose". She thinks I'll come back harder than ever this season.' I shrug, feigning indifference that clearly comes out not so indifferent. I think my mother needs to be pickier about how she thinks second chances are dealt, but in her eyes, I'm totally off-base. 'I told her the road back from binning an entire season and missing more shots than you score isn't an easy one.'

'Lord, no,' quips Jordan. 'Of course it's not easy. But neither was all the shit you guys went through last year.'

The mere mention of last year makes my throat feel as dry and ragged, as if I've just swallowed a whole saltine cracker. 'Guess that's fair.'

'You *know* it's fair.' Jordan waves knowingly as she opens the door to her car. 'As long as you lock in this season!'

I snort and wiggle my fingers in a goodbye before flinging myself into the driver's seat of my truck. Maybe I'll give optimism a go. But the way I move through life, it wouldn't last me longer than a week before the truth catches up with me. Rarely in my life do things come up roses.

I was born in the aftermath of an EF-4 tornado that ripped the roof off a house in Saint Albert and dropped it on a frat at the University of Oklahoma City – almost twenty miles away. Mumma's water broke mid-tornado. She had no idea she was in labour till the adrenaline of the disaster had come to pass. It was the shittiest birth story a person could ask for. But if you asked my mom what she thought about it, she'd call it a blessing. Lilavati Velasco, all silver linings and second chances, would tell you that – as much havoc as the storm wreaked – it spared us for the most part. Other than five of our cattle and a fence on the far end of the ranch, our entire house, property included, was intact. My grandmother called me a lucky charm. You could tell where Mumma got her painful positivity from, not to mention why she loves Jordan and her optimism so much.

Then there's Adan Velasco, her polar opposite. My lovely papa, who is currently trying to form words about what Mumma deems a 'second chance'.

'Well . . . last season wasn't great.'

'It *really* wasn't.' I peer at him from under the brim of my hat, and I'm instantly glad he's got the same look of nervousness on his face that I have. This shit isn't easy. Sometimes, I just need someone to sit in the trenches with me, and that's my Papa.

'But May, listen,' he hums unhappily. 'You can't let that indicate where you go this season. Junior year was . . .'

'Papa.'

'. . . not a great time . . .'

'Go on.'

'But it doesn't mean you deserve to beat yourself up over it. *Even* though I think it wouldn't have been half as bad if the refs hadn't been playing for the other team every game you guys had last year.' He has this little moment of fuming, which looks even funnier since he's sitting on his horse swaying back and forth. He does the same thing I do, puckers his lips in upset thought. 'But aside from that. You know it was hard. Lots of athletes have those hard seasons. Lots of the *best* athletes have those seasons.'

'Did you ever?' I ask him.

Papa, an ex-bull-rider, just throws his head back and laughs. 'Mayday, I'd be lyin' if I said I didn't.'

'God. What, were you just gettin' thrashed around and stomped on for a year?'

'Basically.' He grins, the wrinkles at the corners of his eyes from all his sassy smiling creasing. 'Does a number on a guy.'

'Yeesh.' We cross a small bridge that goes up and over a tiny creek running through our crop, the horses' hooves creating a dull clopping sound on the wood. 'How'd you get out?'

'Told myself no distractions for the next season. No flings, no booze, no parties. Just the sport.'

'Got it. No flings, no booze, no parties.'

Where my mom would cluck her tongue and shake her head at me, my dad cracks up. 'You got it, *mija*. Especially with . . .'

'Money on the line,' I finish for him. It's been my biggest dread: scholarship. It's not the most, but it's been putting me through school all these years. Without the Riders, I don't have my scholarship. And if I want my degree, I need every cent of it.

'You don't need to concern yourself with that, Mayday,' Papa reassures me. Always trying to bring my worries upon himself. 'We'll take care of you, no matter what happens. You just play your best. Promise me that?'

'Hmm.' A moment of sheer silence passes between us, nothing to hear but the sound of the creek. 'Mumma thinks it's gonna be some kind of magical comeback, you know. A big second chance.'

'I'll tell you this.' Papa beams warmly at me. 'I agree with your mother on that. Lila may be unrealistic sometimes, but she's right on this one. You've learned from last year. You've dealt with something difficult – we all did – and now you've got the defences to cope if it happens again. Right?'

'Right,' I echo.

'You know the drill, *mija*. Southern hospitality ain't always worth it. Open your door for two seconds, and next thing you know, a storm's tearing through your house,' my dad muses. 'But when that house gets shredded up, you rebuild it stronger. So yeah, I do think that this is your big second chance.'

'Jordan wanted it all last year.' I adjust my hat on my head, shielding my eyes from the striking rays of the sunset. 'Is it crazy to think that if I do enough of that no flings, no booze, no parties, we can have that? The championship?'

Papa and I trot together in thought for a moment as we approach the stables, slowing our horses down and hopping off.

'Championship's a high bar to clear,' he says.

'Exactly.'

'But there isn't anyone in this town I could see leading this team to one of those other than May Velasco.' As I remove my helmet, Papa ruffles my hair. 'I think if you put your mind to it, *mija*, you can have whatever your dreams desire.'

# Chapter Three

Homecoming

### Colt

I think JJ's going to cry. I'm not sure if I'm just imagining the glassiness in his big blue eyes, but it definitely looks like he's fighting back tears. He clamps a hand down on my shoulder and gives it a shake. 'You could stay, y'know.'

Rod sighs, reaching over to deal JJ's hair an affectionate ruffle. 'I get it, Colt. But we're still sad to see you go. You're gonna miss that crazy street lacrosse game they make us do in March.'

'You can't leave!' JJ tries again. 'If you're not back before pre-season, Stephen will have to come back.'

'Stephen won't come back,' I assure him with a laugh. Stephen, the man in question, got kicked off the team last season, getting caught doing whippets in the janitor's closet. He definitely won't be coming back.

My teammates' words bundle themselves into a big rock that

settles in the pit of my stomach. The guilt of leaving my guys behind – even if it's just for the off-season – is second to nothing I've felt in my life. Especially when you realize you've made an unserious frat boy reach the verge of tears.

Connor presses a big woodchuck plushie into my arms. 'Take him.' With a sombre look, he nods. 'Remember who you are, Coltie.'

It would be just another one of Connor's goofy childish gestures of affection (in his winding, chaotic way) if it weren't for the fact that that sentiment cuts deeper than he intends.

'But what if I'm not back for—'

'Doesn't matter.' Rod smiles his dad smile, the one that makes you feel like he's just made you a part of the family. It's a special talent, the mature schtick of his, considering he's not too much older than the rest of us. 'You're always gonna be one of us. Don't let JJ gaslight you. CJ and JJ will live to ride another day.'

JJ, all forlorn and dramatic, just pouts. I know I should feel bad, but his little kid expression is exceptionally entertaining.

Rod claps my shoulder. '*You* put in the work, man. Don't forget that.'

I feel a sudden rush of gratitude for the dude. Maybe I led the team, but Rod was always – is going to be – the backbone. If I do have to sit out another season, and Coach has to choose a new captain, I personally couldn't think of anyone better for the job.

'Oh captain, my captain.' Drew strikes a salute my way. 'Take care of that knee, alright?'

'You know I will.' The mention of my knee immediately laces the air with tension, at least for me. It's not on Drew – I should be past it all by now. The surgery, the brace, the exemptions, being off the field since it happened. I should be getting ready for next season, but instead, I feel like I'm still picking up the pieces.

I needed somewhere – anywhere – to lay low and figure things out, and the first place my mind went was OKC, where the coaches know me well, and I could pick up a legitimate gig without it looking like I'm just trying to disappear.

And where, maybe, I'd see May again.

Honestly, I should probably be facing this head on, not running and hiding at home. Though it's been so long I'm not sure that I can even call it home any more.

We huddle the same way we had at playoffs that night, one more time. It's a quieter moment; the kind of moment we don't have a lot of in a sport as rowdy as lacrosse. It's the kind of moment that hammers the gravity of what I'm doing into my brain, thudding away at a stubborn, bent nail. You're always told that when you pick up the crosse, you make a promise to the sport: never walk away. And although I'm not walking away, it still feels like I'm breaking that promise.

Arriving home, the first thing I notice about Oklahoma is how worn everyone's boots are.

They started to become a trend during my senior year of high school in Boston, when our whole family moved there for my mom's year-long visiting professorship. The girls would wear shiny white cowboy boots with their dresses, and guys paired Stetsons with their plaid. At that point, I'd already stopped considering myself Oklahoman. What'd it matter, I thought, that scuff-free snip-toes now made multiple appearances each year at 'Western-out' high school football games, carried over to the college bars, worn from frat formals to Halloween and everything in between?

I forgot how boots looked here – how, according to my dad, they were supposed to look. My eyes jump from shoe to shoe in the airport, leather that looks like you could bend it back on itself toe to sole, dull, creased, specks of dirt. The reddest of red flags that New England spoiled the hell out of me is the internal aversion that fills my body when I see worn boots. I hate the feeling immediately.

I pick up my truck, delivered in one piece, from the parking lot, and begin the drive to my family house. I pass through sprawling Oklahoma City proper first, before taking the exit off the highway to home: Prosperity, Oklahoma.

A lot of people questioned my decision when I first moved to Boston. Everyone in Boston wanted to get out of Boston, and everyone in Oklahoma wanted to get out of Oklahoma. It took me nearly blowing my knee out to realize I wasn't totally sure which category I fitted into: I didn't know where I wanted to be any more. All that I knew for certain was that it would be a minute before I could go back to playing pro lacrosse.

And, if I had to spend time elsewhere, Prosperity, college town to the nines, wasn't a bad choice. This would've been my home school in another universe. It's expansive, flat, with a brick sign at the orange-flower-adorned entrance proclaiming that I've entered the University of Oklahoma City, Organized 1864, named for the major city fifteen minutes away in classic American college fashion. The age of the school is evident in the older Gothic campus buildings I pass on my way to the residential area. Swarms of students flood out of lecture halls as classes let out, some wearing those boots that look like they've seen enough stables to last a lifetime.

I weave through narrow downtown streets lined with college

apartments and parallel-parked sedans to find the Bradley house. It's not quite what I'm used to back in New Haven, but it'll do the job. It's the kind of building I'd miss if I blinked: antiquated, brownstone, three floors, surrounded by overgrown trees, with a screened front porch. Ma's favourite talking point about the house is that it was apparently built during Prohibition, and the basement used to be a hole-in-the-wall speakeasy. My sister's favourite talking point about the house is that the speakeasy must have had terrible business, because said basement smells like shit. But what can I say? It has that small-downtown charm.

I park the truck in the gravelly driveway and clamber out, unloading various bags as I go.

'That's all you got?'

I peek up from my mass of luggage with a chuckle. 'Hey, Pop.'

My dad, arms akimbo in the Southern stance of keen observation, cracks a smile. 'Has to be less than half of what Sav had.'

'How does one person own all that stuff?' I huff as I lug a particularly large bag to the side, and my dad saunters down the drive to help me out. 'Makes me glad I missed move-in.'

'She wasn't so glad.' Pop raises an eyebrow. 'Don't know that any of us were. We wouldn't have let it fly if you weren't, what'd you call it . . .'

'On the road,' I finish for my dad as he rolls his eyes with a smile and brings me in for a huge hug. He's where I get my height. Ma is so short that she once baked a cake for the state fair whose top she couldn't even reach.

'On the road,' echoes Pop. His eyes cut towards the lacrosse sticks poking out of one of my duffels, and then to the long pieces of kinesiology tape still gripping my knee, just visible below my football shorts. I think for a moment he's going to ask about that, the injury, the last time we saw each other, but instead, he takes a totally different route. 'House looks just about how you remember?'

'Oh . . . well, couldn't tell you.' I chuckle half-heartedly. I'd love to say it's exactly how I remembered, but the memories are like strands of thread I struggle to weave together. 'What, last time I was here was junior year, right?'

'Junior year of high school.' Pop smacks his lips, gazing up at the roof of the house. *And here it comes.* 'Everyone else came back, Ceej, I just struggled to understand what kept you up there. Oklahoma's perfectly nice, isn't it?'

'I dunno.' I shoulder the bag with the crosses and try my best to hide the exasperated sigh that threatens to leave my body. 'It's nice, but you guys missed it more than I did. It was kinda obvious, to be honest. Still is.'

It was true. Going away to Boston for Ma's visiting professorship in Gender and Women's Studies at the University of Boston itself was a rough adjustment for my small-town family. They hadn't planned on staying at all. They rented our house out to a couple of college kids for the year, full well knowing we would all be back.

Except after Ma's year in Boston, when the family moved right back to Oklahoma and reclaimed their beloved house, I stayed behind. Somewhere in the grungy chaos that was New England, I'd found my home for the next four years at U-Boston. I stayed the summer for lacrosse camp, picked up for UB's Division One team, and I didn't look back. I was the only one in my family who didn't come to hate Boston in some capacity.

Savannah, my sister, was a different story – the University of Oklahoma City was basically her dream since day one. My parents were beyond ecstatic that she'd decided to stay, and, I think, a little relieved.

Now Pop, stubborn as he is, pretends he doesn't hear a word I say. Instead, he moves on to the next excruciating topic. 'You know who plays for OKC now?'

I can smell it in the air before he says it. I don't need him to say it. My cheeks threaten to go red before I can control the reaction. The fucking traitors are already warming up. 'Where's Ma at? Sav?' I ask in hopes that it'll stop him from going off on this tangent before he's even started.

Too late. Pop answers my question in two snappy sentences before moving on to his favourite topic. 'Ma's in lecture. Sav's also in lecture. Listen, Colt. Have you been watching her?'

I've seen every stat, every match, every highlight, every brilliant play and every not-so-brilliant play. I watched last year happen like it was a semi-truck steamrollering a car in slow motion. And she's all I've been thinking about since I took my dive on the field in August. She's all I've been thinking about since the idea to run home struck me. What I'll do when I see her again, what I'll say to her after all this time.

So yeah. No shit, I've been watching her.

I say, 'I guess.'

# *Chapter Four*

### Y'all Had Your Moments

**May**

'Let's work behind the crease, ladies!'
Cleats rustle in the grass as midfield and attack line up behind the net for today's lesson, one we hope will give us some edge when we start our season.

Coach Dillon claps her hands. 'I want a shot on goal from each and every one of you! Let's see it!'

I watch as Maddie, in full Mad Dog mode, cradles the ball effortlessly, flicking around the net to land her shot easily. My hands feel slick against my crosse as our coach beckons me forward. I keep my ball steady in the mesh of my stick when I come up from behind the crease, eyes on nothing but the spot I want to shoot into. That exact spot. I won't let my gaze stray.

And as much as I know it's just practice, the satisfaction that fills my chest when the ball slaps the back of the net is nothing short of what I'd feel in a game. It's got me dizzy. I whoop as the girls howl excitedly. Pre-season is in full swing.

We share a hearty scrimmage after the drill, followed by a slow cool-down session of conditioning. By the end of it all, we're shucking off cleats like they're work boots. We love the field, but after practice, it's a relief to be off it.

'God, I think I have civic duties tonight,' Maddie groans, blowing a strand of perfect blonde hair from her face.

'I think I'm scooping *shit* tonight,' chirps Paige sarcastically, earning a grumble of agreement from many of us in the bleachers. She's our strongest defender, but she, like the rest of us, has every right to be tired of the double life.

'Don't get me started on scooping . . .'

Jordan's quip vanishes into thin air as she's stunned into silence, her head swivelling towards the chain-link fence separating the fields from the parking lot way down ahead of us.

'Jor.' Maddie gives her a shake, but no response. We follow Jordan's stare to the empty lot, where a dark blue Dodge Ram pickup truck has made itself at home. Its owner swings himself out of the cab. The hiss of air that escapes my lips, sneaking between my teeth in exasperation, is completely involuntary.

The girls are in a silent frenzy. Huge eyes meet one another as immediate recognition passes from teammate to teammate. Maddie's the first one to look my way, and she says, in a voice as hushed as a rustle of wind through the tallgrass, 'Bradley.'

Anyone who's anyone in this state knows him, which is funny considering he doesn't give a rat's ass about this state. Anyone who plays lacrosse certainly knows him. Much of this team idolizes him, so Maddie's reaction doesn't surprise me. Jordan stabs an angular elbow into my ribs with a look of shock.

'He's back,' she mouths.

My body goes rigid. I hope my eyes go cold. I move to stand, to get my butt off the grass and get out of here before he comes over to make that dumb, smiley small talk of his, but Jordan grabs my arm, her eyes still trained on Bradley as he enters the field with a giant grin pasted on his face, all the way up to his grey eyes, creased happily in the corners. He runs a hand through his unfortunately stunning, windswept light-brown hair that sneaks past his ears, all overgrown and wavy. For a fleeting millisecond, I can't blame Jordan for staring, but the millisecond is over almost before it begins.

I turn away, attempting to take my friend with me. 'Jor. Jordan, it's time to go—'

'Hey, May!'

*Great.*

I swivel back and make sure I shoot a glare at Jordan on my way around before my eyes land on the man himself.

'Manmayi Velasco,' he calls, still wearing that dumb grin.

He's significantly taller than I remember, which is not unexpected, considering it's been just about five years. Last we'd met, he had just started to get taller than me. I don't love the fact that even if he sat down beside me now, I'd have to tilt my chin up to look him in the eye.

He saunters over to the bleachers where we're packing our things up, and the rest of the girls, unhelpfully, are about as gobsmacked as I am. Someone has to say something before I burst a blood vessel.

Unfortunately, that someone is CJ Bradley.

He rocks back on his dumb polished boots. *Boots*. He can't have been on Oklahoman soil for more than twenty-four hours.

With a tip of his head, he says with a smile much bigger than this situation calls for, 'It's been a minute, huh?'

Well, hot *damn*, it's been more than a minute, and this fool is acting like we just saw one another last month. I'd like to call him out on it, but I'm not sure if I'm capable of forming words in my anger right now. I don't think it'd benefit anyone even if I did try to form words.

'You stayed,' he continues with an air of pride. Pride? Who gave him the right? He didn't stay. He jumped ship the second he got the option. He had the chance to come back, and he deliberately turned it down. What the hell is he so proud of?

I grit my teeth. 'CJ—'

'Everyone who's anyone in lax knows about you,' he begins with a charming smile – the trademark Bradley smile, the smile that caused me all my problems to begin with. That's how he gets you. It's like one of those ridiculous fish with the dangling light in front of its face. 'Can't wait to see you play in person, May.'

'I'd prefer Manmayi.'

Jordan elbows me, although Bradley seems to ignore it completely.

'Well,' he says, beaming in that blissfully indifferent way of his, 'you sure you wouldn't want to scrimmage together again sometime? Just once? For old times' sake, y'know.'

'I'd rather not,' I reply tightly.

It's true. If I were to get on the field with him again, I wouldn't trust myself to overcome the uncontrollable urge to rip out his hair strand by strand.

With that deeply uncomfortable thought, I give him a courteous parting nod (too courteous, if you ask me). I tap Jordan's hand, snapping her out of her stupor. 'I gotta get going. I got chores to take care of,' I tell him stiffly.

I clamber to my feet, duffel over my shoulder, and haul my ass out of the crime scene as quickly as I can with Jordan in tow, leaving Colt looking over his shoulder with a hint of something that might be regret in those normally unfaltering eyes.

'Colton James Bradley,' says Jordan once we're well away from the field. The allegedly fierce attacker has a dazed quality to her voice, all starstruck.

'Thank you *so much* for giving him a beat to open his big mouth.'

'Oh?' She turns her wide-eyed gaze to me. 'What happened to junior year? When Manmayi Velasco said she was "grown up now"?' Jordan throws air quotes around the final three words to ensure they hit their mark.

'Doesn't count when you're dealing with *him*,' I mutter, focusing on the airbrush strokes of the HOME OF THE RIDERS mural on the wall outside the field to distract myself from the conversation Jordan has boxed me into. 'If he can't grow the hell up, why should I?'

'Yeah, that'll happen when guys go pro like that.' She tilts her head at me in that same spirit of curiosity.

I run my hand through my ponytail of straightened hair with a heavy sigh. The last time I had any contact with Colt was when he was leaving for New England, and I hadn't heard from him since. The definition of a teenage boy who never grew up.

'Y'all had your moments.'

'Damn if we did,' I snort. *Moments* is one word for it. *Moments* is the wrong word for it.

## Chapter Five

### Coach Cockamamie

**Colt**

Manmayi Corina Velasco.
 Her eyes drilled holes into my forehead when she turned to look at me. I forgot just how much anger May always had tucked into her small frame – anger that would come out on the field. An endless stream of yellow cards peppered with the very occasional red when we were younger, the product of numerous stick checks and smack talk that toned down as we entered high school. Even in her most recent televised matches with the Riders, I watched as she jogged over to the bench during a time-out, stick and voice both raised when she rounded up her team.

But much more than the anger, I remember the softer side of May, fleeting moments where I got to see rare parts of her that she hid behind lacrosse, a few minutes here and there where that angry furrow in her brow disappeared, and she let herself relax. Though yesterday, when she drilled those holes into my forehead, any trace of her softer side was nowhere to be seen.

And yeah, there are definitely more than a couple reasons she's totally entitled to that reaction. But maybe, just maybe, I'd been holding out for a slice of happiness. A little 'welcome back'. The smallest of smiles.

Today, I toss the Riders lanyard and whistle around my neck. 'I don't think your captain is gonna react too well to this one,' I remark.

Coach Bianca Dillon lets out a sarcastic laugh that echoes off the walls of the storage shed. 'Oh, you're spot on – but you'll be good for her. What you're consistent with, is what this team struggles with. It'll be humbling. Bi-weekly shot-on-goal clinics will have them well-rounded by that first game.'

Shots on goal. Trick shots, specialty goals – the stuff I used to be really good at, unusual for a midfielder, but that was my thing, nonetheless. At least up until last October happened.

'They set a date for that game yet?'

'Something towards the end of the month, maybe the beginning of the next. It's coming up soon.' Coach Dillon passes me a bag of lacrosse balls. 'Hold onto these for a moment.'

I oblige, and I can't help but notice the state of the equipment. This isn't anything like what I remember playing at Boston, and it's a sinking, acute realization that fills my stomach with guilt. This stuff's definitely been around longer than my college equipment had. These girls are playing with balls that probably witnessed the creation of Facebook. I'm not sure if it's an Oklahoma thing, or a women's sports thing, but it gets under my skin.

'How's the funding for the programme nowadays?' I try to be as casual as possible when I pose my question.

Coach Dillon looks at me with humoured yet tired eyes. 'Don't talk to me about funding, City Boy. This is a girls' team in the South. Not to mention, we're in a tough situation as it is. Velasco struggled last season. Wasn't a good look.'

'A good look? Her freshman and sophomore seasons were flawless. That game at Mayfair was a masterclass. And everyone's allowed an off-year, right?'

The coach raises an eyebrow at my defence of the captain. 'Didn't realize you were so partial to her.'

I clear my throat awkwardly and shift my bag of balls from hand to hand. 'We knew each other back in high school.'

'Well.' She nods, lips pursed. 'This may come as a shock to you, CJ, but Velasco's one of two women of colour on that team. She may be a star, but the programme's made up of a board of wealthy white men. Her performance this season's got to be beyond flawless if she wants to stay on through senior season long enough to get into the MLL. If she doesn't keep up, it could even spell trouble for the pretty scholarship they have her on.'

'What . . .' I try to digest the words, the likes of which I've never heard in my years playing lacrosse. 'You mean they could tear away financial aid and boot a player from the team, just like that? You wouldn't have a say?'

'Nope.' Coach Dillon shakes her head, and the tiredness in her eyes appears more resigned than anything else. *This is what it's going to be. We have to deal with it.* 'Best I can do with what I have is get her firing on all cylinders that first game. From there, she's a contender for a contract, for sure. Then it's a publicity game. Bring the MLL's eyes over here, all that. Men's team does a good job of drawing us second-hand attention, at least. You know how Okie loves its Riders.'

That I can agree on. Growing up here, football was big, and the university team was well-loved. But for whatever reason, this tiny college town just outside of Oklahoma City decided that it was going to worship its men's lacrosse team. The Riders, division champs for the last five years straight, brought in crowds from across the state. When you give people who are used to a whole lot of nothing a little bit of something, they latch onto it.

'Do your thing,' the coach continues, with an expectant look my way as we exit the shed, and the relentless Oklahoma sunlight beats directly down on us. 'We can't take chances this season. These girls have to play every minute like it's the last game they'll ever see.'

Stepping back onto the grass from the back entrance, I'm optimistic that the energy will be different between May and me, that yesterday's interaction was just a fluke. The team jogs onto the field to do their laps, Coach Dillon calling out instructions. I must have been lying to myself, though, because – as May runs past me – her eyes gloss over me with that same anger, plus a hint of surprise. I don't think she's going to enjoy what comes after warm-up.

The coach rounds the team up after exercises, in a huddle that she ushers me into. I feel like an outsider looking in on a ritual I'm not supposed to be watching when she makes room for me.

'Lady Riders, we're going to be joined by a guest this semester,' she announces. 'Taking a break from playing, we have CJ Bradley from Prosperity itself hosting our team's shot clinics. He'll be helping us out with some of those tricky goals we struggled with last year, sanding some of our rougher edges, so to speak.'

'Call me Colt,' I offer. I sweep my line of sight around the entire team, but my gaze lands on May. Her slack jaw doesn't mirror the same shock as the rest of the players. If I were to take a guess, I'd say it was verging on horrified. 'I sustained a nasty knee injury this past year, so I'm still a little shaky on the field, but I hope some of the pointers I have to offer can be of value to you all. It's really an honour to be back in Prosperity.'

The team is receptive. They help me out throughout our first shot-on-goal clinic, where we run drills, practise speeding up shots, and more over the course of an hour. I give them the technique, and they put it into play. After I've done my time, Coach Dillon takes over, having them pass, scrimmage, drill some more. By the end of practice, every member of the team is more than keen on grabbing their things and hauling their ass off the field. But for my own selfish purposes, I still need answers.

Dillon heads for her office, and I make a beeline for May, where she sits on the bleachers, legs draped over the row beneath hers as she unlaces her cleats. 'May – Manmayi!' I shout after her.

Her eyes flit upward, narrowed and reluctant to meet mine. 'What?' she grumbles.

'Can we talk?' I ask from ground level. I look up to regard her as properly as I can. 'Just a little?'

The dull brown of her irises doesn't look amused. 'Give me one reason why we should.'

I sigh, tugging on my whistle. 'I'm sorry. I really am. I should have—'

'Don't be sorry.' Her voice is deadpan, cold. 'Don't be sorry, Colt.'

Man. The ice in her tone is sharp; it cuts deeper than I'd like. 'I'll strike you a deal, man. Best of three, if I beat you best of three, will you talk to me? Please?'

May is quiet for a moment, her hands frozen mid-untying of cleats, her gaze trained on the crisscross of the white laces. 'It's been five damn years. You don't get to come back and cut deals.'

She shucks off her cleats and replaces them with leather-strapped Birkenstock sandals over Nike socks, bringing herself to her feet.

'Please,' I press on. It *has* been five years. It's been five years, and not once during those five years did I stop thinking about how I screwed things up, the way I left. I've sat with my regret, and now, it's time to do something about it. 'May, I *need* to talk to you.'

'You *need* to.' She drops her bag with a loud thud and turns back around to face me. *Screw you*, her face says, and for good reason, honestly. 'Three,' she says. 'Miss one, and we're done.'

The breath I've been holding finally leaves my lungs, but another sharp inhale immediately replaces it. *Shit*. 'Okay,' I reply slowly. 'Okay.'

'You asked for a scrimmage.' May scoops up her crosse and picks her way down the stairs. I grab one of the demo crosses from the pile I've yet to put back in the shed. It feels foreign in my hands, and not just because it's not my game stick. It's unbalanced. My fingers twitch against the cool metal, my arms seizing up.

'Yeah,' I reply on a dry throat. Sure, I asked for it. I hadn't expected her to agree.

'You're the most *cockamamie* "guest" we've ever had, you know that?' May snaps as she takes her place beside me on the field. We're about a third of the way up the field from the crease – a long, long shot. She holds out a hand without even meeting my eyes. 'Need a ball.'

I toss one her way, worn as it is, and she catches it in the net of her stick, rotating her wrists to keep it there. She brushes a lock of jet-black hair from her face, the loose threads of her red evil-eye bracelet just skimming her cheek, and lines herself up, squinting to get the goal in her sights.

The way she flicks it is so quick, with such a deft movement of her arms, that I don't actually register her stick moving until the ball hits the back of the net triumphantly, leaving the goalposts quivering. No cleats, aged equipment, nothing special except for raw talent.

'You,' says May.

She takes a step back to swap spots with me. My hands are still shaking on the stick. I look her way for just a moment. The only thing I see on her face is the barest hint of expectancy.

## Chapter Six

### Made the Time

**May**

The legendary CJ Bradley holds a women's lacrosse stick as he lines himself up to take on our goal. He's led the league in shot-for-shot midfielder stats since he started playing on the New Haven Woodchucks, drafted in what was technically his junior year. This is where he's most at home. But for all his bluster, something's missing in the way he stands.

I throw him a ball, and he cradles it idly for a moment, eyes trained on the goal. The steely gunmetal of his irises glitters beneath long lashes that flutter against the brutal Oklahoman sun, his well-defined jaw ticking in concentration. I might have stopped giving him the light of day – or at least tried – but I can't deny the fact that he's got skills. Always did, always will.

Colt lunges forward, and I'm ready for it to be an immediate net. Except, it isn't. The ball veers far right, and before I know it, the thing has wound around the goal and clangs against the fencing in the back with a sad *clink*.

What the *hell*?

He's already prepared with another ball for me when he turns back, and suddenly, he's the one who doesn't want to meet *my* eye.

My next shot's an easy one. Coach had me run these time and time again when I was starting. It's muscle memory, and for a lax team captain, not to mention alleged goal-bagging midfielder extraordinaire, it definitely should be, injury aside. Despite it all, I stand back and watch as he takes his second shot, and it flies over the net. Well, *damn*.

'Best of three, you said?' I shrug as I jog to the goal to grab the balls. 'Sorry, cowboy. Looks like that's a game, fair and square.'

'May . . .' Oh, hell no. I can't do more emotion from him. I pause, balls in hand, and stop to listen to whatever he thinks he's got to say to me.

He swallows, removes his cap and smooths down his tousled hair before popping it back on. I watch his Adam's apple bob up and down as he struggles to find words. 'May, do you ever think about what could have been?'

My mouth goes just slightly slack. Do I ever? About what could have been? 'For the sake of my sanity,' I start, the red-hot flame of anger building up in my chest, 'I try not to.'

'I do.' His voice is quiet, gentle. 'And I wanna talk to you. I don't wanna make excuses. I just want to talk.'

I don't know what gets into me. I didn't tell him a lie. I'm being honest. I try not to think about hypotheticals, and I try hard as hell not to think about hypotheticals when it comes to him. I told myself I wouldn't fall back into his fabricated niceties, that I'd built myself up part by part, and yet there's something in the way he almost sounds timid that forces me to crack.

'I gotta take care of chores at home,' I tell him, keeping my tone as even as possible. Give away nothing. 'My mom's got dance classes till seven. You'll have to give it till the evening here if you want a word.'

'I'm willing,' he says far too quickly. 'Where?'

'Moonie's.' I toss my crosse from my right hand to my left and sling the bag of balls over my shoulder. 'Eight.'

My truck rattles over dirt roads as I pull it into the driveway in front of our house, smack in the middle of the ranch. I spot my dad out back, fixing up a fence. Mumma's probably in the barn with her five p.m. dance class chock-full of middle-aged South Asian women from as far as five counties out. I yawn, clamber out of the truck with my gear on my back, and lumber up the porch, nudging past the screen door with a forceful elbow.

There are houses back in Prosperity where Riders banners hang out on the front porch, bearing the logo with the two crossed sticks beneath the skull, old tornado cellars that have been multipurposed into lacrosse-theme man-caves, but our lacrosse flavour is a little less in-your-face. As I thunder into the house, I tap the first sport-adjacent relic you see when you enter: the framed photo of my first game, hanging on the wall in its wooden frame. It was taken way back when we would drive what should have been an easy fifteen minutes to Oklahoma City. Thanks to inner-city traffic, we ended up braving a thirty-to-forty-minute trip several times a week so I could play on a U8 girls' team. I remember my mom had finally accepted defeat when I chose lacrosse over dance (a decision that was for the best, though, because frankly, I was, like my father, the definition of impatience).

I round the cramped hall to climb the narrow staircase up to my room. I'd love to collapse in my bed, but I'm still knee-deep in chores and have Instrumentation homework for days. I chuck my gear and backpack into a corner next to my desk and flop into my chair. It's usually no difficult task to snap into work mode, at least not for me, but today, after the way I just let CJ Bradley back into my life like nothing he caused me in junior year had ever happened, focus isn't in the cards.

'Jeez.' I yawn, dragging my notebook and laptop over. I open the book to numbers and calculations marching across the lined pages. Measurement error and wind shear and precipitation swim before my eyes.

'MAYDAY!' my dad's voice yells from downstairs. 'Don't worry about the fence, *mija*, it's fixed! Finish your homework!'

'Thanks, Papa!' I yell back, still on the verge of slumping over all the math in front of me. I love what I'm studying – it'll set me up for a fantastic career either after graduation or after lacrosse, whatever happens this year with my precarious situation on the team – but these numbers are a colossal struggle. I need all my attention for this stuff, and it's just not there.

Clear as day, I still remember him walking backwards and waving as he disappeared down the gym hall of Prosperity High School to cheers and chants. That's the crap everyone else saw: the man, the myth, the legend. When someone asks me what I last remember of CJ Bradley, I don't tell them about his triumphant send-off. I tell them about the text. And the strawberries. I refuse to glorify him the way the rest of this sleepy lacrosse town does.

\* \* \*

'Where you going?'

I grab my purse off the hook by my vanity and shoot a smirk my mom's way. 'Meetin' up with my sneaky link.'

'Your *who?*' Mumma's jaw goes slack for a minute before she detects the fact that I'm clearly working overtime to *not* laugh my ass off. 'You're gonna give me a stroke, May.'

'It's what I do.' I grin. 'I'm going to Moonie's. Feed the cows tomorrow morning, I know. I'll be back by midnight.'

'Mm-hmm.' Mumma doesn't look convinced, but she cracks a smile, patting my cheek. 'Have fun. Be smart.'

I often hear people tell me I'm 100 per cent my mom – down to the types of jeans we both wear, currently different fonts of the same Wranglers – but I like to think the bit I didn't inherit was her sense of responsibility (and her unfaltering kindness). I have my father's snark and penchant for poor decisions. Like the decision I made regarding Colt today.

'I will.' I give my mom a little hug, and her quiet chuckle tells me she knows as much as I do that 'smart' is probably the least apt word to describe some of my choices.

I say a little prayer as I get into my truck and do the short drive over to Eagle Rock's only bar and dance hall. My toes feel stiff in my boots, as if I've just thrown on a brand-new pair without properly breaking them in first. Why am I nervous? I shouldn't be nervous. *He* should be nervous.

By the time I've pulled in, the music is already thrumming from inside the bar, some twangy Brooks and Dunn. The dancing has clearly begun, but I'm here on business only. I push the door open and keep my eyes peeled for the problem at hand.

I wish I could say that uppity CJ Bradley is too city to understand the assignment. Unfortunately, he blends in effortlessly, with a Henley that fits a tad too well and a pair of bootcut jeans. Somehow, he's managed to acquire a cowboy hat, and it rests in his lap as he makes happy conversation with at least five people at once, three of whom are certainly loyal female fans, two of whom are guys from the men's team at Okie. I almost laugh out loud. He's still such a big jock it's not even funny. It was the same in high school – he always had a clutch of admirers floating around him – and it's the same now. Unfortunately, unlike most people I know who peaked in high school, it seems like he never experienced the subsequent plummet to rock bottom.

His eyes flit my way the moment I'm in his radius, and his entire face lights up. 'May!' he calls.

I try not to harrumph too hard as I join his circle of conversation. I give everyone, including Colt, a curt smile. 'Hey, y'all.'

'What's up?' He slides his beer towards him and takes a sip, and I don't miss the attempt at a concealed once-over that he gives me. It's awfully similar to the looks we started to exchange freshman year – days I'd personally love to forget.

'Well, I'm here on a Thursday night,' I remark, beckoning the bartender. 'If that ain't something to talk about, not sure what is.'

'Interesting.' Colt's biceps flex against the fabric of his shirt as he sets the beer on the bar. He rakes a hand through his dumb lax hair. It's something I've known few guys to pull off well, but it's also a stupid lacrosse superstition. Dudes who play never shut up about their 'flow'; something to do with a superstition surrounding the length of their hair. More than a few of the guys on the Riders have hair long enough to stick out the back of their helmet, a style dubbed 'lettuce'. Colt has always had tousled dirty blond hair approaching brunette. It's always been overgrown, and it has *always* been infuriatingly effortless. Now, it makes a frustratingly perfect swoop and sticks out well past his clean-shaven jawline. 'You don't go out often?'

'Making the time's tough.' To the bartender, 'I'll do a rum and Coke, please.'

'But you made it.' He smirks his smug smirk, jesting, daring me to give in. God, he's always made it so easy. He leans in and meets my eyes as if he wasn't talking to a substantial group of people just moments before. 'You made the time.'

'Maybe.' I lean in, returning his gesture, and glare right back up at him. I pretend I can't smell every note of his cologne from this close. 'I made the time 'cause I felt bad when I watched you bin shots any pro should've been able to make blindfolded.'

## Chapter Seven

Scuff Your Boots

**Colt**

Well. She still likes to go straight for the jugular.

May sits back, either exasperated or smug. I could never tell which one was which. That, among other things, it seems, hasn't changed.

I attempt a flawless recovery that doesn't come off so flawless when I clear my throat awkwardly. 'So. Your senior year.'

'Yeah,' she says tightly. 'Last season here.'

'That's . . . big. Coach and I were talking.'

'Great.' Her tone is dry as the Sahara. 'Isn't this supposed to be your senior year?'

'Doing an MBA.' I gulp down a sip of beer. 'I wrapped up my degree early once I got drafted.'

'Nice.' Another empty one-word May-ism. She crosses her arms with a sharp exhale. 'I'm not here for chitchat. Go on.'

The whiplash this conversation is causing me throws me off for a minute, but once I register what she's asking of me, the words tumble right out.

'I meant it. When I apologized.' I don't have to pour every ounce of my effort into it, because it comes out anyway. It comes out whenever I talk to her. The hint of alcohol trekking through my body makes it even easier. 'I am really, truly sorry, May. I really am. I know my words aren't a reason for you to excuse the way I left. The way I left *you*. But—'

'We were young. Shit happens.' She thanks the bartender when he slides her drink to her and takes a liberal sip, turning her body towards him. 'Good stuff, Cain.'

I find it funny that she says that. Shit happens, but at least to me, it's still happening. Definitely still happening when I start to notice things like the way her jeans hug her thighs, cinched by the gold-buckled belt around her waist, the way her black tank top exposes her strong arms and clings to the curves of her torso, edges both soft and defined, the way dimples etch her cheeks when she smiles at the bartender – smiles at the bartender? The *bartender's* getting smiles? I tune into the conversation with a cut of my eyes.

'. . . play Mayfair this year,' he's saying. 'You're going to kill it.'

'Thank you!' The smile again. Dimples. She raises her glass. 'Here's to it.'

'You know it.' He shoots her a sly grin. 'On the house.'

'Oh, I couldn't—'

'Gotta treat royalty right when you're in the presence.' A wink. He *winks*. Her smile broadens. My chest goes stiff. What? *What?*

They exchange parting nods as the guy rushes off to help

another patron, and May turns back to me, the smile disappearing as quickly as it had crossed her face. 'Anyway. Like I said. We were young.'

'Yeah. We were, but . . .' I sigh. Her exterior, frosty as it is, is proving impossible to crack. 'May, did those years mean anything to you?'

'What, other than the fact that we were two steers with our horns locked any time we got on the field?' She chokes out a laugh, sweeping her ponytail off her shoulder. I spot an elaborate piece of ink, what looks like flowers, on the back of her arm. 'It was a rivalry. That's what it was.'

'It was – yes, it was a rivalry. Something else was there, though,' I blurt. May looks at me like I've sprouted the horns of the aforementioned steer. 'Wasn't it? And I left without a word . . .'

'You had words,' she corrects me. Her tone is biting, acidic. 'Do you remember that text you sent me, Colt? That fucking paragraph?'

Ah. The paragraph.

'I didn't—'

'"Hey,"' May recites, voice a dull drone. '"Hope your senior year's amazing. Been great playing with you all these years. Take care. Sending you strawberries from Mom's garden. Keep in touch."'

'May . . .' There's so much I wish I could tell her. Like, 'Do you ever feel like it'd be easier to cope with the fact that something will never happen by pretending the spark never existed?' Or, 'I'd never been more terrified to lose one of the most incredible parts of my life, so I just messed it up instead.' Eventually, I can't come up with my own words. I choose hers. 'We were young.'

'Sure. And the only person who benefits from that excuse is you.' She takes a big swig of her rum and Coke. 'Once someone runs you over, Colt, why the *hell* would you let them back up over you again?'

'Please, May. I just wanted to talk.'

'There's nothing left to talk about.' She smiles tightly, a much less open smile than she'd previously given the bartender. 'Tell me about your illustrious career in New Haven or something. Anything. I just can't stand to hear you rehash crap that's been exhausted in my head for *years*. Nothing to talk about.'

Whoa.

I'm quiet for a minute. I fill the silence with a sip of my Bud Light. And once that's done its job, I fill the silence with something so much worse than talking about high school.

'I mean, if there's nothing to talk about, there's gotta be something to dance about.'

May blinks. She sets her glass down. 'To *what* about?'

'You know, dance. You used to throw down at these things.' I gesture to the crowd laughing as they step along to the twangy music the DJ is spinning. 'You knew every single dance forward and backward. Even those ridiculous ones where you used two walls or whatever they call it.'

Something flickers in her eyes, even if it's just for a moment. That soft side to her that I haven't seen yet, it's hiding; I can see it. But it doesn't come out. 'You're going to ask me to *dance* after all of that? Who—'

'I'm not here to talk about myself.' Now I feel my guard go up. It's easy for everyone else to say that whatever I've done up in New England has been "illustrious". I don't love the topic. 'I'm here to spend time with you, May, and if you want to put the past behind us, that's fine. If you think what was going on between us ended a long time ago, I'll take it, but man, we're friends first and foremost, aren't we? Aren't I allowed to give a shit about you?'

Friends. The word should come out more mangled than it does. We had a complex connection from the very beginning. Maybe from an outsider's perspective, it made sense to call it a friendship, but neither of us ever had.

May sighs, a sigh that I watch make its way through her entire body, wearing her out. 'When you put it that way, I'd be a craptastic person to say no, you know that?'

'Why else do you think I put it that way?' I give her an impish grin that she returns with a roll of her eyes, but she hops off her barstool.

'Let's get it over with.' She hums, but I can tell she's itching for a dance. In Eagle Rock, where she's lived as long as I've known her, there's a tiny, cosy downtown, and that's it. Your feed supply store, your farms, maybe a few scattered places just outside of Main Street. It was a shock the first time I saw it. Small-town kids run out of stuff to do pretty fast, and unless you're a fan of cleaning the pen or kicking it on a four-wheeler for longer than an hour at a time, you're probably going to end up at the dance hall.

The tune that starts up as we join the floor is one that's familiar to almost anyone from down here: the bagpipe intro to 'Copperhead Road' by Steve Earle.

'Oh, light work,' I chuckle, and a little smile darts across May's face. *Finally*. It's just a fraction of what I know her face is capable of, but it's more than enough for me.

'Of course.' She hooks a hand in her jeans pocket and sways

as the music picks up, and we arrange ourselves behind the nearest dancers. Her dark hair swishes with her. I still remember when it was so short she couldn't put it in a ponytail. Now, it falls all the way to her waist, the same waist my dumbass can't keep my eyes off when the first step hits, and we kick with our right leg, then our left. She'll tell you she's not a dancer, but when she's on the floor, her feet tell a different story. Her butterfly-embroidered boot-tips tap the wood floor with sharp clicks that follow the music perfectly.

'You still remember it?' she shouts over the bass. 'City Boy?'

'Who told you I didn't?' I shoot back with a wink.

'Copperhead Road' is the dance you grow up doing before you can walk. An easy sixteen steps that are heavily debated from region to region, it'd probably be a sin if I'd forgotten how to do it. New England didn't screw me up completely.

I match May's step tap for tap, my unmarked Tecovas boots in sync with her well-worn ones, careful not to kick so hard I aggravate my knee. She grins when she sees me peeking at her shoes. 'You gotta scuff those up, you know!'

We dance the entire thing by each other's side till the song comes to an end. We're hunched over and laughing as the crowd cheers, raising their drinks as the DJ, a teenage guy controlling the AUX, yells that he's looking for requests for the next dance. May beams as she holds out her hands. 'Nice goin', New Haven.'

It's an unexpected show of amnesty from her, but I accept it happily, knowing how sparing these moments have been. I give her double high-fives, and for a brief moment, our fingers lock, our eyes meet, and something, some unsaid piece of the spark that I know was there in high school returns, an effortless warmth passing between us.

May quickly unlinks her fingers from mine with a sharp clear of her throat. 'I think I'll have a drink,' she says brusquely. She beelines straight towards the bar, and honestly, she leaves me mystified. What the *hell* just happened . . . and what the hell am I gonna do about it?

## *Chapter Eight*

### American Treasuress

**May**

The big yellow high-school bus thunders down the dirt road past the ranch, the chattering of teenagers just distantly audible. PROSPERITY HS, the boxy black lettering on its side reads.

The bus, affectionately called Old Yeller, has shuttled all the small-town kids into Prosperity for the past decade. Similarly to the bar we'd been at a week back, it is a relic of Eagle Rock and speaks volumes about just how isolated this place is.

Once Old Yeller is out of earshot, the ranch is silent save for the sounds of the animals behind me, cattle lowing and horses huffing. People know our Veracruz Ranch as some sort of oasis in the middle of the endless Oklahoma plains, an untouched space where we live off the land and ride our horses to get to the feed store or something, but I like to think it's not much different from any other way of life. We've got our chores, our friends, our family dinners, and our community. All that's changed is the context.

At least, that's the way I'll run things when the responsibility of the ranch eventually falls to me. It's part of the reason I chose to study meteorology. The work will keep me at home, where I can have an eye on the ranch at all times.

I finish putting the feed out for the cows. Later, my dad will graze them – our cattle are pretty spoiled, to be honest – but for now, my job is done. I grab my backpack, toss it into my truck, and head to campus for my first class of the day. I wish I could take it all lightly, like it's any other day of my college career, but I can't. My hands are shaking when I clutch the steering wheel of my Ram. It's the morning of my last college lacrosse season opener, and I'm not sure quite how to feel. After Coach had us doing Colt's goal clinics for a week, honing the very skills I'd struggled with last year, I should probably be feeling more confident. But I can't decide if this is an end, a beginning, or both.

My dreaded Instrumentation class takes place in the University of Oklahoma City's Department of Meteorology. One of the newest buildings on the otherwise aged campus, the Meteorology Hub looms both tall and long, copious amounts of glass coupled with brick. I elbow my way through the double doors that lead directly down to the main lecture hall, already packed with just under eighty Meteorology students. Our programme is small but prestigious. We started with full lecture halls of two hundred plus freshmen, and in unfortunately typical STEM major fashion, have come down to fewer than a hundred seniors getting ready to graduate this coming spring. Like most science-based majors, rough weed-out classes, and later on, upperclassman research projects, are designed to thin out the crowd.

I toss my bag in front of me and push my seat in the third row with an overly dramatic squeak. At first, I think it's the fact that I've come in rattling and thudding that causes a couple of people to glance my way.

But as I unzip the backpack and pull my laptop and tablet from the big pocket, stragglers from the row ahead of mine start to turn around with not-so-hidden looks that'd make you think I'd sprouted horns. *What the hell?*

Before I can even start to theorize about what's going on, Dr Stearns starts the lecture with a curt, 'Good morning,' and the class starts scribbling down notes. I replay all my movements from the last twenty-four hours. What could I have done? Practice. Chores. Bar. Home. And now class. No room for committing any serious crimes.

I make it through Stearns's monotone lecture before packing up my stuff at the end of the fifty minutes, hustling out of my row to avoid any more weird stares. Unfortunately, I'm not fast enough.

'May!' Hailey, one of the girls in my research lab team, rushes towards me. I have a great amount of respect for Hailey Marrero, who rightfully earned her nickname 'Hailstorm' by driving straight into an EF-2 tornado and capturing some sick data for the lab while she was at it. The look of surprise on Hailey's face right now, though, doesn't look to have anything to do with research. 'I can't believe it. You know, he's basically a *legend* out here . . .'

'Who?' I feel my jaw go slack and my legs go numb as I start to register just what might be going on. 'What?'

'Girl, you did that,' gushes Hailey. 'You guys are *so* cute.' She turns her phone my way, and my horror is pretty damn immediate.

On the screen is a shaky video clip from last night. Colt and I kick and step to 'Copperhead Road' and, as the dance ends, he holds his hands up, and we high-five. Except that our high-five turns into a moment. I don't remember the elongated period for which our hands stay in one another's, and I definitely don't remember our eyes meeting the way they do in this video, but they must have, because it's unmistakable. And clearly, to everyone else, the eye contact wasn't the only thing that was unmistakable.

Unfortunate. The man could have chemistry with a plank of wood.

'That's not—'

'Can't wait to see him cheer you on at the game tonight!' Hailey grins, waving as she walks around me to leave the lecture hall.

Oh, no.

It takes me a moment to get my bearings, but as soon as I do, I rush out of the Meteorology Hub and immediately call Jordan. This cannot be happening.

My heart thuds against my sternum. The dial tone drones. *Pick up. Pick up.*

There's a crackle, and then my friend's voice, no hi, no hello, just, 'You didn't *tell me?*'

'Jor, I *swear*, it's nothing—'

'Oh, girl, it sure looks like something, and I'm afraid the entire internet seems to think so.' There's a heavy pause before she speaks again. 'You gotta talk to him, dude. This is going to blow back on him, too.'

'On *him?*'

'May . . . you gotta understand. Whatever you're feeling right now – pissed, confused – that's probably also what he's feeling. And as much as you don't like the guy, it's not fair to leave him to deal with that PR mess on his own. Y'all have to decide how you'll take care of this.'

Jordan and her big mouth. Sadly, she's as wise as she is yap-happy. I groan, tossing the phone in a pocket of my jacket and popping in an earbud while I walk to my next class. 'He's got PR people. This is gonna be my mess to clean up, not his.'

'They'll clean up the mess,' says Jordan with a sigh, 'but they definitely won't clean up whatever feelings were obviously running loose in that video, May.'

'You're kidding me.'

'I am *not* kidding.' I can practically see my friend's interventionist expression, eyes wide and brows raised in *I-told-you-so*, lips pursed. 'We'll debrief at practice. See you later, girl.'

'See you.' As I queue up my spring playlist, I try to tell myself this will blow over just like everything does in this flat, stormy state. Unfortunately, every attempted reassurance only makes me realize just how wrong I am, and how right Jordan is. We *definitely* need to talk.

The first words out of Colt's mouth when I run into him before the game are, 'Coach told me about your season.'

To be honest, that's not what I expected to hear. I stop dead in my tracks in the hall of the dingy locker room built outside the field.

He clears his throat awkwardly and shifts the cones he's holding to set out for warm-up from arm to arm. 'She told me about last season. Your place on the team. The scholarship. Her looking to get you a spot on the MLL. All that stuff.'

I make a mental note to terrorize my coach about this later. For now, it's damage control. The things that happened during my junior season were more than just a bad run. I'd rather it didn't make the rounds. I'd *really* rather this guy had never found out. And as for the MLL . . . what Coach wants is one thing. What I want, I don't even know. 'How much did she tell you?' I ask through gritted teeth.

'Only that.' He looks confused but plods on. 'The thing is . . . May, I'm willing to do whatever you want to do about this.' He gestures between the two of us. *This*. 'Your career is the priority here. You know?'

I cough out a laugh. Suddenly I'm the priority, about five years too late. 'The whole school won't shut up about it. It's spreading like wildfire. If your PR team can fix that, I'll take it.'

I'm not sure if I hallucinate the tiny flash of disappointment in Colt's eyes, but he gives me a curt nod. 'They'll be on it within the day. I'm sure of it.'

I walk the rest of the way to the locker room in silence, Colt striding off in the opposite direction with his cones. As I pull on my jersey and kilt, slap some kinesiology tape on my calves, and lace up my cleats, I ready my explanation to the team once the questions hit – 'Someone took a video that got blown *way* out of context,' I mentally repeat. I'm not ready to address it yet, and maybe that's why I decide, in a move out of the normal, to haul my ass to the field a full half-hour before the team's usual call time.

I grab my goggles and mouthguard and leave my hair in its loose ponytail for now; Brianna is the member of our team that does everyone's matchday hairstyles. I shut the door to the lockers behind me and start the walk from the tunnels out to Chester Johnson Memorial Field.

I had prepared my speech to the team, but by the time I've reached the tunnel, I start to realize I won't need it.

The bleachers, normally empty save for our bags during practices and small crowds during home games, are filling up fast. I've never seen the front rows as full as they are, and from the glimpse I get, plenty of phone cameras are out and at the ready, prepared to capture the source of all the lore that's infected Okie campus.

'Spreading like wildfire.'

Colt leans against the left wall of the tunnel, eyebrows raised, and brushes a stray lock of hair back with a dismissive hand. 'That's what you said, right? You weren't kidding.'

I guess he also found time to change out of his usual shorts and sweatshirt. He wears the Riders coaching staff half-zip with a pair of well-ironed khaki pants. It's a weird contrast to his usual frat-boy demeanour.

'Guess I wasn't.' I tip my head towards the tunnel exit. 'Better stay in here. They're waiting for you outside. Might jump you if you're not careful.'

'Aww.' The corner of his mouth tips up, etching a dimple in his cheek that stabs at a button in my chest I thought I'd long since destroyed. 'You'd care if they jumped me.'

'Yo!' I've never been more grateful for Jordan when she barrels into the tunnel. I wish I was exaggerating, but the girl is quite literally bent over, out of breath, still in her street clothes.

'I *know* you're not playing in those jeans!' I start to scold her, but she holds up a hand, the olive complexion of her face starting to go red.

'Tell me *whose* parents are at this women's lacrosse match?' Jordan scrunches her eyebrows in confusion as she drops her duffel beside her sneakered feet, pointing a stubborn arm at the exit. 'Look at that. That has to be the Harrisons. Serial lacrosse fans. You think they called all their friends or something? Never gave a shit about women's, but here we are.'

'I think it has an awful lot to do with the conversation we had earlier,' I mutter, and widen my eyes at Jordan by way of a cue. She mouths an *oh* as her gaze shifts towards Colt, and another silent *oh* comes out.

My best friend tugs me aside, voice lowered to a whisper. 'So. I take it we aren't coming clean to the entire team right now, American Treasuress? You know we've never had a crowd like this in our *lives*. This is crazy, May. We couldn't even dream of this.'

I glare at the stands, and when I peer at Colt, who's now migrated towards the tunnel exit and is waving at the audience with his dumb, glowing smile, I make sure to add a little extra sting. 'Peanut gallery's full. That's all we could ask for right now.'

'Did you talk to him?'

'Hmm.' I clench my jaw. 'It may not be happening this instant, but we're shutting this down. He knows it.'

## Chapter Nine

### The Deal

**Colt**

The looks of wonder on the team's faces are all I need to know that they've never played in front of this kind of crowd.

Coach Dillon and I make our way over to the sidelines as they jog out onto the field with their sticks and goggles. The shouts of the audience we've drawn is unmistakable – it's obvious what they're here for, but a crowd is a crowd. May gazes up at the bleachers, at the nearly full student section, already getting rowdy in their game overalls, orange towels in hand, and then turns to shoot daggers from her eyes at me, framed by the hot pink of her goggles. The Dutch braid done for her by Brianna whips around over her shoulder, and if I were someone less acquainted with May Velasco, I'd probably be scared for my life. Instead, I manage a cheeky grin and a shrug. As much as May sees the video as a PR nightmare, one I'll have to tell my team to erase sooner rather than later, it's certainly secured the Riders a hell of an opening game, and it's given Captain May a very, very amped-up team. We'd better enjoy it while it lasts.

'You come with quite some sway,' remarks Coach Dillon, scratching at her clipboard with her plastic stick pen. She looks up at a poster with squinted eyes. 'God, these kids work fast. What's that even say? "Bradlasco Lives On",' she reads. 'Have the both of you got some sort of history I'm not aware of?'

'Uhhh . . .' Coach watches my face phase through about five different versions of confusion, and knowledge dawns on her slowly.

'I've heard some insane stories in my time on the lacrosse circuit,' she quips. 'I have time for one more.'

'Um, the thing is – you gotta understand this much first. We aren't together,' I start, adding a couple extra-dramatic waving motions with my hands to really sell it. 'But someone took a video of us a few days back – and there's been some speculation.'

Coach Dillon just raises an eyebrow at me for a minute. Then, she jabs an insistent thumb at the quickly growing crowd filling the stands. 'Clearly! That's the whole damn town out there!'

'And so – they think we're . . .'

'Hmm.' The coach hums in thought. 'I just love the rumour mill among young people nowadays. The things it churns out. Priceless.'

'It's not real. I swear . . .'

'Ah-ah-ah.' She holds up a hand to stop me. I blink, taken aback. *What is going on?* 'That's the *whole damn town* out there,' she repeats slowly. Her gaze falls on me, and then back to the bleachers. 'Maybe they came for you. Or *Bradlasco*. Or whatever it is. But maybe . . . they'll stay for these girls playing lacrosse.'

We watch as the team jogs onto the field to hearty cheering and chanting. They're definitely not familiar with the atmosphere they're experiencing. I can see it in the tension in their shoulders, the way their heads swivel, fully alert. I remember going through the same thing when I started playing in Boston, and years later, last October. I still feel it now – the same tension they do. Crowds are, at their core, terrifying. I think of every single person who watched me go down on the field. Eyes everywhere.

In the girls' case, though, this crowd is a good thing. People stay for lacrosse. And that means lacrosse stays for the people. Budget improvements, bigger and bigger crowds, and the best bonus – an edge when it comes to Major League Lacrosse visibility.

'If May and Jordan finish the senior season out with all eyes on them?' Coach reads my mind, shaking her head. 'By the time they declare for the draft, it's open season.'

Ideas, all kinds of them, kick up a dust storm in my brain. When the first whistle blows, and the draw is on, the ideas are swirling. But it's the moment that May captures the ball, passes straight down the middle to Maddie, and then to Jordan, and at last, when the ball smashes its way into the net, that it all comes together.

'HOLY SHIT!' someone yells excitedly from behind me. The field vibrates with the thrum of the chant – 'RIDE ON, COWGIRL!' Coach was right. Maybe this started out about me, but it'll have brought this town together for something much greater.

'May will never buy it, you know,' I shout over the cheers to Coach Dillon as the girls set up for their next formation.

'I wouldn't be so sure,' the coach shouts back.

\* \* \*

The Riders coast through the first game of their season against Arizona at Sedona, sitting pretty at a cool 12–7. It's no secret they're going to take this one home by the third quarter, but the audience hangs in there until the final buzzer sounds, and then orange and white towels go flying as the Oklahoma City Victory March plays, and the girls embrace on field. May, whose expression had been stony as a wall at the beginning of these four quarters, grins broadly along with her team. Coach's hypothesis is great, of course, but May's smile is the added perk I really, really wouldn't mind.

It fades when she meets my eyes as the team separates and they head back towards the tunnel to the lockers once all the festivities slow down and fans start to trickle out. May's one of the last to head back in. Coach Dillon stops her for just a moment before she hits the entrance to the tunnel. I can't hear what they're saying, as I'm somewhat occupied congratulating the girls as they file inside, but I have a little bit of an idea.

Then she comes my way, May, her braid only slightly matted, her pink goggles in hand, jersey and kilt dotted with grass stains, but attitude perfectly intact.

Said attitude is the reason I don't expect anything at all when she jogs right up to me where I'm standing to the side of the tunnel about halfway inside. She gets close enough that I can make out barely discernible freckles across her nose, can count the empty piercing holes on her ears. Her dark eyebrows knit, and through gritted teeth, she chokes out the magic words.

'Tell your PR team to back down. I'm in.'

## Chapter Ten

### The Game Plan

**May**

I wish I could blame the adrenaline, but it's clear I made the shitty decision myself. For the team, I remind myself. For the women's lacrosse programme Okie needs, according to our coach. For my career after college, I try to ignore the uncertainty surrounding that last part. Either way, it sounds dumb when I realize that this shitty decision has brought me to an overly expensive pasta restaurant in downtown Prosperity, where I sit across from the menace himself.

I don't even like pasta. There. I said it.

'We need to lay down a game plan,' says Colt, swallowing a bite of ziti. 'We need to set a couple of guidelines, for how this is gonna go.'

'A game plan,' I echo in disbelief. This can't be real. I spear a piece of lasagne, attempting to silence my particularly judgemental thoughts that might accidentally manifest themselves aloud. He's such a *man*.

'What? It's true,' he points out. 'If we're going to do this, we need a strategy.'

'Colt . . .' I'm not sure how to react, so in the end, I scoff. 'Dude. It's a relationship, not a lax play.'

Both his eyebrows rise at that. He tilts his head in inquisition, all curious golden retriever-esque, and a lock of light brown hair falls from the rest of his 'do, which is effortlessly swept back from his forehead. 'What's the difference?'

*And that's why no 'spark' between us would've ever stood a chance.* 'So much. There's so much difference. Didn't you have a girlfriend at some point in Boston?'

'Uh, yeah. I did . . .' The confusion on his face quickly turns to a teasing, overly satisfied smirk. 'Why, were you keeping tabs on me?'

'No.' Ugh. I bite down on my tongue. 'People date. They learn from their relationships. I just thought you'd finally have figured out that feelings aren't as premeditated as playbooks.'

The silence that comes after that is deafening.

Colt, always the kind of person who couldn't stand a moment's lull in conversation, clears his throat. 'Anyway. This is technically premeditated. So, we could use a playbook.'

I resist the urge to roll my eyes. 'Fine. What's in the playbook then?'

'Well, we gotta look like a couple,' he starts with a little wave of his fork. 'We need to feed the press nuggets every so often, make sure they think the relationship is still a thing. Keep pulling in crowds. Maybe even expand our crowds.'

'*Nuggets?*' I echo in disbelief.

'Yeah, you know. Like how we were at the bar that other night.'

'Great.' If it isn't enough that he'll be at every team practice, I have to give him quality time, too. 'We can do fake date nights, like, once a week or something. Next.'

'Well, I couldn't miss a game,' he continues. 'That'd include road games. Which means I'll be travelling with you, which means more eyes will be on us, and we'll have to keep up the appearance wherever we go, whenever we're together.'

Road games. I hold back a sarcastic laugh. I'd forgotten my favourite part about the season. The travel games, my usual escape from the tiny-town chokehold that was Eagle Rock and Prosperity, would now be an experience I'd have to share with Colt.

Not to mention the variable I had yet to contend with: how seriously Colt would take this whole thing. What if when we went to Albuquerque for the rivalry game, he strolled out on the town after a little too much to drink, and he woke up on the floor of some random Alby-U dorm room? I only entertain the idea because I'd done it once before and lived to regret every second of it. Anything is possible once we factor in road games and I don't particularly want to think about that.

'Honestly, though,' Colt says way too quickly, once he notices the vacant expression on my face, 'I'm only committed to doing what you're comfortable with. You're writing the playbook, at the end of the day, not me.'

His cheeks are going slightly red. He messes with the silver chain around his neck, glancing at me all anxiously, his eyes darting like caught prey. He's definitely flustered. It would be more amusing if our fake relationship and my real career weren't at stake.

'I appreciate that,' I finally reply. It's not a lie. 'Colt, I'm going to be real with you. I don't know where to start here. I saw the full crowd, and how happy the girls were because of it. Jordan and I are graduating, and we need to figure out what kind of role lacrosse will have in our lives after that, and this publicity, this attention, it helps. It attracts scouts. It attracts options. You know that.'

He nods, fiddling with his fork. He meets my gaze through ridiculously long eyelashes. 'Yeah. I know. I get it, May. Trust me, I do. Breaking into the pros is a big decision.'

*A decision as big as where you chose to go to college?* I want to retort. *A decision as big as leaving Oklahoma behind?* I wonder if he remembers the faces of everyone who was disappointed that, as much as Prosperity wanted Colt, Colt didn't want Prosperity. I wonder if he saw all the shit that happened here just a year ago. I wonder if he knows how much small towns need anchors. How much this place needed him and his talent, and how the ease with which he made the choice to turn his back on the people who made him who he is today – and, I guess, on me – was a knife to the chest.

I count my losses and let it go, though. 'It is. But as Coach has apparently made clear to you, you're also aware I'm personally in a tough situation. I have a dogshit year to make up for if I want to stay on this team. I don't need distractions. This is the means to an end for me. Let's keep stuff separate.'

Something changes behind Colt's eyes, just a hint, and he

nods in acknowledgement. Crap. Maybe I'm being too blunt. 'And when I leave?' he asks tentatively, before I can get too caught up in my own head.

'That's curtains, isn't it?' I reply, drumming my fingers idly on the table. 'We stage the great big breakup. Call it quits because you're leaving, yada yada. Works out well for both of us. No one leaves this thing tied down.'

'Fair.' He smiles, but it's far less eager than his usual grin. 'Makes it all the more important we have a nice outline to get this thing right, then.'

He takes a napkin from the centre of the table and extends a hand my way. 'You got a pen?'

I shrug and pull one out of my belt bag for him. 'Sure.'

Unfolding the napkin, Colt uncaps the pen and starts writing a big number '1' with a dash beside it. 'You tell me what to put on here, I'll write it. Our playbook.'

The ache in my chest is dull and nostalgic, and it's a feeling I thought I wouldn't feel again. It's a feeling I squashed after that spring when I watched Colt walk down that hallway with his cheery waving. After his half-assed text message and his mom's infuriatingly good strawberries. It reminds me that there's a hole in there, and that hole, only one person was ever able to fill, rivalry or not.

I swallow hard. I want to say, 'Hiding. Our first play is going to be hiding. You continue hiding things from me, and I'll hide them from you. Don't let this get too real. I don't think I could survive everything you put me through a second time.'

Instead, I say, 'Unless the circumstances demand otherwise, how about keeping our distance?'

**May's Plays**
– Keep our distance. Unless the circumstances demand otherwise.
– Minimal PDA. We refuse to be *that* couple.
– When in doubt, do as our overly romantic parents would.
– No deep conversations about deep life things (henceforth).
– These terms end when Colt leaves.

## Chapter Eleven

Talk of the Town

### Colt

'If we're going to pull this off, you'll need to know the team backwards and forwards, inside out. The Riders are May's whole thing.'

Jordan Gutierrez-Hawkins hefts her lacrosse stick to point at a photo on the slide deck she's showing on the lecture hall projector. We're somewhere in the business building, I think, where she's taken over one of the biggest auditoriums on campus to walk me through what she's deemed crucial information for me to know in order to succeed in this fake relationship.

Jordan, with enough personality for a twelve-person team, uses her whole body to gesture avidly as she gives me her rundown. I remember her pretty well from our time at Prosperity. She and May were joined at the hip from the first grade, the earliest we all went to school together because Eagle Rock was too small to have one to itself. By the time we got to high school, I had my group, primarily consisting of the guys from my team, and Jordan and May had theirs, primarily consisting of the girls from their team. A couple of the dudes would try to shoot their shot with the girls' team, but oftentimes to no avail.

I'm trying to pay attention to what Jordan's saying, but my brain is still hooked on the 'fake' in all these terms – fake relationship, fake boyfriend, fake date nights. Sitting in that restaurant with May, I had to spend the whole dinner forcing down the feeling in my gut that just wanted it all to be *real*. I craved again that shred of enjoyment she'd shown at the bar that night, but I could see it on her face, and how she'd laid down the law with her voice: this was all business for her.

'COLT!' Jordan calls from up on the stage, voice bouncing off the high ceiling of the auditorium, her brow creased in disappointment. 'Are you listening?'

'Uh, yeah!'

'Sure.' She narrows her eyes in disbelief, but continues with her spiel. 'We'll circle back to May shortly. As for me, you'll get to know me pretty well, considering I'm the only one on this team besides Coach who knows what's going on. This is—'

'Wait. Pause.' I raise a hand. 'You and Coach orchestrated this thing?'

'What, you think we wouldn't?' Jordan shakes her head. 'Coach is more than just an authority figure for us, Colt. When we're not home with our families, she's Mom. For the record, the two of us had a whole talk about Bradlasco last practice. We can't tell exactly how May's feeling about it all, you know she's hard to get a read on, but she's letting it fly. For the team, I think, considering she has so much weight on her shoulders after last year.'

I still don't know the entire story about May's junior year, but from what Coach told me, I can put some of the pieces together. It's not the kind of thing you ask to dig deeper about.

Jordan clears her throat for dramatic effect. 'So. I continue requesting your attention. This is Maddie. Attacker. Miss Bellmare. She spends most of her day in classes, spends some time with us, and whatever time is left is spent doing her duties. Civic title, technically, so not really your traditional beauty queen. She's a political science major. She has thoughts, and she lives to make them known.'

In similar fashion, Jordan takes me through the Riders' starting twelve: the midfielders, attackers, defence, and the goalie, Lexi, who frankly terrifies me more than any other member of the team (except maybe May).

'She's definitely walking, talking fear,' Jordan ends triumphantly, wagging her stick at Lexi's team photo – which is more like a mugshot – complete with a glowering stare. 'Brianna – quick, pop quiz, who's Brianna?'

'I – uh . . .' I'm notoriously terrible at pop quizzes, so I wiggle uncomfortably in my seat. 'Um. Midfield. Hair?'

'Good. Hair Brianna starts shaking when Lexi asks if she can braid her up for a game.' Jordan clucks her tongue. 'That's what you call bad energy, if you ask me. And there's your first-string twelve. We'll start there. Know us well. You'll travel with us cross-country, probably body some buffets with us, a couple of college dining halls across state lines. You'll definitely get asked about us in relation to May in interviews. You'll definitely get asked . . . about May. Segue.' She raises an eyebrow, then puckers her lips in thought. 'Let's do some more trivia, Colt.'

Oh, no. The mischievous look on Jordan's face tells me all I need to know about the upcoming trivia I'll have to endure. I'm literally about to start biting my nails. 'Um. Sure?'

'Question!' She clicks forward in the slide deck, to a giant photo of May with the Riders' mascot, a comedic-looking horse standing on its hind legs. Even with that thing next to her drawing attention to its googly eyes, May's stunning grin is what captivates me. She's a knockout, always has been.

'May's favourite colour.'

'Hot pink.'

'Wow, cowboy.' Jordan nods in approval. 'Bare minimum. May's horse's name.'

'Uh . . . Rocky?'

'Okay!' Jordan taps her lacrosse stick against her palm with a grin. 'I see you. You got chops. If May could eat only one food for the rest of her life?'

*Damn it*. I gulp, trying to call back something – anything – from high school. Or even now, honestly. I'd take it. In the end, I come out with, 'She doesn't like pasta, does she?'

'Ugh, Big Time!' groans Jordan. She throws her hands up in despondency. 'You were on a roll! And you *know* the way to a woman's heart is through her stomach, don't you? What if she asks you to grab a plate from the buffet? What're you going to get her? Repeat after me, champ. *Nashville hot chicken*.'

This monstrosity of a trivia match goes on for another thirty minutes before Jordan finally clicks to a slide of the entire team, leading to a large-font THANK YOU. 'You did good,' she says sternly. 'Hope you took some notes. But you did good.'

'Thanks.' I shoot her a grateful smile. Then, I wonder, maybe I *could* get some context on May's last year from Jordan. Not reasons. Just context. 'Jordan . . . could I ask . . . everyone seems to mention May's bad last season. Off-seasons happen, though. It's not something horrible . . . right?'

'You gotta ask May about that, you know.'

I raise an eyebrow. 'Is it something I should know?'

'Well, I think part of the reason she can't stand the sight of you is because if you'd stayed in Oklahoma . . .' Jordan shrugs, her expression one of slight pity. 'It would *one hundred per cent* be something you would know.'

*But you didn't stay.* The words she doesn't say are louder than the ones she does.

Savannah slides the breadbasket my way, crossing her eyes. 'All that's left is wholegrain, dingus.'

'Thanks,' I grumble, but I still take a roll from the basket. It's fresh, still warm. Wholegrain be damned, I'll take one of my mom's homemade rolls in any form. Sav can have her all-purpose flour.

Ma, happy and content with my healthy choice, shoots me a smile. That's definitely not all she's keen on, though, and it's certainly not all Pop's keen on, judging from how glowing and excited they've been since the game. They know as much as the rest of the town – the rest of the state, possibly – and are riding a wave of satisfaction because of it.

'How's May?' asks Ma, setting the salad bowl down on the table as Pop comes in with the steak. How they put this stuff together every night after Ma's full day of teaching and Pop's twelve-hour days performing trauma surgery at the hospital, I'll never know.

'No practice today.' I take an aggressive bite of roll to shut myself up before I can say something stupider than that. *Fuck.* What's so special about practice? We're supposed to be in a relationship. How the hell would I *not* know how she is? *Damn it, Colt!*

'He's so secretive,' Ma teases, nudging Pop, who swings around from the stove with a skillet in hand and a smirk on his face.

'You know, Colt,' says my dad as he serves me my steak, 'I was the same way when I started dating your mom. Right in this very town, you know. Reluctant, quiet, didn't wanna admit what was happening between us. Say what you like, but magic happens in Prosperity. It's a good thing you came back.'

Sav, out of the corner of my eye, rolls hers dramatically. I resist the urge to flip her off. *She's* the one who stayed here for college. 'Colt Bradley, homecoming king,' she singsongs sarcastically. 'Ooh, damn. That reminds me. You're lucky you weren't here for homecoming. They would have paraded you and your girlfriend around like nobody's business.'

'Shut up,' I mutter with all the energy I can muster.

Savannah and I have always been at odds. It's kind of a sibling thing, but it's kind of also a thing that's made worse by distance, especially during your sister's formative years. I missed her prom for a New Haven home game, but made it to her graduation – so technically I have been back in Oklahoma since I left – but it all moved so fast. The only reason I didn't miss that, too, was because I had training in Houston the next day. I flew into Oklahoma City, drove straight to the high school, sat for the ceremony, took a few pictures, and went right back to the airport to catch a tiny domestic flight to Houston. But then I missed her freshman year move-in because I was playing in New York City. I honestly wish May would be as outwardly angry with me as Sav is about the whole skipping-town thing. It would hurt a hell of a lot less than the disappointment.

'Well, make sure you're treating her right,' Ma chides me. She's using her professor's voice. 'Walk her to class. Buy her dinner. Listen to her when she tells you how her day's been, how she's feelin'. Bring her around here at some point. We'd love to have her. And for crying out loud, go to her games – that one ought to be easy – but Colt, you left that girl on her own for *years*. You're lucky she's even talking to you. You have a lot of lost time to make up for.'

Sav snorts. 'If he tried making up for all his lost time, he'd still be doing it by the time he was in the grave.'

'Savannah,' sighs Pop with his best tired-parent voice. He's adapting pretty fast. I've only been back for a few weeks, and already our parents have gone from excited to have both kids back home to quickly becoming sick of our bickering.

'What?' my sister whines. 'He's no exception just 'cause he's *famous*.' She puts on a high-pitched voice for the last word. Ma and Pop exchange a pursed-lipped look. They're definitely holding back laughter now.

'I'm trying my best!' I protest.

There's a moment of silence before our parents finally lose it, leaning on each other and laughing like they're still our age, and everything is unserious again. Their infectious energy is one of my favourite things about them, but at that moment, it's my ma's advice that rings in my head.

*You left that girl on her own for* years.

## Chapter Twelve

### Puppy Dog

**May**

By the time I arrive at campus, I've already had a long morning so, with a groan, I swing myself out of my truck, cursing the work boots still on my feet. I never wear them out here if possible. It's like wearing your house shoes out to buy groceries. That's not accounting for the fact that – as much as Oklahoma is a major agriculture state – it's still uncool to show up in boots unless it's Thursday, Friday or Saturday night. I'd have remembered to take them off if it hadn't been for Mumma and Papa.

The two of them have never really been social media users. So when Mumma held up the video of Colt and me at the bar the other night, stopping me in my tracks on my way out of the house, her eyebrows rising curiously, I honestly wasn't sure what to say.

'What should I make of this?' She had smirked the sly sort

of smirk that told me she'd already made something of this. 'May, after all these years!'

Baffled, the words 'It's not like that' had started to form in my throat before I remembered the game plan. My parents, naturally, would be the sort of weak link that could break the entire chain by telling the whole town what was going on before the last of the explanation had left my mouth. I, against my instinct, would have to uphold the lie.

Through gritted teeth, I had fabricated some sort of mangled response about us testing the waters, before I quickly headed away from the scene of the crime, realizing too late I still had my work boots on.

Now, by the time I start the walk to the Meteorology Hub, backpack in tow, and see a familiar blue Ram sidled up in street parking, its familiar owner leaning against the side, I'm ready to start swinging fists.

'Morning.' Colt adjusts today's backwards cap, so his hair sticks out from behind. The weather is chillier than usual, so he wears an orange OKC hoodie and jeans. If I didn't know any more about him, I'd think he actually went here.

'Morning,' I grumble in return. He shows no sign of noticing that I look like I've just rolled out of bed to be here, or that I have zero shits to give at the moment. He just beams brightly. What a goon.

'The nice thing about doing my master's online is that I get to make my own schedule, so I thought I'd walk you. If you're okay with that.'

*Walk me?* I want to say. *How can you act as if it's so easy to walk with me when I watched you turn your back on me like it was light work years ago?*

'It's . . .' I check my watch. 'Nine-twenty, and pretty much everything that has happened so far today has been a series of events I was in no way okay with. Might as well up the ante. Add a sprinkle of fake girlfriend duty to the mix.'

Colt's face looks like it goes through about fifty different emotions in trying to decipher the blunt sarcasm I've thrown at him. Okay, so maybe the guy's trying to be nice. Maybe I feel a smidge of remorse for being a menace. But after all the bad days his departure caused me, I figure he owes me enough that he can put up with one of those bad days, live and in person.

Silently, I turn towards the quad, he turns towards the quad, and I hike up my backpack. We walk side by side, matching our steps without a word. It's the start of the ten-minute lull between classes when the campus fills up with students cramming sidewalks to the brim, and as we near the Diamond, our four-pointed quad named ever so originally, the exodus begins, college kids filing down the walkways with headphones on and coffees in hand. The stares are inevitable – some calculating, some gleeful. I glance at Colt, far enough away from me that you could put a May between us.

God, screw this.

Against my better nature, I close the space between us so our shoulders just barely brush. Colt's gaze skims my arm before sneaking up to meet my eyes.

'I know play number one is supposed to be distance,' he whispers with a half-smile, 'but it seems an awful lot like you're using my nuggets tactic right now.'

'Can't use one play for every single match, can you?' I retort. I push aside the way his little smile, right beside me, inches away, could make the coldest of hearts thrum with warmth, and I sure as hell shove down the urge to return the smile.

'You got me there.' Colt shrugs, all exaggerated, his muscular arm flexing against mine. 'So what class are we going to?'

'Synaptic Meteorology and Forecasting.'

'Meteorology,' he echoes, wide-eyed. 'Damn. Well, pretty fitting for the girl who was Jo Harding for three Halloweens in a row.'

'Oh, my god.' The laugh that he finally manages to get out of me is primarily embarrassment. The Jo Harding costume isn't something I like people to know about. 'That was *elementary* school. You can't hold it against me.'

'May, what kind of first-grader is watching *Twister* once a month?' He laughs with me, grinning so hard that his eyes narrow happily, the corners etched with crow's feet from years of unbridled smiles. 'Best part was that your parents enabled it. Your mom dressing up as Melissa . . .'

'And Dad as Dusty.' I snort, shaking my head. 'Please, please never share this knowledge with *anyone*. I swear, if you open your mouth to a single human being—'

'I won't!' Colt traces an imaginary 'X' over his heart. 'I promise. But truly. Other than the extremely oversize jumpsuit—'

'Seriously!'

'—other than the jumpsuit . . . Meteorology's a great major, right, but, and this isn't to say you shouldn't pursue it – you're a powerhouse – but you're fucking great at lacrosse,' he points out, and the compliment really shouldn't make me feel as light and airy as it does. 'You'll go all the way to the MLL. Hell, you'll probably play sixes in the Olympics some day. You won't be working a nine-to-five for a long time if that happens. So I guess my question is, why this nine-to-five?'

The light and airiness has faded by the time he gets to the end of his so-called encouraging spiel. The anger is back. Anger at all the stuff he missed, good and bad. At all the times we just picked up our sticks and played without a word. At all the long, late-night talks we slowly started to share. And at all the trust I placed in him.

I told Colt the sorts of things no one else knew about my family, about how even with all my parents' hard work, we still had debt from the ranch, and how I felt responsible because the place would be mine some day. I told him I was scared I wouldn't be able to make it out of Prosperity, and he listened. Then, he told me the sorts of things no one else knew about him. He told me stories about his grandfather, a former Ivy League athlete, and his grandmother, one of the first women to compete in the women's College Lacrosse Championship, who'd inspired his love for lacrosse. He confessed to me he was scared that if lacrosse fell through for him, he didn't know what else he'd really want to do with his life. No one had ever talked to me that way, been so raw. And certainly no one had ever listened so intently. Hell, he was still doing it, right now.

Well. All those times I thought something was different apparently didn't mean all that much to him. And now, with his nine-to-five question, he had no business trying to change the narrative years after it'd been written.

Colt is fortunate. We reach the Meteorology building right as the word 'five' leaves his mouth, 'I should probably head in. Class starts in, like, three.'

His mouth makes a quiet O, and he nods. 'Gotcha.' The silent acknowledgement of my deflection is clear as day.

'Appreciate you walking me.' I smile tightly. I do. I really do. I just don't know if I can stand having this puppy dog of a man by my side for the rest of the semester. I can't decide if I despise his ignorance, or if I envy it, but whatever it is, it's eating me alive.

## Chapter Thirteen

### Run It Back

**Colt**

'GET INSIDE! THROUGH TO THE CREASE!'
It's deep into the third quarter, and Coach Dillon is at the point where her clipboard is about to fly out of her hand and achieve terminal velocity. The girls are down just one goal. We've had a shot clinic since the opener last week, and our performance – especially against a team like the Mattison Marauders, from Kentucky, second in the league – has been much improved. But as Coach loses her shit when Maddie misses an open shot, I can't help adding a big fat brick to the giant pile of blame on my chest. *This is because you aren't teaching them right, Colt. You gotta pick up the stick and get over yourself.*

'She's tryin',' Coach Dillon says aloud, definitely more to herself than anyone else, as she brushes a dark brown curl from her brow and adjusts her jacket.

'They'll get there,' I add, and the coach nods in agreement.

It's not looking great, though. We've tried every formation up to this point, and somehow, the Marauders' defence is five steps ahead every time. Our enormous student section, which feels as though it's breathing down my neck, is bleachers and bleachers deep with a sea of orange and white. Silver bead necklaces and sparkly black eye glitter as frat guys throw their hands up in dismay with every missed shot. An empty shooter bottle flies through the air and lands in the benches.

'DUDE!' a guy in orange and white striped bib overalls shouts from the front row, pointing right at me as he leans treacherously far over the rail, just in case I didn't realize who he was trying to address. 'GET YOUR GIRLFRIEND IN LINE!'

I get it. Everyone has the right to get pissed during a rough game. I've got pissed at my own team during a rough game. At that moment, though, it doesn't matter that I'm just posing as May's fake boyfriend, I'm up to the rail before I can register it. The flare of phone-camera flashes point straight at me as students let out calls of 'ooh' and 'oh, shit'.

'What'd you say?' I brace my foot on the step up to the front row. This guy's maybe two inches shorter than me and has the dumbest college-bro attempt at a cross between a fade haircut and flow I've ever seen. Is that supposed to be a mullet? What *is* that?

He has some nerve, because he gets further up in my face, lifts the beer in his right hand, and says, like I can't hear him clear as day, 'I said, YOUR GIRLFRIEND'S SHIT, bro!'

'I might be three concussions deep into my career' – I push myself up onto the ledge so I'm now a good foot above the guy – 'but I can tell you that between you and my *girlfriend*, one of you's a self-made Division One athlete, and one of you's sittin' on your ass shotgunning beers in the stands calling women "shit". Find a *fucking* mirror and check yourself. Bro.'

The crowd in our immediate proximity hoots and shakes their phones in satisfaction, and before I grab a practice stick and check this dumbass myself, I hop down from the front row ledge and make my way back to the coach. For someone who's supposed to discourage violence during games, she appears strangely satisfied, hiding a little smile of appreciation on her face.

'Well, well,' she says, 'for a faux beau, you're holding on tight.'

I feel my greatest enemy, the deceptive flush of red, make its way up my neck. 'I'm just doing my due diligence.'

Coach Dillon hums her assent, and we turn back to the game, where the girls are picking up the pace double-time. Shouts of plays sound as May takes the draw – and with the whistle, pushes her stick up in a bid for the ball. She wins out over the girl opposite her from Mattison, and Coach and I whoop.

'LET'S GO!' I shout. 'GOOD HUSTLE!'

May gets the ball over to Maddie at the first shout of 'GOT BALL' from the defender guarding her. Maddie darts around another defender and passes the ball clean back to May. From there, it's May Magic that'll take us the rest of the way.

She dashes towards the goal on impossibly light feet. Coach clutches my shoulder, eyes wild, clipboard extended, and we lean forward in anticipation as a unit. This is it, this is it. It won't get us up, but it'll tie us, and pressure is pressure.

'COME ON, MAY!' I shout.

She lunges forward to take the shot, and the ball soars. Our eyes follow it, until a defender dashes up towards May and, before we know it, the defender's crosse has made a sloppy arc, at the end of which her stick nails May square in the back of the head.

I've seen way too many of these in men's games, but the danger here is that women don't have helmets. If you take a hit, it's straight to the skull, and when May goes down, clutching her head, the medics move instinctively.

'CRAP!' I hear someone yell from behind me, and I'm not gonna lie, I feel much the same way. My heart thunders like it wants to pop right out of my chest. I lunge forward and Coach, who'd been frozen mid-hype, recovers her composure, tugging on my arm with a shake of her head. 'WHAT THE HELL?' she shouts, the most she can do in this situation. 'COME ON, REF!'

The referee subsequently shows a very appropriate red card, but my eyes are still on May. She's not getting up, and I can't see much through the crowd of medics, but whatever is happening doesn't look good.

Right in front of me, I watch as the entire scene morphs into something I recognize far too well. Surrounding May are a group of guys in blue jerseys and shiny helmets, and in agony on the ground is me. Calling out her name in vain. In tears.

My hands go clammy. No way can I just watch this happen. If my heart was thundering before, it feels like it's about to burst now.

'Can't we go check on her?' I'm practically pleading with the coach, who looks as helpless as I feel.

'Colt – you're not the head coach. They could eject you for the next couple of games . . .'

Whatever. I've already fought a frat guy. I have nothing left to lose. The ref can show *me* a red, for all I care.

Before Coach can hold me back again, I bolt onto the field,

sneakers crunching in the grass, my breathing ragged as I weave through the crowd of players, into the inner circle of three medics. The pounding of my heart slows when I notice that May's eyelids are fluttering, lips forming words. *Thank God*.

'What's goin' on, man?' I crouch down next to her and look to the lead medic for some sort of declaration.

'She's gonna be groggy for a minute,' he tells me. 'We'll definitely need to get her checked out further in the tent to rule out a brain bleed or anything severe, but I'm pretty confident it's just a concussion.'

I groan. It's never 'just a concussion'. May's gonna be devastated. That's at least two games she'll have to miss on concussion watch; that six-step protocol they put you on will definitely take her out of play for the Riders' first away game – her last first away game. Sentimental value is a major factor, of course, but missing games won't look good to the school either. For her scholarship, her spot on the team, just one concussion could spell trouble.

'May.' I try to meet her eyes as if it'll get them fully open, get them to focus. 'Hey, May. Hey, hey, hey, look at me.'

She squints, her vision still wavering. 'Colt?' Her voice is a whimper, probably the most helpless I've ever heard her, and I immediately hate it.

'I'm here.'

With an unsuccessful heave, May pushes herself just barely off the grass and, as she slumps back against one of the medics, I cradle her head in my arms. 'Whoa, hang on. You're concussed. Give yourself a minute.'

*Shit*. The entire team's around us, more staff. May's out of it, and even in this situation, we have face to save. The dumb lie has to live. *Dote, damn it, Colt!*

Fortunately, even post-concussion, May's intuition beats mine. She gives my hand a squeeze, as if to nag me, *Play the role, dude*.

As much as it's in keeping with the role, it doesn't feel like one when I reach down and sweep a strand of her hair off her cheek, tucking it behind her ear and into her headband. 'You're gonna be just fine,' I whisper.

'That was a smart move.'

May holds an ice pack to her head, legs dangling over the side of the PT table as she winces. 'The run onto the field.'

Post-game, it was straight to the tent for May, even though she was able to get up on her feet. The Riders ended the game with a draw against the Marauders, and May learned she would be out for two weeks, at the least, and in for the six-step concussion protocol.

From the pained look on May's face now, it's clear to see she's not happy about it. But there's another expression, perhaps a hint of curiosity, that dances across her face. It could also just be the concussion. Or simply the fact that I've never been great at reading emotions.

She uncaps an electrolyte drink and takes a long swig. 'It was admirable. Definitely helped our case. I mean, I ate shit, but at least we got something out of it. You didn't have to do that, though,' she adds quickly.

A twinge of nerves, the most emotion she's shown openly, flashes across her face and then disappears, and she's back to her straight-faced, nonchalant usual. She's a little too good at this.

'I know.' I lean back against the doorframe and watch as her eyes search me for some sort of tell. 'It's just . . .'

Honestly, where do I start? That I believed I could undo all the mistakes I had made, that I understand all the ways I went wrong when I could've had something with this phenomenal girl? I believed that yes, she was gonna be just fine, but also, that there was some kind of hope that *we* would be just fine some day?

But the second we got off the field, I realized just how dumb I was to so much as entertain the thought. Like May had said a month back, no one asks to have their heart backed up over again after somebody's already flattened it.

'It was the right thing to do,' I finally finish, and the weight in my stomach is as dense as lead. 'It's what everyone expected, right? Just keeping up appearances.'

## *Chapter Fourteen*

Out of Hiding

**May**

My mom charges into the PT room like a hurricane of a woman, bringing her very full clear stadium bag and my dad with her. She swoops in so abruptly that my team, all of whom have now gathered alongside a ridiculously awkward Colt and a quite relieved Coach, have little time to react to her arrival.

'It's just a concussion . . .' I'm literally in the midst of assuring my teammates when she gasps loudly at the sight of me.

'May!' Clucking her tongue, Mumma rushes up to me and tilts my head every which way, groaning unhappily when her fingers run over the bump. 'May, what's this? Why don't y'all wear helmets?'

'We're not supposed to whack each other over the head,' I grumble. 'The other girl got a massive penalty for it.'

'But *our* girl is the one we care about.' She sighs, clearly unhappy. Mumma always thought I'd follow her into dance, her high-school sport, and I think she was glad that I first befriended Jordan, who'd been a dancer from a young age, hoping some of it would rub off on me. Instead, we had only strengthened our allegiance to lacrosse, and although I know Mumma is proud of me, I'm sure every game we play creates a marked increase in her blood pressure.

Papa clears his throat. 'We're just glad you're okay, *mija*. You gave us a scare. And we're glad we could count on Colt to be there for you.' He throws a proud-dad smile Colt's way – interesting. As concussed as I am, I recall immediately that even our parents are living in the lie. The stern nudge that Jordan gives Colt doesn't escape my notice.

'Absolutely – um, absolutely,' Colt finally replies, returning the proud-dad smile with a wobbly little one of his own. 'Nowhere I'd rather be than by her side. I'm as relieved as you are.'

Oh, so *that's* easy for him to say.

I beam up at Colt, the most plastic grin I have. 'It's once in a blue moon that you'll get a boyfriend who'll run onto the field for you.' Then I turn to my mom, and with a raise of an eyebrow, 'See? I'm all good. Colt will be the first one on the scene if anything happens.'

Mumma doesn't look persuaded, but nods anyway. She exchanges a look with Papa that I don't particularly love, and as much as I can feel her next words coming, they still strike terror straight through my chest when she speaks.

'Colt, we really do appreciate you. I'm not sure what we can say or do to thank you. Especially considering you've been so close with May so early on. It's so wonderful to see things are finally . . . coming together,' she tells him. 'And really, do drop by our home when you get the chance. We'd love to have you for dinner sometime. Just as a thank you.'

I am *mortified* on the inside.

As if it wasn't enough to let myself absorb the blowback from the concussion, the games I'll miss, and the way Athletics is going to look at me after this, my parents are being beyond cordial. They're treating this guy like *family*.

I try my best to channel 'confused concussed woman' while continuing to plaster the empty smile on my face.

Colt, for all his bluster, looks like he's holding back panic when his eyes dart from me to my mom to my dad, the both of them, at least, waiting expectantly. 'Well – I couldn't impose—'

'You wouldn't,' Papa puts in with a good-natured chuckle. 'We've already known you for years, son, it's no skin off our back to feed you a meal. It's the least we could do. Clearly you're beyond good for our daughter. It'd be our pleasure. No rush at all. We'd just love to have you come home. Back to where it all started, one might say.'

*Damn it, Papa.*

After all that, there's no way Colt can say no. Shit. He blinks a couple times as if digesting everything he's heard. Finally, he stutters out, 'Oh, sure.'

'Beautiful.' Mumma finally loosens up a bit (the only positive to come out of this situation), giving Colt a relieved smile. 'We really do appreciate you, Colt. Tell your mom and dad we're so excited to have you back in town. They've raised you well.'

The *irony*. I could laugh the bitterest of laughs at everything she says, but I hold it in till the hugs are exchanged all around and my parents leave us to excited team chatter about boyfriends and dinners and cooing over Colt's gesture. 'Don't be a stranger, son,' Papa even goes so far as to add. 'Come round when you get the chance, alright?' *Son?* He's gone all buddy-buddy.

I get the point. It was a kind gesture, Colt's heroic run. But it was for the sake of the game plan. There's nothing to coo about. Is there?

Coach Dillon hops up onto the PT table next to me, and instead of the same warm smile I've been seeing for the last hour from spectators and paramedics alike, she purses her lips, her eyebrows rising. 'You know something, May?'

'Know what?'

'Well.' She shrugs. 'How do you feel about what Colt did today?'

I go slightly slack-jawed. 'Coach. You know what's going on.'

'Oh, honey, it looks like *you* don't.' She cuts her eyes towards Colt, who's going all red and gooey amid a conversation with our defenders on the other side of the long room. 'That boy could've taken a pretty severe penalty for running after you like that. You remember what the penalty is for being on the field, don't you?'

Maybe, but I try not to let on. Instead, I swallow hard. Guilt buries itself in a pit in my stomach that I refuse to acknowledge.

'Could've been fined *thousands*. Barred from our next few games. Even a subsequent penalty waiting for him in the MLL, sitting out a few games. But when he saw you out there . . .' Coach shakes her head knowingly. 'He didn't do that to put on a show. I couldn't hold him back. Didn't listen to a word I said about the penalties. Just . . . ran.'

Coach waits for some kind of response, and I really can't find one.

I scratch my nose, my biggest tell, a crack in my perfect poker face, and she laughs aloud. 'Take a good look, May. You can't hide from it for ever.'

# Chapter Fifteen

Albuquerque

**May**

I busy myself picking out each type of cloud as they pass the windows by. *Cumulus. Nimbus. Stratus.* Jordan, on the other hand, wants nothing to do with clouds.

'. . . *really* famous football team, and maybe now, we'll get to see some of the players at the game—'

'Girl, you are *too* much,' Maddie hollers from the back of the bus.

'Shut your mouth!' shouts Jordan in return. 'You don't wanna see Ronny Casamento?'

Sounds of agreement fill the bus, and up front, Coach shakes her head exhaustedly. Beside me, in the aisle seat, Colt's brow furrows. 'Ronny who?'

'Ronny *Casamento*,' Jordan says with a little extra 'oomph'. 'Last year, when Albuquerque came up here for the yearly match, we met him at this massive party Lambda Alpha Delta hosted. I thought Maddie was gonna pass *out* when he complimented her game. Sayin' all these things about how she was scoring and then something real cute about her smile. She *ate* it up. And him? He wouldn't stop following her around like a lovesick puppy all *night*.'

'He'll looove to see her again this year,' Brianna jumps right in.

I can't help but laugh. The lore around Ronny Casamento goes deep – especially because after the Lambdas' Jungle Gym party, he followed Maddie on Instagram, and rumour has it they've been in touch over the past year, waiting for the next Albuquerque game to have their adorable little reunion. As it goes with all rivalry games, we alternate between away and home each year, and this year, we're travelling to Albuquerque to play the Armadillos in one of our most anticipated matches of the season. I'd be more excited, but the eight-plus-hour bus ride and concussion protocol have kind of ruined the mood for me.

'He's guaranteed to be in pro football within the next two years,' I point out, raising an eyebrow at Maddie, who's got her quickly reddening face in her hands. 'That's wealth management. Capitalize on that while you got the chance, girl.'

'Noooo!' she groans. 'Guys!'

'Hold on, now.' Colt grins, that dumb, lopsided grin that has the ability to make your heart skip about a million beats. A dimple etches itself in his left cheek, and I find myself wishing he'd turn the smile he directs at Maddie my way. *Gross! What?* 'Are you looking forward to seeing him, though, Maddie?'

'I . . .' She slowly removes her hands from her face, and sheepishly, like a shy bride, nods just slightly. 'I guess I am.'

'You guess?' teases Jordan.

'Okay, fine!' Maddie blurts. 'I'm counting the fucking hours!'

The bus explodes into laughter and jeers and shouts as Maddie swats away the girls' grabby hands. There's something fun about being young and in love. But I've learned that when you've done it once and staked everything on it, you can't quite replicate the feeling ever again. At least not for anyone else.

We reach the Albuquerque Memorial Union later in the evening than we would have liked. It's nine p.m., and we've been on the road since noon, with the game T-minus eighteen hours away, and a boatload of starving lacrosse players ready to demolish the welcome buffet. We immediately lug our bags up to the only room they've prepared so far, form a mountain of twenty-plus duffels, and head down to the buffet. By the time we return to the room, we've stuffed ourselves full, and many of us have our hands full with additional plates of pizza.

'Keys are right here!' Coach Dillon announces, with a stack of cards in hand. 'I have Brianna, Jordan, Lexi and Maddie in 409; I have Nyla, Paige, McKinley and Kassidy in 11; Cameron, Johanée, Bea, Allison . . .'

The coach makes her way through the roster, and then she brings the hammer down. She extends a key card my way, and with a knowing smile, says, 'May, we were gonna put you in one of the rooms of fours, but we had a booking situation with Colt traveling with us.' She turns to Colt. 'The school books us exactly nine team rooms of four girls each, covers all thirty-six of us, and then I get my single room. That gives us ten rooms total. But considering we have one extra coach now, I think it may be best you both share. Will y'all be okay with that? I'll be in Charlotte's room.'

'You're sure?' Colt asks, ever the gentleman when it counts.

We exchange a nervous look. This *definitely* wasn't in the cards when we decided on this fake relationship thing. In fact, May's Plays number one is to keep our distance. This is very much not keeping our distance.

'It's either that or put Colt in a room with three college lacrosse girls getting ready for a noon game tomorrow,' she says with a shrug. 'That's a sort of chaos none of us are prepared to deal with. I know you guys have that entire press thing going on, but . . . our alternatives aren't great. It makes the most sense for the rest of the team. It was Jordan's idea, for the record.'

Damn it, Jordan. I'll have words with her after she plays tomorrow. I grit my teeth and paste a smile on my face as best as I can. 'Sure. We'll make it work.'

Five minutes later, Colt and I are staring down one solitary full-size bed. We are, after all, staying in the AMU Hotel attached to the Memorial Union. It's school-owned and operated. I don't know what I expected, to be honest. A California king? A hide-a-bed couch, at the least?

'Thoughts?' Colt finally says after a long, awkward moment.

We exchange a look of pained confusion. Colt looks remarkably put-together in his hoodie and training shorts for just having suffered a nine-hour drive with thirty-six raucous girls in an abnormally toasty bus, and I hate myself for noticing. I hate that I register the way his lashes flutter in thought, and the dimple appears in his cheek again, this time as he tweaks his mouth to the left. 'I can sleep on the floor.'

My line of sight immediately travels to the kinesiology tape slapped all around his bad knee. 'You're *not* sleeping on the floor.'

Colt's eyes widen, lips parting just slightly. 'No, I can—'

'I've slept on the floor before in way too many shitty hotels, and I know you have, too.' I chew on the inside of my cheek and regard the bed with disdain. The elephant in the room. 'We'll figure something out.'

'Yeah.' He idly cracks a knuckle before reaching out and grabbing one of the forty different pillows on the bed, tossing it in the centre. 'Make a wall?'

It's our best bet. Maybe it will stop my heart from thundering like a herd of horses at the mere thought of sleeping in the same bed as Colt Bradley. *It means nothing*, I remind myself. Except that high school May would probably have passed out at the thought.

We busy ourselves in filling the tentative silence with the whispery *whoosh* sound of pillows hitting sheets as we form our wall. By the end of it, there's an obvious division slicing through the middle of the mattress.

'I think I'm gonna hop in the shower.' I yawn. I feel like crap, and I figure the shower will help me fall asleep instead of staying up all night in a state of hyper-awareness. 'Unless you wanna go?'

'Oh – no, you go ahead, I'll go after,' Colt replies quickly, sheepishly.

With a curt nod, I unzip my duffel and grab my PJs, and I try not to notice the hint of pink that creeps up Colt's neck as I pass him to get to the bathroom.

I try really, really hard.

## *Chapter Sixteen*

Fighting Chance

**Colt**

May emerges from her shower with her hair twisted into a towel, and wearing an oversized peach T-shirt with the Riders' skull-and-crossed-sticks logo on the front. She undoes the towel and pats her hair dry, and the entire while, I do my best to pretend I'm just super, super focused on the reels I'm scrolling through at the half-desk situated across from the window. Dumb little things capture my attention, though, like the way her biceps flex as she reaches for the back of her head, or the way her eyebrows furrow in concentration when she pulls at a stray knot in her hair. 'You can go ahead,' she hums, her eyes fixated on a random spot on the wall as she intently attacks her hair with the towel. She tosses it back, and it falls so long it's almost to her waist, even in loose curls.

'Yep. Yeah.' I clear my throat awkwardly. *Cool it, Colt.* There's no way I'm gonna be that guy that makes this more awkward than it needs to be.

My shower is a sobering, desensitizing kind of cold. It doesn't completely rid my brain of thinking about May, with her wet hair and her bare legs, but it does enough to keep all those thoughts at bay. I usually just sleep in shorts, but I tug on a Woodchucks shirt to keep things civil. It's a poor decision. The shocking cold wears off the second I step out into the room, and I realize it's going to be way too warm in here to get to sleep like this.

May looks to be having no problem. Her naturally curly hair is piled into a messy knot on top of her head, and she's swapped her contacts for a pair of tortoise-framed glasses that would look tacky on anyone but are ridiculously cute on her. She even has a book in her hands that she seems to be deeply engrossed in – Jane Austen's *Emma*. It doesn't take me long to imagine that she's in my apartment in New Haven, in my room, and she smiles when I walk in, puts down the book, and . . .

*Stupid. Stupid, stupid. You missed that shot a long time ago.*

'I'm going to finish the chapter,' she murmurs without looking up. 'I won't keep you up, I promise.'

A warm tingling fills my chest as I shrug, pretending to be totally and utterly indifferent, skirting the bed to hit the desk, where I pop my laptop open and busy myself checking the class pages for my masters' courses (like I have work to do, I'm already ahead by a week).

My phone vibrates, and I spare it a quick glance that turns into a much longer glance. It's a text from Rod Wilson, complete with an attached social media post. *THIS YOU??*

Oh, God. I open the link. Someone in the stands at the home

game the past weekend took a video . . . of the whole thing. The run onto the field, everything. *Oklahoma lacrosse power couple*, reads the caption, closed out with orange and white heart emojis. Tens of thousands of likes, inching towards hundreds of thousands. All the comments. It's instantly overwhelming. I knew what starting for the Woodchucks, the most notorious lacrosse team in the country, would mean for me, and I knew what captaincy would mean, too – my personal life would no longer be my personal life, my private matters becoming public business. But this is different. This time, I'm bringing May with me, as my *girlfriend*; a blatant lie, and it makes my chest clench.

I want that lie to be true, man. And the fact that the whole world gets to believe it is a truth, while I have to live my life knowing it isn't, is a cruel thing.

'What is it?' May asks.

'Look.' I turn the screen her way, and she immediately winces.

'I get it. I took a hit . . .' Her eyes travel to the caption, the likes. 'Oh.'

'Yeah.' With an overly aggressive shove of my phone back onto the desk, behind my laptop, I shrug. 'People will forget about it in a couple days, though. It's how the internet works. Go ahead and finish your chapter.'

The time she takes to finish is the longest moment of my life. I force myself to fixate on the screen of my laptop, but my gaze has a mind of its own. It wanders to May's strong arms, to her fingers turning the pages with special care, to the wrinkle in her brow that forms as her eyes dart from word to word. I literally have to kick myself. The second this charade is over, we're back to arm's length, plus or minus a day's drive, away from one another.

'Didn't know you had glasses' comes out of my *dumb* mouth the moment I see May put her book on the bedside table.

May just raises an eyebrow. 'Chalk that one up to all the shit you didn't notice when it was right in front of you in high school. I used to wear them all the time.'

Well, *damn* you, Colt. I curse the fact that Jordan's trivia session couldn't have covered this very critical detail.

With a silent nod, I rise from my chair with a little stretch. 'I think I'm gonna head to bed.'

'Me, too,' says May. She swallows hard enough that I notice, the first indication of some kind of nerves on her part, gesturing vaguely to the other side of the bed. 'Wall's sturdy. I'll stay on my side if you stay on yours.'

'Yep.' I put myself down on the left side, May on the right, and let out a heavy exhale as I lean back against the pillows. 'Night.'

'Night,' she echoes and flips the switch on the lamp. We're plunged into that immediate black-out-curtain hotel darkness, and it becomes very, very obvious when there's nothing to see that there is *definitely* a palpable tension between us. I can hear May's breathing as she rolls over to face away from me, sheets crinkling around her, a slight tug on the comforter alerting me to her need for a little more warmth. I surrender it gladly, turning away on my side.

I'm on the verge of sleep faster than I'm prepared for, my eyes lulling shut, at least until I sniff to keep a sneeze at bay, and the smell of May's peach shampoo is the first fragrance in the air. I suddenly remember something Sav told me once when we were still in Prosperity, way back when she was in middle school. 'People like you and May Velasco can never be *just friends*, idiot.'

I figured I'd try to fix it when I first got to Boston. But all I felt was this deep, stifling sensation of being uprooted, of missing a limb. I needed May. I'd picked up my phone, drafted a text message, missing home – missing her – more than anything else.

> *May. I know I messed it up, how I left, but I can't do this without you. I guess that's what I was so scared to tell you. You've been by my side for years, on the field and off it. I don't think I can stop now. I need you.*

And then I saw the last text I'd sent her. That lame shit about 'Been great playing with you' and 'Mom's garden'. Those strawberries I left her with.

I thought about Sav's stupid advice again. Thought about the fact that I'd left things this way, and how I'd been expecting her to just text me back like we were still totally cool. Like I hadn't up and left without so much as a word to her. Just that text.

Instead of fighting the fear, I gave in. I had played chicken for years.

Now, in the dark, with nothing to look at, nothing to distract myself, it all rushes back to me in an enormous wave. I don't know what gets into me, or why I let it get into me, but by the time the first fateful words are out, it's too late.

'Hey, May?'

She grumbles groggily into her pillow before turning to the wall between us with a muffled, 'Hmm?'

My voice is floaty, quieter than I've known possible, like I'm listening to myself talk from out of body when I say, 'I really fucked up. Fucked a *ton* of stuff up.'

The crackle of the slightly shitty air conditioning is perfectly clear. I don't dare breathe for fear of the noise it'll make. The cat's finally out of the bag.

From May's side, sheets rustle, and then, a barely audible hum. Is it shock? Is she shocked? I can't completely make out the sound. Part of me hopes she doesn't totally hear me, but I keep going.

'I never said anything, you know. When I had the chance back then. Sometimes I wonder what things would be like if I had said something. If maybe we wouldn't be pretending right now.

'And I came back, and it's just . . . It's so messed up, and I feel like I keep making it messed up. I . . . May, I wanna make it right by you. You deserve that. You're owed that. I'm so, so fucking sorry.'

I wait, I wait in hope that maybe she'll say something, maybe she'll say what I want her to say. Maybe this is my do-over, this dumpster fire of a confession in a mediocre college hotel room in Albuquerque. But all I hear is her breathing, steady, quiet, even. No words.

I tell myself she's probably fallen asleep. She probably didn't hear any of that stuff at the end. And if she did, she'd have been too sleepy to remember it. She might think it's a dream. Maybe.

I roll back over to face the wall to my left.

I don't fall asleep for another two hours.

# Chapter Seventeen

Mayday

**May**

'Sometimes I just wonder what things would be like if I had said something. If we wouldn't be pretending right now.'

I think about it all the time. There have been countless nights where I've stayed up living in a world where CJ Bradley and I addressed our feelings. I spent weeks bouncing between wanting him to have an exceptionally rough practice and take a mean crosse to the face, wanting him to have this 'eureka' moment where he figured out he screwed up a good thing, or even wanting him to have the biggest of big goals at his first game simply so that I'd know he was happy and content. Only now, years later, I find out that he's been thinking about the same things. It's a damn cruel twist of fate.

I pray he stops talking then and there, but the fool is getting emotional, and I don't know how to feel about it when he says, his voice a quiet rasp, 'I'm so, so fucking sorry.'

I hold my breath with every word that comes out of his mouth. At that moment, I have no idea what to say. I've imagined a million scenarios where Colt comes back and finally realizes he made a mistake by leaving me the way he did, and I've imagined a million more where he's rich, famous, and doesn't give a crap about me any more.

It took a couple of wine-and-cry sessions, but I got past those alternate universes, and I moved on. I did. But never, in any of those universes, did I imagine I'd get what I'm getting right now. This confession. These feelings.

A moment passes, and I decide for the sake of my sanity that hopefully Colt thinks I've fallen asleep. I'm not concerned with getting the best sleep possible since I'm not playing tomorrow, but my eyes stay open for the next few hours as I contemplate everything I just heard, everything I never thought I would hear. And somehow, I think that maybe Colt is doing the exact same thing.

Next morning, my eyes flutter open to bars of sunlight cast through the room by the slats in the so-called blackout curtains. I'm quite warm and cosy . . . toasty, even. Getting out of bed would be a crappy move right about now, I think to myself as I hum contentedly and burrow my way back into Colt's arms.

COLT'S ARMS.

OH MY GOD.

I recoil so fast I think I'm going to knock Colt out cold, throw a punch right at his very muscular chest. There's no match for us to worry about, but suddenly, I've never wanted a game to arrive sooner. I need something to take my mind off whatever the *hell* I've apparently got myself into.

Oh my god. Oh my god. I try my best to disentangle myself without waking Colt up. Our legs lie across one another's, and there's a mess of pillows every which way, not at all resembling the wall we'd put together last night. Colt's arms are ridiculously strong and ridiculously difficult to move from. His hair is all tousled, sticking up in funny directions, a crease mark tracing its way along his cheek. He mumbles in his sleep just as I'm finally creeping off the bed, and I freeze in my tracks, eyes wide. Shit.

Thankfully, the guy doesn't stir, completely passed out as he is. I let out a quiet sigh of relief and head towards my bag to grab a sweatshirt and running shorts. What he doesn't know won't hurt him.

Albuquerque has brought out cheerleaders and a full student section for this match. It's never drawn too much of a crowd – after all, it's a major rivalry game in a women's sport, which means virtually no one makes an effort to learn about it, except maybe the lovesick Ronny Casamento – but I think I know the reason the school's suddenly rolling out the red carpet. The reason, unfortunately, stands right beside me with eyes wide and arms flailing, a crowd of admirers behind him in the stands with phones out.

'THROUGH!' Colt and Coach yell in unison, pointing in the exact same direction. 'RUN IT THROUGH!'

Maddie obliges, and in a split second, has made it through the defence to smack an absolute bullet of a goal into the net. She raises her crosse, and although the Albuquerque home crowd isn't having it, our team cheers harder than anyone on the field.

Colt whoops, his wavy hair rustling about in the warm wind, as he claps loudly. 'Go get 'em, Maddie!'

'You make a good team player when you try,' I can't resist prodding him.

He smirks, getting one last clap in. 'Maybe that's something *you* didn't notice back in high school.'

'Oh.' I cough awkwardly and raise an eyebrow. As if I'd buy that. 'You were a ball hog. I watched enough of your games to figure it out.'

'You watched my games?' His incredulous tone is so obviously exaggerated, but it does its job, flushing my cheeks.

'Only so Deena could see Michael play,' I cover up my momentary slip cleverly. Those two were all over each other. The Romeo and Juliet of the Prosperity lacrosse programme, we called them. The girls and the guys didn't get along for shit, but Deena and Michael would sneak little hushed conversations during practice, when we were supposed to rotate off the field. 'We weren't about to send her in alone.'

'I see.' Colt clicks his tongue, turning back to the game. 'You know, Deena and Michael just got—'

'Engaged. I heard from her,' I finish before he can try and make a point. 'That's young.'

'Yeah. But hey, they're high school sweethearts.'

'We are not high school sweethearts.'

'Did . . .' Colt does this awkward little choking cough that immediately alerts me to what he's about to bring up. Oh, no. 'Did you hear . . . any of the stuff I said . . . last night? I was out of it, I honestly didn't mean to . . .'

'What stuff?'

My poker face is exceptional. I grew up in a Texas Hold 'Em household, not to mention one that is half-South Asian, half-Mexican. He won't get me to crack, I can promise that much. I keep an impassive expression and mirror his glances at the ongoing game.

'Ah. Okay.' He seems a little relieved, his brow less tense, but a look of disappointment flashes across his face. It's gone before I can single it out. 'It was dumb, anyway.'

It was absolutely not dumb. It was earth-shattering. He doesn't need to know, just like he doesn't need to know that—

'This morning, we . . . that was totally unintentional,' says Colt quickly. 'I'm so sorry that happened. I swear, the fucking pillows must have just . . .'

'Hmm.' It's my turn to shift awkwardly now. I had hoped this one wouldn't make its way out of my treasure chest of secrets, but even Colt, as dense as he can be, has the keenness to recognize we somehow slept like a married couple last night. Fine. As long as he doesn't realize that it was my leg that ended up splayed across his. My head that found its way to his chest. 'I guess. It happens.'

## *Chapter Eighteen*

### The Ballad of Hot Rod

### **May**

'Today, we hit on the no-look twizzler, something a close friend of mine particularly excels at back in New Haven . . .'

Colt, with the whistle and keys around his neck, commandeers the clinic like he's been coaching for an eternity. I'm afraid it's a good look on him, Rider Orange. The thought is unwelcome in my brain, and I immediately shove it right out the back door the second it enters. He does a good deal of pointing, a couple of waving gestures towards the goal. Were his arms always that jacked? Was he always that jacked, Colt? And *sweet mama*, how are his calves still *stunning*? For crying out loud, the man was in a knee brace for two months. There's still tape all over his leg. Stunning calves. Beautiful quads. Quads that could probably crush a watermelon—

'May!'

'Huh?' My eyes snap up from calf-level to meet Colt's stormy ones. 'I was asking if you'd like to demo for us.'

Demo? It's *his* shot clinic. I blink, waiting for Colt to call me on my BS or turn this into an opportunity to flame me for being off my game, but the switch-up doesn't come. One of the most complex goals out there, and the MLL's star scorer isn't demonstrating it himself?

'Yeah.' I slowly adjust my grip on my crosse, stepping up towards the goal, although I've still got an eye on Colt. He steps away with a nod towards me. 'Jordan'll set you up.'

*What?* There's no way he can't even set me up. It's our fourth shot clinic and the pattern is striking. When has Colt *actually* picked up his crosse and demonstrated or passed or anything of the sort? I can think of maybe one instance, other than for our bet when he'd first arrived, and for said MLL star scorer, he'd done a piss-poor job.

'Sounds good.' I try to give Jordan a dramatic wiggle of my eyebrows to convey my thoughts, but my goggles do me no favours. I probably look like I'm having five different kinds of facial spasms.

Colt blows the whistle, and Jordan flicks the ball my way as I run past the goal. I cradle it in the net of my stick, spin back, and – without looking – fling it towards the net. It's a frustrating attempt, and one I'm not at all proud of when the ball clears the goal, just barely brushing the side of the net.

'Shit!' I groan, crosse raised. 'Dude, how do you expect me to make this? That shot's my weakest point!'

I'm about ready to stalk towards Colt, who's readying his composure for the storm, when someone else's damn voice saves him.

'Whoa, what's this?'
*What the hell?*

An unfamiliar guy jogs towards us from the right entrance to the field, from the fence. Is this CJ Bradley, part two? I wonder what estranged Oklahoman son has returned to cause us misery this time.

But as he draws near, I realize he is very much not one of ours. However, he's not unfamiliar, either, and I share a look of recognition with my team. Distracted from our trouble in paradise, heads turn towards the newcomer with wide eyes. He's not in a Woodchucks jersey, but for anyone who keeps up with the MLL, it's evident this is none other than Bradley's right-hand man, Rodney Wilson.

Rod Wilson grins, definitely not reading the room, as his deep brown eyes crinkle in the corners and he runs a hand through his unruly black waves of hair. He looks older than Colt, although I know from stats that they're only about a year apart in age. People like to say it's probably the shadow of a beard, something the clean-shaven Colt's never dared to attempt, or the fact that Rod became a (now single) dad at eighteen, at which point Colt probably still needed someone to strap up his shoulder pads for him. 'Won't you say hey, Coltie?'

The tension in Colt's body immediately leaves it as he cracks a smile. 'Hey.'

Our entire team watches in shock as the guys embrace so enthusiastically you could hear the back thumps from a field over. Jordan's jaw is literally on the floor. *Oh, my idol*, her eyes scream.

Once they've got over their reunion, Colt introduces Rod. 'This is Rodney Wilson, my pillar on and off the field. You've probably seen him in games, but I'm excited and pretty surprised you get to meet him in person . . . Bro, when did you even fly in?'

Rod smiles slyly. 'I planned it all out. Came in yesterday. That awful street lacrosse game just got done in Chicago, so I figured why not drop by and check out the scene. Connor and JJ came, too. Either way, figured it'd be a good time to watch you all play at home. Tali's here, with your mom. She's probably being a nuisance in office hours right now.'

No way. No *way* does Colt just get to hide behind his star teammate right now, ever so conveniently. I want to know why I just had to humiliate myself on the field so he could go on some ego trip. 'Great. It's nice to meet you, Rod.' I smile tightly. 'But back to the problem at hand. I'd love some explanation about why you just had me demonstrate a shot everyone here knew I wouldn't make?'

Rod's eyebrows fly upwards almost comically, and he takes a step back, hands raised in surrender. Colt shoots his friend a murderous look. Good. He deserves to muscle through a struggle alone, for a change.

'We will talk about it.' Colt's voice is low yet stern, and it's a far cry from the happy-go-lucky I've got tired of over the past few weeks. It's strained.

Then, in a tone so quiet that only I hear it, 'You're not playing by the plan, May, and it's gonna get us shot in the foot.'

'Maybe I'm not,' I mutter, 'but neither are you. Like you said. We *will* talk about it. For now, though. Why don't we . . .' I return my tone to a fairly normal volume. 'Why don't we make sure your friend enjoys his time in Oklahoma?'

# Chapter Nineteen

In the Doghouse

**Colt**

She's so onto me. And it doesn't occur to me what kind of implications my personal life might have on our public one, until that practice.

Rod, for his part, isn't experiencing any sort of stress. In fact, the second his ass hits the chair at the dining table in my parents' house, he starts yapping with them, and they, of course, have been immediately hooked in by his ever-so-social personality since the day they met, two years back. He's the kind of guy who, as far as I know, has never needed media training, and has the propensity to chat up a pile of dirt. It doesn't hurt that his daughter, Talise, is the sweetest angel of a pre-schooler that ever walked the earth, and is currently happily asleep in the guest room, something my mom mentions with delight more than once in between talk about what an 'easy' child Tali is.

'. . . and I was always so sure there was something brewing between the two of them,' my dad is going on and on; all of this shit about May and me in high school. 'And then Colt here chose Boston. That's what you call missing one train to catch another, if you ask me, because, you know, Boston was good. Boston brought us a lacrosse legend. But if we're talking about May, he got lucky, and here we are.'

'Mmm-hmm.' Rod nods. 'Though at least today, they weren't behaving much like a couple. I don't know if it's how the two of them get over lacrosse, but you could've cut the tension with a steak knife. Horrific.'

'Really?' Connor Dean, momma's boy of the Woodchucks, leans forward inquisitively, his big blue eyes the size of our dinner plates. 'That true, Colt? Trouble in paradise?'

I roll my eyes at Rod, the snitch. 'It wasn't *that* bad.'

'Oh?' Ma is unconvinced. 'Is that why May isn't here tonight? You know we invited May along with the guys, don't you?'

'I was pretty excited to meet your girlfriend,' JJ Kovacic – our team's child in a college grad's body – adds unhelpfully, all crestfallen. 'Not to mention future MLL player, I hope.'

'I know,' I grumble.

'No sass at the dinner table,' my sister cuts in. Sav crosses her eyes my way to punctuate her point.

'Savannah.'

'Colton James.'

'Dude, stop!'

'Sav, Colt, come on. We have *guests*.'

'How does it feel when your girlfriend bails?' smart-mouths Sav.

As if on cue, the doorbell rings, and as much as I don't want to face May right now, I *pray* it's her just so I can shut my sister up.

'I'll get it.' I scramble to my feet and, before anyone at the table (especially Rod and definitely Sav) can give me any shit, I rush over to the door to see who's there.

As I open it, relief and terror simultaneously flood my body. She's standing on the porch in fresh Wranglers and a tight long-sleeved grey Henley after my own heart, her hair braided over her shoulder, that same pair of brown boots embroidered with butterflies peeking out from the hems of her jeans, her favourite pair. She holds a big glass container covered in cling wrap, which she extends my way, totally deadpan. 'Dessert. We made tiramisu. If you're into that.'

'Thanks – um, thank you.' I step aside and usher her in, closing the door behind her. I try my best to slap an expression of upset onto my face. I mean, I should be pissed. We absolutely have to strike this dumb relationship balance unless we want to be found out, and that's not even accounting for the fact that May's anger at practice started prodding at some of the reasons for coming home that I haven't been so keen on sharing. Instead, I find myself leading May to the kitchen, where we're at least somewhat secluded from the hubbub of the dining room.

'We're not actin' much like a couple, are we? Going out there and starting arguments in front of the team?' May sets the tiramisu on the island and leans against the counter, crossing her arms. Guarded. 'But forget the relationship end of things for a moment, actually. We wouldn't even be worrying about that if you'd been a fair coach out there. I'm not asking for special treatment, Colt. I'm asking for *fair* coaching.'

'May, I . . .' I'm keeping my voice way more hush-hush than

she is. The May I know well, with the relentless affinity for red-card games, is starting to creep in. 'I swear, that wasn't my intention at all. I know last season wasn't the best, and it wasn't fair of me to—'

'To put me in a situation where I had to make the sort of shot I missed a million times over last year?' she finishes, eyes wide in disbelief. 'Really, Colt? It's not just about learning how to move. It's about learning how to *think*. You have to teach that. You can't expect me to just *know*. Does it make sense for me to say that?'

*It's about learning how to think.* I kind of wish she weren't right all the time.

'Trust me, I get that.' I train my eyes directly on hers. It's the only way I can find to steel myself for the confession I'm about to make. I've hurt her and hid enough from her, and if I keep doing it, I'll burn the last bridge I have with May Velasco for good. 'That's why—'

'Oh my word, May!'

I almost slump over the island in despair when Ma hustles into the kitchen with her flailing hands and hugs, and that's the end of that. 'Ma,' I groan, but it's lost to all the cooing and embracing going on at the island. My mother, quintessential lacrosse mom through all the ups and downs, has never missed a game since May and I started playing in elementary – and being a professor of what she is, she never missed a single boys' *or* girls' game. May got to know her pretty well as our rivalry turned to one-on-ones and pickup down in Eagle Rock, to staying late on the field at Prosperity High, to bets on milkshakes, to bets on dinner. And my mom, of course, *loved* May.

'It's so good to see you, Mrs Bradley.' May's voice is muffled, crushed by Ma's shoulder.

'May, I am *so* sorry.' Ma holds May at arm's length, a little frown on her face. 'Despite whatever our reckless son does, you're always more than welcome to come around, you know that. You'd also be more than welcome to take a GWAS class next semester' – at that, May lets out a laugh – 'if you weren't graduating, young lady.' My mom beams. 'I'm so proud of you, honey. And *so* glad Colt finally came to his senses.'

Ma's eyes scream, *FINALLY*. For everyone else, this fake relationship is about playing along with a lie, but for my parents, it's very much their dream come true. The breakup at the end of this is going to crush them. And me, to be frank, but I'm trying not to think about that.

With a happy, 'Let's go eat,' my mom sweeps us towards the dining hall, where Rod, Connor, JJ, and Pop are waiting with massive smiles, and Sav with a smirk.

'May!' the three of my teammates proclaim happily in various cadences. *Naturally*. I don't recall them giving me that kind of cutesy welcome.

'You made it!' Rod grins. 'Glad we get to properly meet.'

'So am I.' She sits down and shoots him a smile. 'The team's all huge fans. We're thankful you could drop by.'

'Likewise,' chirps JJ.

Sav looks evilly gleeful as she reaches for a piece of focaccia bread. 'May, I thought you *hated* Colt. Which, I don't blame you, but . . .'

I grit my teeth and clear my throat, glaring at Savannah. 'My sister doesn't mean that.'

'No, I did hate you!' points out May. 'We were rivals in every way.'

'Some weird head-to-head turf war between boys' and girls'

lacrosse at Prosperity,' Pop says with a nod to the guys. 'This place is a lax hotbed.'

'Interesting,' Connor hums. 'It's gotta be kind of nice, though. I've lived up on the East Coast all my life. I never thought a tiny town in Oklahoma would be so obsessed with lacrosse.'

'Don't get him started,' I warn. 'If you provoke Pop, he'll talk your head off about Prosperity lacrosse history.'

Pop raises his hands in disbelief, but Ma, Sav, and I just shoot him knowing looks. My dad is the original Division One yapper.

'Well, May.' Rod fully turns to face her. 'I know all about Colt's story. How'd you get into the sport?'

Her face immediately lights up, and I kick myself when I realize just how *shit* I've been doing at the fake boyfriend gig. How can Rod do that in a split second, and I haven't managed it yet at all?

'It's a strange story,' she begins, as a wistful laugh – one I'd probably give my heart and soul to hear for ever – leaves her lips. 'My mom wanted me to dance, same as her and her mom before. A very safe pastime. But my father was her polar opposite. He'd ridden bulls in his youth, stopped right before he got married. I was four when I started training for barrel racing. It was everything I wanted as a kid, but soon, I realized I wanted to feel the same thrill my horse got to feel when he ran round the course. I wanted a sport where I could run free and still get to cause a little chaos, and Prosperity was just starting to shape its youth lacrosse programme, feeding into the frenzy of the college leagues. You can guess the rest of it.'

'She was the captain of the high school lacrosse team. And even then, she's still been in the annual rodeo fifteen years running,' someone blurts. That someone, tragically, is me. The implication of my stupidity doesn't hit me until all the heads around the table, including May's, have turned my way. Am I fanboying? I'm fanboying.

Ma is the first one to croon, 'Oh, you two are just the sweetest.'

May's cheeks go pink, but there's a hint of gratitude in her eyes that I return when I grin. 'Almost makes me wish I hadn't moved up to New England so I could've seen every year she'd run in it.'

Not a single word out of my mouth is a lie, and I hope May knows it. I hope she knows I used to sit at every rodeo, listen to the announcer call her name over the booming speakers and join in the applause after she and her horse had done the cloverleaf perfectly – effortlessly – her braid thumping against her back, a tip of her hat as she finished the run.

At the end of the dinner, May's tiramisu sits completely cleaned out, the glass container empty on the table, and the two of us help clear dishes. At the sink, she hands me a plate, meets my eyes, and says, 'You wish you hadn't moved. But you moved anyway.'

A lump grows in my throat at the glancing hint of pain in her voice. It's the first time I've really heard it so quietly, tentatively. What my actions did to her.

I take the plate, and I turn off the water so I can make sure she hears what I tell her next. 'Yeah, I did. I got a lot of things out of that move. College, the Chucks, lacrosse, all that. But May, man, I lost you. And there's not a day that's gone by since I left that I haven't thought about that.'

This time, she has to hear me out. She's definitely not asleep. She definitely heard it all.

Gaze lowered, May brushes a wave of hair behind her ear, tucking it into her braid. I have to fight the urge to weave it back in myself. Then she looks up at me, and it's unnerving how vulnerable she seems. The familiar red-card chaos look is gone, replaced with big eyes, welling with tears. The only other time I've seen her like that was after her first concussion, way back in middle school. Manmayi Velasco never cried.

She says, voice so quiet it could be a whisper, 'It really, really hurt, Colt. It still hurts.'

## *Chapter Twenty*

Foul Play

**May**

I don't give away emotions easily, and I'm still not completely sure why I surrendered to Colt in the way I did.

Even at the end of the week, as we warm up on the field for the home match against Mayfair, my first one back from concussion watch, it feels like a source of shame when he looks at me from the sidelines with this new air of guilt. It's clear that if we keep going on like this – unable to meet one another's eye, awkward, decidedly loveless – Rod Wilson, who I can tell is already suspicious as he watches the warm-ups from the sideline, may just find out we're lying about our relationship, but that's a whole other can of worms.

Fortunately for Colt, my focus right now has to be on nothing but locking in for this game and keeping consistent for the sake of my tuition.

With every ball I whip into the net, that dumb sentence replays in my mind. *I got a lot of things out of that move, but I lost you.*

BAM.

*There's not a day that's gone by since I've left that I haven't thought about that.*

BAM.

'May!' Coach shouts, clapping her hands. 'Save some for the match!'

Oh, I'll have plenty left for the match.

We stand for the anthem as the Mayfair girls shoot daggers at us with their eyes, and we shoot daggers right back, tightening ponytails and goggles to show them we're all business. The Mayfair match was one of the only ones I had a decent performance at last year, and I plan on making sure that's the case again. Hailing from near Austin, Texas, Mayfair is a team of spoiled daddy's-money girls who've had quality gear and expensive energy drinks at every turn of the way. I find it never puts us at a disadvantage. If anything, it gives the Riders a competitive edge.

At the draw, I lock eyes with Marissa Raymond, Mayfair's captain, the backs of our sticks' heads against one another as the ref places the ball in between.

'Get ready to apologize to your little boyfriend,' she taunts through her mouthguard. 'He's gonna regret picking a Riders girl after this shitshow.'

'Oh, and you could do better?' I mumble. Shit talk, *chirping*, is a key component of lacrosse, men's and women's. We'd be nothing without it. It's the most we can manage without whacking one another and taking a severe penalty.

Marissa's a walking Barbie. Five foot nine, with a long blonde braid that has Mayfair navy ribbons woven into it, and big blue eyes that stare straight into your soul. Maybe she's used to guys chasing her around at Mayfair, but I'm not sure what she expects out of us here. She turns Colt's way, to where he's got his arms crossed, all coachlike in his quarter zip and whistle. And she blows him a *kiss*, complete with a dirt-eating grin.

'Trust me, honey,' she whispers conspiratorially. 'We're taking this match. And I'll be taking your boyfriend home, too.'

The ref blows the whistle.

I almost swipe her head off with my stick on the draw, because if she's here to play, I'm going to prove I'm no less. I don't know what surge of jealousy floods my body and I know Colt's not my boyfriend, but I don't care. There's no way this chick is winning.

Mayfair tries hard to keep their promise, but we push back – hard.

By half-time, the scoreboard reads 4–4, and the atmosphere is tense. The girls are in knots but, regardless, they're doing their best to hold the line. We block three attempts that get pretty close to scoring in the third quarter alone. Once the fourth quarter hits, we're getting desperate, and the vibe on the field reflects it.

All it takes for tensions to boil over is Brianna intercepting the ball on a Mayfair drive to the goal with fifteen seconds left and a tie score. Suddenly, the Mayfair girl she blocked drops her stick, yelling a strangled 'What the *hell?*' at Brianna, charging straight towards her.

In a matter of moments, Jordan, Maddie, and I are on the

scene, shoving ourselves between the two girls as the Mayfair girl comes in swinging. The ref tweets her whistle frantically, yelling, 'GIRLS! THAT'S IT! THAT'S A YELLOW!' and waving a yellow card about.

'Get ready to sleep alone tonight, Velasco!' Marissa shouts, flipping the bird my way as her team cackles and eggs her on.

My heart thunders in my chest, and I peer at Colt, who stands beside Coach by the bench.

*You're doing great*, he mouths. His eyes flick towards Marissa, and he shakes his head. *I got you.*

I count to three on the next exhale I make. I can hear Marissa laughing from all the way over on the other end. I tune her out. A lot isn't real between Colt and me, but what's always been real is the intuition we share about the sport, and the determination to get it done. He's one of the only people who's ever understood that, aside from Jordan.

I adjust my grip on my stick and retake my position in the midfield. It's tunnel vision on the goal. A draw will be shameful at this point. We need this to be a *win*.

'SEND IT, MAY!' Colt's voice yells from my right.

When the ball lands in the head of my stick, instinct takes over.

Mayfair is everywhere. One girl is all up in my face as the timer ticks down, and I dart aside, turning my back to the goal. Five seconds.

I chuck the ball around my right side when I turn, all prayers, locked in on the goal, giving it some extra whip with a spin back.

The *thwack* of the ball against the net has never sounded better.

Our growing crowd booms around us, all on their feet, as the screens flash RIDERS WIN in big orange digital letters. The girls on the bench swarm the field, circling our current players, pumping fists and shouting cheers. Out of the corner of my eye, as we break the huddle, laughter all around, I see my least favourite person of the afternoon, Marissa Raymond. I'm trying to keep my temper within its limits, telling myself maybe she's not all terrible off the field, but right now, this woman is *beelining* towards Colt, and in that instant, there's only one thought in my head, and it's that I am absolutely getting there first.

I run for my life towards the goal, where Colt is just making his way to the huddle, Coach not far behind. Marissa has intercepted him, telling him some shit with a dumb, conniving smile on her face, Colt regarding her with confusion. 'COLT!' I shout, and the idiot looks my way, his daze breaking into the broadest, biggest smile.

'Way to get 'em, May!' he calls back.

Marissa touches his arm, bats her eyelashes, doing everything to bring his attention back to her. I've been trying real hard to give her the benefit of the doubt. This show isn't helping.

Colt, bless him, doesn't buy it. He fully turns and jogs towards me, arms outstretched. 'You were phenomen—'

I literally crash right into his arms, full force, and it's a miracle he's still on his feet, but he apparently finds all this amusing, because he bursts out laughing. '*What?*'

'She's been chirpin' at me all game,' I say by way of explanation.

He snorts. 'I saw that much.'

'I appreciate you,' I tell him.

'Is that a lie?'

'That is not a lie, Colt.'

He grins, but as he scans the crowd, his eyebrows furrow. Someone at the lower level of bleachers yells, 'KISS HER, BRO!', sending the Riders girls into a frenzy of giggles.

Colt's cheeks go pink, and he coughs awkwardly. 'Well. The moment we've been waiting for. Does this violate play number two? Minimal PDA? What's minimal?'

I steel myself as I train my attention on him, on things I usually will myself not to notice. The sparkle of his eyes; the way his hair tickles my fingers, interlaced behind his neck, arms draped across his shoulders; the little scar in his eyebrow that I know is from a crosse to the face when we were younger; his nervous dimples and his perfect jawline. 'I think we can consider this minimal.'

Nearly every muscle in my body tenses at the thought, but hey, this is what we signed up for, right? It's true; celebratory kisses just clear the bar. We owe the audience one if we want them to keep showing up – and keep driving sponsors to Prosperity's lacrosse programme. And maybe, just maybe, bring us a scout or two.

I put on a smile. It's too easy. It should be a struggle, right? Why is it easy?

Behind us, I catch sight of Marissa and her team whispering, all hush-hush, with nasty looks our way.

Colt's fingers gently tip my chin back towards him, and his voice is quiet enough that only I can hear when he says, 'She's not even an option next to you, Manmayi Velasco.'

My heart flutters against my chest, butterflies scrambling to escape my rib cage, and when our lips meet, the butterflies go absolutely feral. His words are like honey, sweet, all-consuming. When I close my eyes, I relish every single one of them. This is business, I know, but as easy as the smile was, this is easier. It's so easy for me to fall into his affection, even all these years on. As his thumbs stroke my jaw, his strong hands moving to cup my cheeks, I can't figure out whether that ease of falling is a good thing, or a terrible thing.

The crowds scream around us, but the only thing I can hear is the blood rushing behind my ears as we pull apart, and a corner of Colt's mouth tips up in a little smirk. 'Not bad for no rehearsal.'

The thudding of my heart is still uncontrollable. Adrenaline, certainly. We've just won a game. Of course, that's what it is. This is definitely not a teenage fantasy come true. I'm not losing it right now.

'Not bad,' I repeat.

Well. Not bad, and then some, but you won't catch me admitting that to him.

## Chapter Twenty-One

No Signal

**May**

'You know, I can't get a read on you.'
'Huh?'
I regard Colt's look of confusion with a raised eyebrow as I kick my sneakered feet up on the bleachers in front of us. The entire field's empty now, the crowd all gone home, and the only indication that they'd ever been here is all the ravaged shooters and beer cans lying in the stands, where we're sitting now. 'I mean, come on. First, you leave me in the dust in high school. Then, you throw all these things about "regretting it" every which way. And *then* you put me in what you *know* is the most uncomfortable possible position in practice. And then, *finally*, you kiss me in front of the entire university.'

Colt grabs his backpack, fiddles with the whistle still around his neck. 'I won't lie to you, May, this game plan thing hasn't been the easiest for me. It's . . . yeah, we have a history, and that hasn't helped it.'

'I'm afraid it's been more confusing than anything else.' I clear my throat, running a hand through my now-loose hair. I have to pause before carefully choosing my next words. 'I just want to know, Colt. You'll make it through the rest of the semester, right? Because—'

'Yeah. Yeah, I will, I swear.' I watch a light go out in those deep eyes of his the second the curt words are out of my mouth.

Colt shoots me a tight smile. 'See you tomorrow, May. Good shit today.'

My heart plummets a little at the sight of him leaving the field. It reminds me too much of that memory in the hallway, the last time I saw him. But now, I'm not asking myself why he's leaving any more. I'm asking myself why he's back – and why, this time, I'm driving him away.

'Good shit,' echoes Rod's voice. My head snaps right to the source of his rich baritone, and there's Colt's right-hand man, a couple stair-steps below me on the field, leaning against the bleachers. 'You guys gave it a pretty solid shot. I might have bought it if the both of you weren't so emotional in love.'

'Weren't so . . . um, bought *what*?' I manage to stutter out. I barely know this guy. He's also the last person I expected to start saying shit like 'emotional in love'.

'You don't have to keep playing dumb.' He smiles wryly with a shrug. 'It's *so* obvious you two aren't actually in a relationship.'

My jaw nearly falls straight to the floor of the bleachers. He's been here for less than a week. There's no way.

Concern enters Rod's eyes, and he bounds up the stairs of the bleachers, gesturing to the empty spot beside me. I nod, and he awkwardly takes a seat. 'Okay, so you're clearly falling to pieces right now. May, let me clarify, I'm not going to tell *anyone*. I've been close to Colt for years, and even though I definitely – obviously – haven't known the guy as long as you, I'm not out to ruin your lives, that I promise.'

I met the man days ago. I'm not sure what reason I have to take anything he says as gospel, but there's something about his presence, something genuinely warm and compassionate, that makes me think he'll absolutely stick to his word.

'I think I know enough to put the parts of the story together. I'm not here to do that, though,' he says quickly. 'I'm here 'cause clearly, part of the reason I saw right through you guys was because I know when Colt's bullshitting. And he's *definitely* bullshitting with you.'

'Excuse me?'

'Alright. I'm doing a terrible job at this.' He turns to face me. 'May, do you know why he's here? Like, why he's really here?'

I snort, finding a spot of dirt on my kilt to focus on. 'That thing all the pros do. Probably to keep himself relevant while he's injured, right? So he can get the clout he needs from "back home"?'

Rod's next smile is a little sadder than his typical. 'May . . . I've been debating telling you, but honestly, I want to keep this real. Because I think Colt hasn't, and I think I know why. Has he ever, I don't know, come up with stupid ways to avoid the stick? To try not to—'

'Oh, to try not to *lacrosse*? Yeah, making me bin that dumb shot,' I cut in with a little huff. 'I get the knee injury. But come on. Not being able to touch a ball and stick is a little much. What about it?'

'After Colt dislocated his knee last season,' starts Rod, 'he met a couple of complications that honestly weren't expected to happen at all. We were all ready for a smooth recovery, to have our captain back, but instead Colt got a shitshow, in the form of inflammation so bad it was still fuckin' braced up at Christmas time.'

I wince with an involuntary twinge of sympathy. The understanding that only another lacrosse player can have about how much injury *sucks*.

'But since then, at least physically, he's turned over back to ninety per cent. Well on the way to a hundred. He really should be out there playing next season, captaining the Chucks to our title. Didn't get it last year, unfortunately. Losing sucked, but we were hopeful we'd get it next time, Colt at the helm, except now . . .' Rod shakes his head. 'I can still hear the way the guy was screaming on the ground, calling for his mom. May . . . when he gets so much as near the stick, it's so weird. It's like he doesn't know how to play any more. Something snapped when he got hurt back in October, and no one knows how to fix it. Not even team-mandated therapy. So when he realized it was *really* bad, he decided he was going back to Oklahoma. Not for clout, not to keep his reputation up. He came back here to hide.'

I've never known Colt to be a hider. I know I'm one. I tuck myself away in a corner of campus – i.e. the Meteorology building study pods – after a terrible exam and sob. Colt took every hit when we were kids, and he took them standing. I never saw him falter. But this Colt is, at least according to Rod, scared. That revelation dumps rocks into the pit of my stomach by the wheelbarrow. The guilt is so heavy, I don't know what to say.

'Right now, this is between me, Colt, and the PT and therapy teams. And now you. He doesn't know if he's gonna come back for the next season. Hell, he doesn't know what he's gonna do if the team finds out he's completely recovered. Especially the bosses. I mean, he doesn't know if he's going to play ever again.' Rod lets out a nervous laugh, leaning forward to prop his elbows on his knees. 'It has me scared as shit. We're all pretty young. To have your career end like that is one thing, but to have your mental health – your state of mind – so fucked up that you don't know how to play a sport you've been training in since you could walk . . .'

God.

That was part of why I fell so hard for Colt. He was indefatigable. He was a wall that ploughed through whoever he needed to knock down to make goals. And yet, he always had so much heart. The dumbass had jokes and shit-eating grins alongside the kinds of plays that made college scouts dizzy. He made for a fantastic rival. He made for a fantastic friend.

'Thanks.' My voice shakes when I try to force a grateful smile with Rod. 'For telling me. I . . . I had no idea that's why he was here.'

Rod snorts. 'He's good at hiding things. He gives you the infuriating cowboy pearly-whites—'

'Oh, he *does*,' I agree with a chuckle. 'Like he's trying to flush all the doubt out of your mind, right?'

'It's like being brainwashed!'

Rod and I share a moment of laughter. Colt. What a sweet, clueless, ignorant idiot.

'Guess I have to make amends,' I say once the laughter has subsided.

'Don't let yourself think that.' Rod stops me. 'He did you dirty, May. No one deserves to be left alone with their feelings like that. He's the one who up and left, at the end of the day. I may not know exactly what upset you, but I'll tell you that you have every right to be. People who leave . . .' There's a glassiness in his eyes that tells me he knows a little too well what it's like. 'They shape the rest of our lives, whether we like it or not, and we *absolutely* have the right to put that on them. But we can lessen that impact by looking at what we have now. And what you have now might just be a second chance.'

'After . . .'

*After everything he did to me?* I'm about to say. But it doesn't have the same punch now that I realize he's paying in a different way. His homecoming isn't one of celebration. It's a self-imposed exile. He's helpless here. Powerless.

'Is there anything else I don't know?' I ask instead.

Rod looks up in thought. 'Well – he *totally* doesn't want you to know this, but there's one thing.' He pulls his phone from his jeans pocket and does a little bit of frantic tapping, scrolling, some zooming, as he talks. 'I guess he's dated a few women up in New England, that I know of, but nothing really seemed to last. I'd ask him how it went, and honestly, it wasn't even like he was being a dick, or anything. He just sounded pretty guilty. Ashamed. And I think . . .' He turns the phone my way. 'This might have something to do with it.'

Oh. My.

It's a photo of Colt by his Woodchucks locker, painted this ridiculous blue and full of what's no doubt smelly lacrosse gear. Beside him and his cowboy pearly-whites, though, is a picture taped to the inside of the open door.

My University of Oklahoma City media day photo from freshman year, complete with my name in neon cursive, in case anyone was in doubt of who the woman in his locker was.

MAY VELASCO. #13.

## Chapter Twenty-Two

In for a Penny

**Colt**

I haven't left Prosperity since getting into town, a fact I realize as we drive past the endless fields and farmland that blanket the outskirts of the city. It's a nice break from the chaos of last weekend, an away game in Atlanta. The silence is exactly what I've needed. Okie students always joke that they're the outermost layer of Oklahoma City, but they're wrong – *this* is the outermost layer. Maybe a farmhouse every half mile or so, if you're lucky; the rest of it is for grazing or crop.

We whip past the sign: EAGLE ROCK, POP. 562. With the sun beginning to go down post-Monday practice, the sky is lit up in dusky oranges and pinks in the background. It's fucking unreal. I remember coming down here to play pickup, guys versus girls. A couple of them had grown up with traditional

Choctaw stickball and then moved into lacrosse, and they were lethal. Loss was imminent.

'Wow.'

May turns into the little intersection that takes you towards Main Street. When we hit the tiny strip, it's just as I remember. The church is on one side, the bakery and grocer on the other, and away in the distance are the feed and tractor supply stores, all bracketed by endless clear skies, burning with sunset. God. I'd forgotten what these parts of Oklahoma looked like after years in Boston, and I hate myself for it right away.

May rolls a window down and extends her hand out into the open space, wiggling her fingers against the wind. Her curls dance about in total and utter freedom. Her face, for the first time since I've seen her again after all these years, is truly at peace, her eyes fluttering blissfully. Disturbing her feels like a sin.

We pass the corner café and bar – a true hole-in-the-wall spot – before driving another three or so minutes out to the red-awninged feed shop. A left takes us down a rocky dirt road that rattles the truck, smoothing out when we hit the hand-painted sign that tells us we've reached the Veracruz Ranch.

The lowing of multiple cattle greets us through May's open window when she pulls the truck up the narrow driveway and parks it. May's Birkenstock sandals smack the asphalt, and she yawns with a stretch. 'Might need a nap after this, but hey, best get it over with.'

I remove my cap, unfortunately allowing the setting sun to beat down on the top of my head. By Boston standards, it's way too early in the year for it to be hot like this. 'Is this us finally making good on your mom's dinner invitation? Why are we here, exactly?'

'We're more making good on my dad's invitation. They're out for the market, so . . .' May scratches her shoulder, squinting at the sun and towards her house. 'Maybe not so much the dinner as the "back to where it all started".'

'Back to where what started?'

'Us.'

If it weren't for the way she fidgets nervously, toeing the dirt driveway as she inspects my face for a response, I would have thought the word was easy as pie for her to let slip: 'us'. The thought entertains my delusions, the fact that maybe she feels just a *fraction* of what I do. That would be enough hope. Because I've had girlfriends, but I've never, ever known a girl like her.

'And sure, my parents aren't home,' she says to me, 'but some of the ranch hands are. We have a bit of a walk.' Under her breath, she mumbles, 'Take my hand.'

I freeze in my tracks at the notion. Take her hand? She'd probably take off my *head* if I so much as tried. But she takes a step forward, glowering back at me with an insistent raise of her eyebrows. We've already had to kiss in public, right? What could this hurt?

I reach out, and gingerly, my palm meets hers, our fingers effortlessly weaving their way around one another. The hesitation I feel at first touch becomes more comfortable as we walk, side by side, around her house and down the dirt path towards the ranch. Hand in hand.

'No *way* you guys kept this.'

'Well, where do you think the Eagle Rock kids play pickup on the weekends?'

'Good point.'

My sneakers stir up dust as we approach the half-size lacrosse field mowed into the back of the ranch. A fixture of Eagle Rock itself, ever since the Velascos decided the local lax and stickball kids needed somewhere closer to home to practise, the field is quite literally the lacrosse analogue of *Field of Dreams*, except – instead of mid-cornfield – it's just fences that divide us from the cows. You can hear the cattle even more clearly here. The sound brings me right back. Way, way back.

'I was ready to call you a liar when you first told me you had a lacrosse field in your backyard, back in, what? Elementary?' I remark with a laugh.

We cross onto the short-grass field, with its dull white markings, and May smiles wryly. 'For once, I can't blame you. This is the most ridiculous small-town shit ever. I told Papa it would be weird. He did it anyway.'

'Do you still think it's weird?'

'Not a bit.' May jabs a thumb back towards the house. 'I'm gonna grab some sticks and balls.'

'Sticks?' I stop in my tracks where I'm walking around the goal, one foot in the crease.

'Uh. Yeah.' She raises a sceptical eyebrow. 'We're on a lacrosse field. It's not a school trip. We're not just here to grab concessions, take photos, and hit the road.'

Without any further explanation, she heads off to the garage, leaving me outside with just the field, *so* many questions, and a singular memory.

May came around the ranch house from where they kept the horses. She had on worn jeans and a pink equestrian jacket. Stomping over wearing the chunkiest boots, she eyed all five of us, myself and four friends from Prosperity and Eagle Rock, with exasperation. Even at ten years old, she had an attitude like a barbed whip, an attitude that I felt the full force of when her analytical gaze fell on me, and the corner of her mouth twitched sassily.

I shifted my stick from hand to hand. 'We were gonna play, if you are.'

May's brow furrowed. She tightened her ponytail, which, back then, had been a big poof of curls that she hadn't yet managed to tame, and grabbed her matching hot pink lacrosse stick from where it leaned against the fence. An insistent snap of her fingers in Michael's direction got her the ball. She tossed it up in the air and caught it and, in her boots, marched towards the face-off circle her parents had drawn in the field.

'I'll play.' She pointed to the spot across from her. 'Draw, Colt.'

I was doubtful. May was a whole foot shorter than me, and definitely more than a couple pounds lighter. I thought I'd tip her over, but what I didn't realize at the time was that May Velasco didn't just have the uncanny ability to lead a team. She had the ability to lead herself, and that allowed her to push the limits of what everyone else thought was possible. Including me, I learned when she planted her booted feet across from my sneakered ones, met my eyes, and propped the back of her stick's head against mine. That was the first time I ever played her in lacrosse, and it certainly wouldn't be the last.

'Colt!'

May's voice, from the centre of the field, snaps my wandering mind to attention. She waves my way. 'Well? Right into it!'

This is a different time. I don't know why she's trying to start a one-on-one, I don't know what she thinks I'll do, but we're not young any more; and for my part, I can barely figure out how to cradle the ball. I jog towards her, and when my fingers close around the stick she holds out to me, it's a grip of uncertainty. Embarrassment. I try my best to mirror her draw position, but the second I get low, bend my knees, my injury flashes before my eyes, the pain scorching my entire leg. I feel the scratch of the grass against my arms, the sting in my throat when I hold back tears, even as I yell in agony.

'Colt!' May calls again. I think she's going to whack me upside the head with her stick for a moment, but instead, she lowers it. She removes a hand from her stick, then the other, letting it fall to the ground next to her. And she does something that makes me forget all about the pain.

She presses her hands to either side of my head, her thumbs at my temples, and she looks me dead on. 'I will not hurt you, Colt. I promise. There is *no* stake in this game. You are not being held to anything.'

I blink. She doesn't budge. Her face is so close to mine that I can feel her breath caress my cheeks when she exhales shakily. 'I just . . . I just want to play a round with you again. Just once. Semi-properly. I fucking missed you, idiot.'

I swallow hard. The air between us is electric, silent but for the sound of the cows and her last sentence hanging in the air. I would find the mooing comedic in any situation but this one.

'Missed you, too,' I manage.

She nods, and the moment is over, just like that. She turns away, re-arming herself with her stick. 'Go for it. Let's do a face-off. You know that better than the draw.'

May readies herself close to the ground, bottom of the

head of her stick touching the grass, right by the ball. With unsteady arms, I do the same on my side. 'How . . . how did you—'

'Rod told me.' She smiles apologetically. 'He didn't need a second glance to figure out we were lying about the fake dating crap, apparently. But that's not your biggest problem.' Her smile falls right off, giving way to a new emotion – a very new emotion, one I've never seen in May, at least: sadness. 'Is it?'

I cleverly duck her question, and instead try my best not to focus on all the things Rod could have told her about me, pressing my stick's head closer to the ball. 'In for a penny, I guess.'

'Alright.' May clears her throat. 'On three. One, two, three!'

On three, we push our sticks against one another's, battling it out for possession, but even with May's sobering moment of emotion, it doesn't help what Dr Mendoza called my 'yips'. I keep pushing, but I'm not sure exactly what I'm doing. My arms go numb, and suddenly, I'm not pushing any more. I pull my stick back, and May immediately takes the opening. She snatches the ball up easily, starting a play for the goal, but her beeline slows right away as she looks over her shoulder.

I've come to hate the look. The pity, the moment when people figure out that a guy who could have been an MLL champion can't even push his stick in the right direction now. It's easy to blame it on an injury. They get that. When something physically hurts you, it gives them something to look at. Maybe that's why I don't want to call it what it is. Because when they don't have something to look at, it becomes an excuse.

'Oh,' May finally says, but it's not pity on her face. It's a certain type of pain.

The kind someone only reveals to you when they've been exactly where you were before.

May's junior season. Lifeless games. Dead passes. Goals that most youth players could have made.

'This isn't new to you,' I exhale, letting my stick hang carelessly in my hands. 'Your junior year.'

She purses her lips. 'Guess not. Wasn't just my junior year. My life crept into my game plenty of times. When you left. And then when . . .' With a twirl of her stick, May gazes up at the clouds, and then back at me. 'Anyway. To answer your question, no. This isn't new to me.'

'How the *hell* did you come back from it?'

'I don't know exactly how.' She shrugs, and she does that little combination of things again, the purse of her lips, the look up, a blink or two. Holding back her emotions. 'I found the right reasons to move on, I think.'

## Chapter Twenty-Three

Personable Guy

**May**

It was the June after my junior year at Prosperity High. Hot, dry, and heavy with nerves. First game of summer league. I picked up my stick just like I did before any match, but this time, something was glaringly different.

I couldn't stop seeing him across from me, him with his crosse, me with mine, opposite sides of the field, just like it had always been. Opposite sides of the country.

Emotions were supposed to be easy for me. I got my dad's stoic nature, rather than my mom's out-loud empathy. I had never struggled this way before.

'MAY!' I heard Jordan's voice yell, and suddenly, the ball was coming my way. A crucial pass – and I flinched, my stick flailing instead of preparing for the shot. The ball whipped right past me. I watched the entire thing go down in slow motion, down to the moment that ball landed square in the net of an opponent's crosse, and that was that.

That match was the first time I'd ever had to be benched. Understandably, after a few of these incidents in the fourth quarter, the coach had had it up to here. 'I think you ought to take a break,' she said with a sigh, subbing me out for Teresa Ingold.

The silence in the locker room afterwards was deafening. I felt so deeply ashamed of myself. How could I let a man come between me and my game? He had allowed me to let my team down.

My hatred for him doubled in size and, as for my heart, it shrivelled up. I had no room left to cosy up with my sympathy for CJ Bradley.

I don't think I ever truly came back from it. The way you feel when you realize your entire team is watching you, witnesses the very moment when you send all their work to shit because your personal life gets into your head. It really, really sucks. Which, maybe, is why I can't bring myself to feel like Colt deserves any of what's been coming his way. I guess I know just how horrible it is to stand there and forget everything you thought you knew so well.

The most I can ever do about it is to practise. To make sure, like Papa says, that your house is stronger the next time the storm comes. Which is why showing up to practise Thursday, with a home game coming up Saturday, only to hit brutal traffic, puts me in an awful mood.

'What the hell?' I groan as my truck inches forward in the

lane. The traffic light for the field is literally *right* up ahead. Almost there. Please stay green.

It does. I make the turn into the Chester complex . . .

'No *way*.'

The entire parking lot is full, rivalling game days out here. Every spot is taken, and I have to circle the place like a vulture until I find one parking space so far out I'll have time to listen to half a podcast on my walk to the field. I completely forgot this was today. And unfortunately, so did everyone else.

They're gathered at the far equipment shed, well outside of Chester, where we keep the golf carts. Even Coach is there, jaw slack in shock. 'May!' she yelps. 'This was today?'

'I had no freakin' idea.' I stare down the chaos happening inside Chester, visible through the chainlink fences. The grass, our field, is completely full of adults and kids and families all together, and the thud of the bass shakes the ground all the way out to where we are. The whistle of water guns is loud in the air as coloured water and powder fly above the fences.

'What's today?' asks Colt, squinting at the field.

'Uh. Some context.' Coach clears her throat awkwardly. 'We are *kind* of stretched thin for money here. As you know. So we rent the field out.'

'You do *what?*' Colt's right eye twitches in confusion. 'For who?'

'May's mother has some contacts.' Our coach winces as a bomb full of colourful powder explodes above the field. 'In the South Asian Association of Oklahoma. Their Holi celebration is today. Which we did not realize. At all.'

'Wait, wait. So what's going on with practice, then?' Maddie holds out a hand. 'Is there another field we can use right now?'

'I'm afraid not.' Coach looks like she's literally sweating bullets as the entire team glares nervously. 'I know your game is Thursday, girls, but the soccer field is taken, and you know sure as hell we won't be able to get into Benson.' She's unfortunately right. Athletics would never let women's lacrosse onto the precious football field just to run a practice. 'Why don't we go see what time it ends? Maybe we can postpone? Or ask if they could wrap up early?'

'Coach.' I shake my head sadly. 'They're Desi. They probably got here two hours late. There's no way they'll leave a minute early.'

'Well, negotiation is our only bet!' Jordan calls, already jogging towards the field with waving arms beckoning the rest of us. 'Worst case, we party!'

'That's easy to say,' I grumble. 'We have a match Saturday.'

'I mean, it's not all bad.' Colt perks up. Holy golden retriever. He's bright-eyed, gazing at the celebration going on right across from us. 'This could be fun, right?'

'We're going to get eaten alive by aunties.' I used to go to this thing with my parents every year (who, more likely than not, are already inside, getting sloshed and fighting kids for their water guns). Unfortunately, I stopped around the time I turned fifteen. It sucks to step away from that side of my culture for such a stupid reason, but I cannot stand the community judging every breath you take and every choice you make. My mom had much the same to say about the story when she married my father. It took her, quite literally, over a decade to finally re-immerse herself into South Asian culture.

By the time we reach the door to the fence and sneak in, the music is so loud my eardrums might just burst into about a million pieces. Someone's water gun fires, and I wince as the droplets fly.

'It's fun!' Brianna chirps happily, moving her shoulders to the beat of the invasively booming Bollywood song playing in the background. Ever so eager to make conversation no matter where we put her, Brianna taps a nearby girl's shoulder. 'Hey! Do you know what time this thing ends?'

The girl just shrugs and laughs. And then proceeds to throw a fistful of pink powder straight at a shocked Brianna.

Our cheerful midfielder spits out bits of pink with a strangled, 'Oh, okay!' Then, to me, 'May? Is this normal?'

'Yes.' I can't help but laugh. 'Holi is the festival of colours. The whole thing is that you throw these coloured paints and water at each other. Or—'

I don't get to finish. An arc of bright blue soaks my entire left arm. My mouth slowly falls open as I turn to absolutely storm down the offender. 'Water cannons,' I mutter through gritted teeth, getting ready to hit the warpath, Smurf-blue and all.

Colt stands a couple of paces away with a group of young boys, all of whom are exchanging smirks and giggling. A big grin spreads across his face as he holds out a cannon happily. 'Retaliate!' he shouts. 'It's fun!'

I absolutely refuse. I won't be retaliating anytime soon, considering I'm already turning into a blueberry from the left side. But the urge to get Colt back for this attack is stronger.

Jordan is already at my side with an entire bag of purple colouring. 'Get 'em,' she jeers, grabbing a fistful herself.

I reach in, take as much powder as I can hold, and make a run for it. Colt's eyes widen, and he reacts far too late. By the time he's dodging, I'm already throwing the entire mass of purple right at him. The cloud of it erupts every which way, and once it dissipates, he's standing there with purple all over his hoodie and face, his cannon at the ready.

This time, when he fires it, it's straight on. Nearly every part of me that's facing him is dyed blue in less than a second, and those damn kids he's got to do his bidding take their shot at the same time, spraying me with red and pink and orange while I struggle to run from these ridiculously fast boys, dodging disappointed aunties and drunk uncles.

'An *army?*' I gasp through coloured water. 'Of *children?* How, Colt?'

'I'm a personable guy,' he chuckles as he jogs towards me, but when he pumps the cannon, a sad little spray comes out. 'Aw, come on! Dude, Rahul! Hit me!'

Rahul – one of the members of Colt's newfound army, a little Desi kid who can't be more than twelve – chucks his gun Colt's way. Colt snatches it, basically spamming the trigger, only for a weak spurt of green water to come out.

'Nice going, Captain Personable.' I grab some more purple from the bag of some passing aunty, and I don't hesitate to smear it all across Colt's cheek, completely unaware of how close we're suddenly standing to each other until my hand comes away from his clean-shaven jaw. 'And for the record, happy Holi.'

A smile spreads across his face, as spattered with colour as it is. He spins the little water gun on his index finger. 'Happy it definitely is.'

I roll my eyes. He's so damn tacky. Except he uses my moment of ignorance as an opportunity to steal some colour, because I feel the sprinkling of powder on my forehead, and my gaze snaps right to him. With a laugh, he opens his hand, revealing a massive mound of red powder. 'I'm not gonna throw it. That'd be cheating.'

'You don't need to be chivalrous.' Or does he? There's something sweet about it: the patient look on his face, laced with longing. 'Looks like anything goes here.' I gesture to the full-out colour war going on around us.

Colt, even so, flicks his gaze to the rest of the red in his hand. 'May I?'

Oh, honey. You're a couple. Yeah, of course he may. For the narrative, I remind myself when I nod yes.

His fingers brush my cheek, leaving behind a trail of coloured powder, and my eyes find his light-hearted smile. It takes some effort to remind myself that this is for everyone else's benefit.

'Happy Holi, May,' he whispers, stormy eyes glimmering. His touch traces tracks of red down the side of my neck before dropping off. Goosebumps spread all over my body at just that much. No matter how many times I force my mind to put the brakes on, instinct just has to have its way. Maybe all signs are trying to tell me something, but I can't afford to read them.

I turn my attention to something I can actually control instead.

'You're easy to distract.'

Palming Colt's tiny water gun, I trigger it straight at his chest, the barrel pressed right against him, and he looks down in alarm, and then amusement, as the green spreads across the fabric of his beige hoodie.

'That's *actually* cheating,' he practically chokes out, clutching his heart all dramatically.

I raise an eyebrow. 'Funny of you to say.'

'Sure. But considering you're the one distracting me, I think it's fair.'

My pulse pounds double time when his eyes trace their way across my body reverently, even though I'm a hot mess covered with every colour of the rainbow. My wet T-shirt clings to my body, my running shorts the only water-resistant article I have been fortunate enough to wear.

'Colt!' shrieks little Rahul from a couple of paces away. I'm instantly thankful for the kid's presence, ending my contemplation. 'Come here! We're going to get Aryan's mom next!'

'Aryan's mom is next,' Colt says to me, ever so seriously, like this is a mission of utmost importance. He slides his gun from my hand, his palm just brushing mine. 'Don't think we're not coming back for you.'

He runs off with a clutch of at least eight kids, fitting for the man who, at least in my eyes, never bothered to grow up. Something about this is different, though. Endearing. I can't ignore it for ever. The thoughts war in my head until he disappears in the crowd of dancing and yelling people covered in colours, and all that's left for me to think about is the feeling of his fingers on my cheek.

## Chapter Twenty-Four

Red Card

**May**

It's a full house at Chester yet again, this time versus Austin, and it's something we've got more and more used to seeing at our games. That and the massive cameras and broadcasting teams that are here to televise this game.

We're also collecting new fans with every game, new Riders loyalists flooding in from across the state as 'Lacrosse Power Couple' goes viral. The bleachers are starting to fill to the tops, brimming like the carbonation threatening to spill over the side of a full glass of soda.

I snap on my goggles. Beside me, Jordan grabs her stick, taps it against mine with a grin. 'Ride on, cowgirl. Let's bring this one home.'

'Let's.' I return her grin, but it's wiped right off my face when

I see Colt heading my way. I can't let him distract me now. Especially not after the moment we shared on the backyard field, and definitely not after the feelings that suddenly overwhelmed me at Holi.

'May, I never got a chance to give you a proper thanks,' are the first words out of his mouth. I'm not sure what the appropriate reply would be. I let him continue. 'Those kids from Holi asked me to play a round, you know. They're probably gonna whoop my ass, but I still want to thank you. For just getting me out on the field that other day. I guess I could say it felt like a first step.'

'You don't owe me,' I tell him, pulling my roll of medical tape from my bag. I focus on picking at the torn end where it sticks to the rest of the roll. 'What happened to you was terrible. I'm not leaving you out to dry after that.'

'For the record, May . . .' He sits down beside me on the bleachers. Jordan raises an eyebrow my way, but doesn't say anything. That girl. We're going to have a chat about this later over margaritas, I'm sure, but I mentally thank her for staying quiet. 'I'm sorry it happened to you.'

I've had ups and downs in this sport. Twice I have suffered momentarily coming off my game. But I've never had to bench myself because I completely forgot how to play. I always bounced back. I had good people around me, a sounding board when I needed one, and other times, a cushion to fall back on.

I watch Colt, and something twists in my gut when I think about the fact that now he picks up a stick and doesn't know what to do with it. This is the same kid who picked up a stick for the first time and *immediately* knew what to do with it. As athletes under stress all the damn time, crashes in our mental health are nothing if not common, and what Colt is facing is the worst kind of crash.

I keep picking at the stupid tape. The end doesn't lift. Colt, for his part, holds out an open palm, expectant gaze meeting mine from beneath long lashes. He brushes a wave of hair back, and the muscles in his forearm do that flex thing that I hate to admit is unfairly attractive. 'May I?'

His dumb forearm muscles have all my attention. I surrender the pink tape to him, and he unrolls it easily. Nice one, May. I stick my hand out. 'It's the wrist.'

Colt makes an affirmative humming sound, and his head dips in concentration, that same piece of hair falling over his forehead as he carefully wraps my joint, his fingers brushing the sensitive skin of my inner wrist, the pad of his index finger smoothing the end that he tears off, tucking it in neatly. 'That good?'

Is that good? *Is* that good?

'Sure,' I say.

*May. You diabolical liar.*

'Get out there.' He pats my hand; a tame little gesture, but I accept it.

Maybe it's the closeness of the moment we just shared, or maybe it's the entire front row of bleachers craning their necks to watch us. Or maybe it's both. Either way, Colt catches on quickly. He leans down and brushes a gentle kiss across my cheek. The tiny wink that follows sends my pulse thudding away so hard I hope he can't feel it in my fingers. 'Grab a red card or two, while you're at it.'

'Why in the hell do you want my red cards?' I resist the urge to cross my eyes at him like a little kid.

'You look awfully pretty when you get pissed. Even prettier when you start to blow your top when the ref goes for the card.'

'Stop playing.' I snort, but that word fills a small part of the gap he left in my heart. *Pretty.* As if on instinct, I give his hand a squeeze. This little ritual – beginning of a ritual? Fake ritual? Whatever it is, it feels so simple. The warmth that spreads across my chest when I think of having someone sitting at the bleachers, a kiss before games, a celebration together after, someone to do your medical tape for you, is unexpected. It creeps up to my face when I realize that the only someone I can picture, at least at the moment, is Colt.

*Miss May. The only reason you're only picturing him is because no one else has ever done that for you.*

But doesn't that mean something? Even if we're lying to the rest of the world? Does it mean something to us?

I watch Colt's retreating back, and Jordan seizes the moment to scooch right on up next to me, batting her eyes dramatically. 'Colt and May, sitting in a tree, K-I-S-S-I—'

'Are you five, Jordan?' I prod her in the side, rolling my eyes, but she just giggles in response.

'Fuckin' rain,' we hear Lexi grumble a couple benches down as she starts heading onto the field. Great. We can't have a proper game if Lexi's upset.

'See? Bigger fish to fry. Someone needs to turn that girl's frown upside down so we win this,' I point out smugly.

'I mean, she's justified.' Jordan tips her head upward, the space between her eyebrows wrinkling with worry. 'Looks like it'll come down any moment.'

For a Meteorology major, I tend to lean optimistic with my weather predictions. I'm not exactly looking to go into forecasting;

my intended area of specialty is a bit narrower. Unfortunately, the current cloud patterns fall under that umbrella.

'Great.' I head for the field, anyway. 'Twenty bucks says we don't finish this game out, Jor.'

'You're probably gettin' your money.'

'I'm almost positive.'

The ref waves a warning hand, insisting we get into our spots despite the clouds overhead, ones I recognize a little too well. It's not just education that gets you to that point, it's experience: seeing it all overhead as a child, knowing when it's time to bring the horses in and start moving down to the cellar. I take classes with students from the city, and they have to start at square one to pick up that kind of intuition. My dad always insists that even if the university tries, they can't teach it the same way farm kids in the South pick it up. Right now, despite the fact that a ton of them are probably wasted, said farm kids in the crowd are starting to look up, grabbing their stuff, their friends, and their bottles of beer.

I set up for the draw opposite the midfielder from Austin, and she gives the rumbling sky the same uneasy glance that I do as the ref blows her whistle. We get right into it. I win the draw, flinging the ball straight to Maddie.

'HUSTLE!' Coach Dillon calls from the sideline. 'YOU GUYS GOT IT!'

We're about to have it, with a play from the attack taking us through Austin's layer of defence, Jordan right at the net with what's going to be a sure goal . . .

The sirens start with a slow, eerie wail that increases in pitch as I count one, two, three Mississippi. Jordan drops the ball, and takes one peek at the clouds before she yells, 'GO!'

No one needs to be told twice. In a town like Prosperity, we know the drill all too well. The stands file out immediately. The warning flashes across the digital scoreboard screens, and the announcer repeats the spiel. 'Folks, that's a tornado warning. A tornado's been spotted a city over, and we advise you all to seek shelter now. Let's clear the stadium.'

'MAY!' Colt's voice cuts through the chaos. I'm in a sea of players and audience members. I look this way and that, my two braids slapping my cheek, but I can't find him. My pulse picks up, sweat from my palms slickening my crosse. Shit, shit. People are starting to head through the tunnel on ground level to funnel out and into the stadium basement. Has he already been swept up in there?

'Colt!' I shout back. There's a panic to my voice that I don't recognize. I've experienced so many of these things, but the last one . . .

*In the moment, May. In the moment.* But my ribs feel like they're closing in on my lungs, and every breath is shallower than the last. The wind whips up around us, creating a tinny whistle when it cuts through the bleachers. 'COLT!'

'Hey! Hey, May, come on!'

'Colt!' I see the top of his head first, his brown-blond hair, and then the bewilderment in his eyes, as frightened as I feel right now. Colt, as much as he grew up here, hasn't witnessed a twister in years. I squeeze past a throng of fans, reaching a hand out and grabbing onto his as soon as I'm within reach. His palm is as clammy as mine. He wraps an arm around me. 'Come on, let's go,' he says, his chest heaving against my back with every word as he shields me from the push and shove of the influx of people trying to pile into the tunnels.

'We won't fit,' I manage, voice breaking. *In the moment.* I try centring myself, imagining a cord around my waist tying me to the ground, channelling all my energy into my therapist's advice, but it's not working. The shouts of people around us, the body heat emanating from the crowd, it's too much all at once.

And then the barrage.

The rain comes in a pounding sheet of water, washing over the stadium in a windy rush of moisture that slaps you square in the face. It takes maybe a minute before we're soaked to the bone, even in the tunnel, owing to the openings on either side.

'I got you.' Colt rubs my back with one hand and holds me to him with the other, steering us to the right, into somewhat dry territory, and then down the set of stairs that leads to the basement. It feels like some kind of dystopia, what with the crammed staircase, the death march of people shuffling into the makeshift shelter.

Chester is just about the worst spot to wait out a storm. We may be D1, but our field is ancient, its shelter meant for crowds half the size of what we typically get – and a quarter of the size of what we've been getting as of late. We are shoulder to shoulder in the basement, cramped around piles of old lacrosse equipment.

My entire body shudders. I'm scared. And normally, I'd pull myself together, but now that I'm afforded someone who doesn't expect that of me, in the way the rest of the world does, I don't bother hiding my fear.

The tears freely trickle down my cheeks, and I bury my face into Colt's shoulder, holding fast to his strong body. The rest of the crowd knows the drill, the Oklahoman procedure of looking for something that's anchored to the earth. That's what they'll try their darnedest not to let go of, but for reasons I know I'll never understand, I refuse to let go of Colt, as if he has roots that reach right down to the core of the planet.

'I'm not scared of storms,' I murmur. Got to salvage some dignity while I have the chance.

'I know,' Colt replies. He smooths my hair down, brushing errant curls from my face, and I swear I hear him say, 'That's why I fell for you.' Or maybe it's the whistle of the wind. Or the pounding of the rain and the crack of the thunder. I could have heard anything.

But I chose to hear that.

## Chapter Twenty-Five

Oblivion

**Colt**

We hunker down in the dingy basement for half an hour, but it feels longer. By the time the roaring wind dies down, and the distant voice of the announcer says the storm has passed over and it's safe to come out, everyone's rattled, quiet, and exhausted. Murmurs fall on the crowd as we start the ascent up the stairs, back to the stadium.

May looks ashamed when she removes her arms from around me, wrapping them around herself instead. She looks a lot smaller than I ever remember her being. She'd probably hate me for thinking it. 'Sorry,' she says as we climb the steps.

'Don't be,' I reply immediately, maybe a little too quickly.

She seems taken aback, but nods, swallowing hard. There's not really much to say. The damp spots on the shoulder of my hoodie are evidence of May's tears, of the crack in her façade that she allowed me to see through. And that moment, as much as I could try to convince myself, that moment was definitely not fake. Fake doesn't hang onto one another like the world is coming to an end.

The light splinters in through the tunnel, as if it's the entrance to heaven or something equally magical, but what we see when we get a view of the field is vastly different. It doesn't look like we were in the tornado's path. That's not saying much, though. There are various leaves and branches all in the bleachers, and the backpacks that were left behind on the sidelines have been tossed every which way, some missing completely. Water and beer bottles alike are strewn across the grass. The scoreboard blinks unhappily, flickering every few moments.

'This isn't the worst of it,' Jordan says to May beside me. 'Where did that fucker go, then, if not here?'

'I don't know.' May exhales wearily. 'But the damage here . . .'

Jordan taps at her phone, raising it in a feeble attempt to get bars. I catch a glimpse of the weather app on the screen. She squints at the reports. 'Looks like we're clear. And . . .'

She stops abruptly and lowers the phone slowly. Her eyes are wide with a hint of pity, as the rest of the girls assemble around us, stragglers coming from the crowd, drawn by the tension among their teammates.

'May.' Jordan regards her best friend with pursed lips, and May doesn't seem to need explanation. She presses a fisted hand to her mouth. That same fear I saw on her face in the basement, the absolute terror, starts to creep back. That's how I realize that the state of the field we're looking at right now is just the beginning.

'We,' May finally chokes out, 'need to go home.'

Jordan pockets her phone and looks to me. 'Do you still have your car keys?'

This drive to Eagle Rock is nothing like the first. Everywhere we look, signs have been blown to the ground, front-yard trinkets lie scattered and broken, plants have been uprooted. When we hit the town itself, it becomes evident that Prosperity was fortunate.

I remember well enough that tornados leave giant gashes in the ground when they plough through, quite literally, and the gash starts to show right away. The Eagle Rock sign is split in two, and from there a massive wound cuts through the earth, raking its way through houses, shops, and storefronts that are carved open so wide you can see the bones of the structures. The church is completely destroyed, and part of its spire lies across the street.

In the passenger seat, May looks out of the window, stony-faced, unreadable. Shutting down.

I pull past what's left of the feed store, and around towards the road that leads down to the ranch. I can't even bring the truck up the driveway.

The minute I hit the brakes, May flings the door open and runs straight across the shingle-littered grass, her lacrosse cleats pounding straight into the muddy dirt. 'PAPA!' she yells. 'MUMMA!'

Jordan, in the back seat, looks like someone's sucked the life from her face. She's pale as a sheet as she takes it all in. 'My parents texted,' she says quietly. 'Spared our place. It's so twisted. The paths these things take.'

The knots that form in the pit of my stomach agree. For your home to be standing, to have four walls and a roof, running water, electricity, it feels gut-wrenching when you see something like this.

We both get out of the truck, and I lock it before we jog down the way May went. My heart thuds double-time at the fear of what's in store, more so about what May might have found. My fingers twitch, hands shaky, but my body is put at ease when Jordan and I catch sight of May and her parents in a shared embrace, standing outside what's left of their home. It's a miracle that the first floor of the house is still quite intact. Much of what's around it – the fencing in the ranch, the barns, the stables, weren't so fortunate. And then there's the field. *Our* lacrosse field. My mouth goes dry when I see it in the distance, grass all torn up, goalposts ripped apart, netting in pieces, covered in shards of wood from the fences.

'Oh, thank God,' Jordan sighs.

'You took the words right out my mouth.'

'Lord.' She kicks a piece of wood, glancing up at the parts that still stick up from the ground like fingers of a hand reaching up to the sky. 'This is completely . . .'

'Yeah.' I crouch down and pick up a shattered photo frame, inside which is a news clipping of May, the calling card of exceptionally proud parents. *UOKC RESEARCH AIMS TO PUT THE 'EARLY' IN EARLY DETECTION.* A group of five people, May among them in a Johnny Cash T-shirt and jean shorts, poses beside one of the dated tornado sirens down in Prosperity.

'Clean-up's going to be an all-week affair.' Jordan nudges me. 'Red Cross will be here soon, but we'd better get a start on it now. C'mon.'

The house is still in a treacherous condition, so we wait on a couple of the Velascos' construction-savvy friends to come over and help get inside so they can look around and grab what valuables they can find. Later on, the Red Cross arrive, joined by teams from the county, to assess the damage. I hear Mr Velasco mention that they're fully insured, against floods and tornadoes, which is a very slight source of relief among all the chaos. The house is obviously their biggest concern, but then there's the ranch – all the grazing land, the fences, the barns. And importantly, the animals, including May's barrel-racing horse and the Velascos' prize cattle, which Mrs Velasco assures May the ranch hands took to the evacuation barn, a town over, the second the tornado watch came on.

'That's good, at least.' May sighs, wiping dirt off her hands on her sweatpants. 'Rocky's safe?'

'Rocky's safe, May, but where will we put him?'

'We can take 'em all up to Tía's, right? She's got room on her farm.'

'May.' Mrs Velasco takes her daughter's hand. 'We are *lucky*. We can't push it. We'll take this a step at a time.'

Her mother heads off to check with the contractors alongside her dad. It's definitely not my place – it's not my scene, and I shouldn't be saying shit considering I'm the guy who decided to turn up again after leaving the state – but I open my mouth anyway.

'We're here for you, May,' I say tentatively. 'If anyone can get back on their feet—'

'Colt, you can stop now, alright?' Her voice wavers, her eyes filling with tears, fists clenched at her sides. The hasty bun she's tied her hair into threatens to fall out from on top of her head.

'Please! Acting like you've been here all this time when you got out of this place as fast as you could and this, *this* is what we deal with while you're up there at your game-night bars and your socials and your after-parties. Okay? I get why you're here. I get it. I am *sorry* for the pain you are feeling. But you aren't helping my pain when you treat me like you're some sort of *gift* to the *simple people* of Oklahoma, right in front of my damn face and this house, our home . . .'

She covers her mouth with a quivering hand, shaking her head. 'Please, please just let us be. Please, Colt.'

## *Chapter Twenty-Six*

### PBR on the Porch

**Colt**

'Don't take her too seriously.'

Mr Velasco's reassurance comes with a cold bottle of Pabst Blue Ribbon beer, straight out of someone's truck cooler. He nods, extending it my way. 'Here. We really appreciate you helping us today.'

'I don't know that your daughter does.'

He lets out a laugh, probably the first someone's laughed in this space in hours. The sun is starting to dip below the horizon, and we watch the teams clearing out for the day from up on the porch – one of the only parts of the house left intact. 'She does. In her strange, Mayday way.'

'Can I . . .' I accept the beer, popping the cap in thought before I finish my sentence. 'Would you guys like to stay at ours tonight? It can be the night; it can be however long you'd like. I just . . . I think . . .'

A weight seems to lift from Mr Velasco's shoulders. He smiles, and it's both grateful and melancholy. 'We'd like that. Can't thank you enough.'

'You don't have to. We can head over soon.'

He gives me one last firm pat on the back, and jogs down the driveway, hopping over rubble on his way out, talking to the contractors. I sip at my beer for a minute. May definitely doesn't appreciate me. And it's not like anything she said was wrong. She had the right to say every word of it.

As if she knows I'm entertaining thoughts about her, a creak of the planks of wood behind me and a clink of a beer bottle signal her arrival. 'Probably an EF3,' she says, referencing the Enhanced Fujita tornado damage scale that only two kinds of people would casually drop: Meteorology majors and Tornado Alley-ans.

Her voice is rough, but it's softened from earlier. 'Almost decimated a town, but there's still worse storms out there. Isn't that sick?'

'Sick's a kind word for it.' I turn to meet her quickly reddening, puffy eyes. This is the circle of life in Oklahoma, and seeing it this plainly, it's obvious May'd resent me for leaving. For leaving everyone behind and saving my own skin from this. Like I said, she's entitled to every word she said earlier. I can't be anyone's saviour when I wasn't around for the past five years. It's obvious she'd hate me because her junior year, the season it all went sour . . .

'Last year, it cleared Pontiac. Just about fifteen minutes from here. My uncle and aunt's . . . I'd be shocked if you saw the news from up in New England.' Her tone is one of bitterness, each word a sting, but she sits down beside me anyway, nursing her PBR with two hands. 'My dad's youngest brother and his wife.'

'Did they . . .'

'Saying they're fine now is probably an overstatement, Colt.' She purses her lips, blinking back semblances of emotion. 'Sure, they survived it. But all their stuff, their cattle, their equipment, gone. The way back from something like that . . .' Hunched over, perched on the porch, all the fire in May's eyes has fizzled out, replaced by a sense of helplessness. 'My aunt cried for days because the storm took her old 4-H steer's heifer. And maybe people say that crying over things like that is dumb because at least you're alive. But when you lose everything you own? The kind of scared you feel? That's like nothing else. It shook our family to the roots. Then we thought we were next. I couldn't play right. My head was somewhere else. I mean, who gives a shit about lacrosse when your house could get ripped out of the ground tonight? Tomorrow?'

She slides her beer to one side, the glass scraping the uneven wood planks. 'They called the first storm "The Widowmaker". Like every tornado name in public media: shitty, crass and insensitive. And accurate. Clocked the highest death toll of any twister in the state in the past ten years. Auntie's farm was fifteen minutes away from us, Colt, *fifteen*. And the fuckers didn't stop. They kept coming, county after county after county. News said it was an epidemic.'

'You could've told me,' I start to say, but I decide to swallow my words. She doesn't need me to try and be some sort of caretaker right now. She just needs me to *be*.

'Personally,' I say instead, 'I wouldn't have given a shit about lacrosse, either.'

'You're not all terrible when you sit and listen.'

'I guess I do that, sometimes,' I joke lightly. 'I'm sure I'm not that mean.'

That gets a quiet chuckle out of May. 'You didn't talk to me for five years. You're pretty mean.'

'I'm sorry.' I set my beer down beside me so I can look her in the eye – really look at her. Past the stunning face I fell so hard for back in high school, and into the brilliant mind that can come up with plays on a dime, but is also so burdened, all the time, with everything that whirls about in her life – a mental cyclone. 'For trying to be something I'm not.'

She shakes her head. '*I'm* sorry, Colt. I took my anger out on you. It's just . . . to be hit by a storm twice in two years, it's a lot. You know? We have seasons where this stuff comes and hits us over and over, but you get desensitized. Not having a minute to think in between the storms is different from getting a year to get your shit right, and then . . .'

'That's fair.' I raise an eyebrow. 'But you're allowed to be angry at me. I hope you know that. You're right. It's not okay, the way I was trying to be something I'm not.'

'I'm not totally right, thought.' May waves a hand out towards the crates of stuff we pulled out of the rubble, crates that now sit on a flatbed attached to the back of my truck. 'You don't have to say anything for us to know who you are. And you're not pretending to be anyone you aren't. You're Oklahoman. Maybe New England turned you into a terrible person, but you're still Oklahoman.' A smile sneaks out from the gloom that had settled over her face throughout the day. 'The Colt I remember, at least.'

*The Colt you remember is the Colt you made me. A better man.*

My cheeks are warm, either from the alcohol starting to fill my body, or from the compliment, but I get the feeling it's the latter considering I've only had a few sips.

'So.' I clear my throat awkwardly. 'On the topic of the Colt you remember. This whole shitshow's gonna get into people's heads. They're going to expect us to get even closer. The crowds are going to keep growing. People love an underdog.'

'That's unfortunate.' May wiggles in her seat on the porch like a fifth-grader forced to sit through a PG kiss at the end of a coming-of-age movie. 'Where's this going?'

'Well. It's going . . . maybe this is a good point for me to ask, you know, for the sake of being a better fake boyfriend or whatever, why . . .' The words tumble out of my mouth, completely out of my control. 'Why did you hate me so much for leaving Prosperity?'

This is the question that's been on my mind since the day she shot me that death glare in the stands when I walked in on practice. Now, though, the question is, will I get an answer?

'Right now, you're here. You saw what just happened to everything within twenty damn miles. This ranch, this place; it's been in the family for generations. It's all my *bisa*, my great-grandma, had when she came here. She built that barn with her two hands and a couple of stable boys. It's where she got married. Had my 'buelo – grandpa. Then he got married here, Mumma and Papa got married here. I've spent my whole damn life here.

'And even then, shit's always been ebbing and flowing. Gotta pay the ranch hands. Never know what a given month of pay cheques will look like. And this weather . . . it can take away everything you've ever known in *seconds*. If I'm not here . . . who'll be?' With a shake of her head, she takes a sip of her beer. 'We don't get lucky here, Colt. We have to suck it up and dig our boots into the dirt. You . . . you left, and you don't have to do that any more. I get it. You have a good thing in New Haven. But I gotta provide before I think about up and leaving.'

I wait for more, but that's that. It sounded like there was a thought there – envy, maybe? – but it ends before it's fully formed, and she moves on to the next. 'There's also the slightly important fact that friends don't leave one another, turn their back, go radio silent, and then suddenly show up again with a sorry and a smile.' She shrugs, the liquid in her bottle sloshing, and my stomach churns as it sinks into my shoes. Looks like I *definitely* just got an answer.

'I . . .' I wince. No easy way to sugar-coat this. 'I really left you high and dry in the middle of Tornado Alley, didn't I?'

May snorts, and then laughs, for real, out loud this time. Her eyes squeeze shut, and she covers her mouth. 'Okay, *Wizard of Oz*.'

It's kind of funny, and maybe I'd laugh in another situation, but my eyes are wide as I take in the aftermath I left behind. For years, I played on this tension between us, and instead of doing something, I dropped a couple excuses and took the first flight out. And maybe it would've made it different if I hadn't done the next part, but I didn't look back. Not once. Because I knew I'd screwed it up.

She picks up on my realization right away, the laughter subsiding slowly. She drums her fingers on her beer bottle, and after a long beat, she says, 'I heard everything you said that night in Albuquerque.'

Wait. Albuquerque? When she was asleep?

Evidently, not asleep.

'Oh. *Oh.*' I scratch the back of my neck. Fuck. That wasn't my brightest moment. My chest tightens with anticipation. I wait expectantly for something to come next, but May pushes herself to her feet with a yawn and a big gulp of her beer. 'Probably a good time for us to start heading back. Thanks, by the way. For having us over.'

'Yeah – um, it's no problem at all.' I blink a couple times. It's not easy to recover from the fact that we had just, almost, had a pretty deep emotional discussion. We had just, almost, touched on the topic I'd been waiting to touch on since I left Prosperity, and then, with a flip of the switch, we're back on neutral ground. I'm jealous of May's emotional regulation, honestly.

With one more glance back at the rubble surrounding the bones of the Velasco ranch home, I stand up and, half-empty bottle in hand, head after May.

## Chapter Twenty-Seven

### All Tied Up

**May**

'There's no way. We can't concede. It's the final game.'

Maddie leans forward, a fist pressed to her desk, firm punctuation after each word. We rarely do team meetings formally like this but, after the storm, we've had something come up that arguably required a greater deal of discussion.

Coach Dillon looks pained. 'Maddie, I understand that. But the school—'

'The school can think *whatever* they want,' puts in Jordan with a passionate wave of her hand. 'They're just trying to save money. Sure, our stadium's still a little way away from being ready to host. But look at men's soccer. They're not telling that team to "take it down a notch", are they? So why us?'

We all know why.

'Roper Rivalry is more than a game,' I add matter-of-factly. As captain, the girls look up to me, and as much as a part of me wants to sit down and admit defeat after everything – everything my father's family built – is now in pieces, we need to stay in this fight. 'It's probably our biggest battle of the year. And besides, we have a shot at the championship, I believe it. This is redemption. I don't see us sitting here and taking the punches while the guys get to do what they like.'

Around the circle of desks, the girls nod, murmurs of agreement tossed about. 'We'll do whatever it takes to get there,' Brianna promises.

'We only have a week.' Coach's tone is warning, but I catch a hint of pride in her eyes. 'Will you girls really be able to pull this together? No one's making you hit the stadium and start repairing it yourself . . .'

She trails off as she looks around at the smirks on all our faces. The Roper Rivalry between Oklahoma City and San Antonio is the stuff of legends.

'It's time to close this season out right,' says Jordan with a raised eyebrow. 'According to the tables, if we beat San Antonio, one of the *final* two playoff spots is ours.'

She exchanges a grin with me, and I egg her on with a spirited, 'And we *certainly* want that, don't we?'

The girls whoop; slaps of desks all around. Storms can screw a lot of things up for us, but this season isn't one of them. We've been there, and we're not willing to repeat it.

Mrs Bradley sighs in exasperation when Colt holds up two more ugly ties. He looks as tired as she does. Both of them are justified.

The options are hideous. They look like they came straight out of a 1990s movie, all weird shades of beige with accents in bright reds and greens, dated patterns, the works.

'You can't be serious.'

'I didn't realize I'd need *ties* here, Ma!' Colt defends himself.

Fortunately, I'm just a bystander. I sit by with my bowl of eight p.m. cereal and watch the entire thing go down. I got lucky with my Rivalry outfit; I keep my formal wear with my dad's sister – Tía Juana – down in Tulsa, and she sent the pantsuit up yesterday. Colt, on the other hand, seems to have left all his ties back in New Haven, which leaves his dad's old relics, allegedly from Mr Bradley's time as a medical resident back when dinosaurs roamed the earth.

'May. May, come on,' the idiot implores me. I sigh extra hard over my bowl of chocolate puffs. I'd ask how we're keeping our parents from finding out this couple thing is a lie, but I think it's working its charm fairly naturally. Even with all four of them under the same roof, they seem to be taking our constant bickering as a sign of affection. Which is dumb.

He takes my hands. Another fairly natural thing. The physical touch between us, something neither of us was prepared for at first, has also become strangely automatic since we talked, out on the porch. I wonder if Colt overthinks it as much as I do.

'May. What are you wearing?' he grills me.

'Same thing every year,' I tell him with a shrug. 'Something you would know. If you had been here. Every year.'

'She got you there!' Mrs Bradley hoots from behind us, where she shoves all the ties into a box gleefully, never to be seen again. 'Why don't you ask your sister?'

'Ohhhh, no.' Colt looks like he's ready to throw up. 'Savannah would laugh at me until her face turned blue from losing oxygen.'

'Are you scared?' I tease him, and gosh, the little tormented wrench of his face is actually kind of satisfying. 'Of your sister?'

'She's kind of . . . like you . . . about the whole "leaving home" thing.'

*Serves you right!* I'd like to cackle. 'And she could get you a tie?'

'She's in fashion design,' he mumbles. 'She could make me one to match you. If she didn't hate my guts.'

I don't know if he thinks *I* think he's low effort, or something, but quickly he says, 'I'll fight Sav to make sure we match, though. Because Pop's ties . . .'

I snort. 'If you show up in one of those atrocities, with respect to your poppa, we might have to kick you off the team.'

'That bad?'

'Worse.' I look to Mrs Bradley for confirmation. She nods, adding a little wince for emphasis. 'Looks like you're gonna have to head into the hornet's nest.'

Colt shivers. Watching a five-ten man who's got an ego the size of a small house get all terrified of his little sister is wonderful. 'I'll talk to her once I'm done outside.'

'Outside? Are you digging up my plants?' Mrs Bradley tuts, dropping the box of ties and stalking our way. 'Colton James Bradley. Get your hands off my begonias.'

'My hands were never on them!' he insists, face going pink. 'I'm just . . . pulling weeds.'

'Pulling weeds,' announces Mrs Bradley. She looks about as unconvinced as I am. 'Right, then.'

Colt takes his leave all awkwardly, darting out through the

sliding back door like his tail's on fire. The second he's out of earshot, his mother and I burst out laughing at the same exact time.

'He doesn't know how to pull weeds for his life!' She chortles. 'And those *ties*! My god!'

'I wouldn't let him out of the tunnel!' I howl, making her laugh even harder.

'Oh, May.' Mrs Bradley lets out one last chuckle before smiling contentedly my way, pushing a stray piece of her greying brown hair back into her ponytail. She has a youthful face, and I can tell she's given Colt much of it – the steely eyes, the dimples. 'You are so good for him, though, you know? He struggled a lot last year. It's good to see him back on his feet. Literally and figuratively.'

I swallow hard. Well. Like every conversation I have with anyone close to Colt, this seems to have taken a turn. Maybe I shouldn't pry, but I think about how patiently he'd just sat and listened when I talked about what happened in Pontiac. The image of my photo taped to the inside of Colt's locker comes back to my mind, clear as day. The direction our conversation had started to tentatively creep in, out of the lines I'd drawn for myself before we started this thing and into territory that more than broke fake relationship play number four: no deep life conversations. Who knows how long that photo had been on there? Since he got drafted? That meant that maybe I was wrong, and maybe he had remembered me in his stupid, no-contact way.

And maybe I'd also never reached out. I hadn't texted or called or anything either, but I remembered him just as well. Clearly my head and my heart remembered him. Because even all these years after he left, I was still talking to him with the kind of candour I could never muster with anyone else. I had never told anyone else about how I felt after junior year, not even Jordan, not completely. Did that mean he'd been more than a friend? What the hell was he now?

In the moment, though, I snap back to reality and repeat Mrs Bradley's words in my mind until they make sense. *He struggled a lot last year.* 'Struggled?'

Mrs Bradley sighs, taking a seat on the couch in the living room. She waves me over and I oblige, sitting down beside her. 'We were in Boston about a year when I had my visiting professorship. Up and moved everything that summer. My husband even found a position as a guest physician at the School of Medicine so he could be there with me. Colt, though, he wanted more from that place. So he applied, got in, and before we knew it, University of Boston. We could scarcely believe it. He struck it big on the UB lax team – Division One. That had done more than enough for his chances to go pro. And then, three years later, the draft came. The offer was literally instantaneous. He was the third pick. New Haven. Suddenly, our son was all over the sports channels, all over social media, an overnight phenomenon, and that was when I knew that boy had given up the Oklahoma in him to become a New Englander. Everyone else loved him so much all at once, but I was in your boat.' She smiles sadly. 'I just hoped he still remembered us. Home.'

'Mrs Bradley . . .' She took the words right out of my mouth, honestly. I remember feeling deceived. Lied to. I had my own problems, but Colt parading around as if this town, these people, hadn't cultivated his talent, made my skin crawl.

'Then the injury happened.' She presses her hands to her

knees. 'It was a long few months. After the complications and all. As quickly as he'd wanted to be in Boston back in high school, he wanted nothing more than to come home now. I wasn't sure what had got into him, but I knew it was more than the bad knee. Except . . .' With a forlorn laugh, she shakes her head, almost guiltily. 'I was *glad*. I felt awful for it, but I was glad he finally wanted to be back. Is that so wrong?'

Maybe not, I want to say. I thought I was pissed he'd come back, and yet there were moments I was, as twisted as it was, grateful he was here. Grateful he'd helped us pick up the pieces of our house after the storm. Grateful he'd taped up my wrist for me. Was I grateful that he'd looked up at the crowd and kissed me, right in front of the whole town? That, I'm still working on figuring out. I think.

'When he left the way he did,' I finally say, 'I wanted him to come back for a couple weeks afterward. I oscillated between this weird sense of longing and this red-hot anger. And then I accepted it. That was the way it would be. So when he did come back, I didn't expect to feel . . . the same way as you, I guess.'

Sure. This relationship is founded on a lie. I'm not really Colt's girlfriend. I've played nice as well as I could. But as Mrs Bradley and I sit side by side and just talk about how much we miss Colt Bradley, the *real* Colt Bradley, I don't need to tell any lies.

# *Chapter Twenty-Eight*

Savannah

**Colt**

'Hold still, dingus.'
I could snap at my sister, but I choose peace, considering her hands are a little too close to my neck to chance pissing her off. She works deftly at the new tie, and flattens it at the very end so the designs show.

'Don't get it dirty. You eat those Chester Corn Dogs like you're not gonna live to see tomorrow.'

'Says you. Remember when Ma had to threaten to leave you at Chester before you ate your fifth one of the game?'

Savannah scoffs. Taking after our dad, she's got what I like to call judgemental eyebrows and piercing green eyes that'll tell you exactly what she's feeling even if you don't ask. And if you do ask, she, like Pop, won't hesitate to be plain about it. 'Yeah, right. That's Ma. *You'd* better be nice to me. I won't be making you any more matching-your-girlfriend ties otherwise.'

I peer at the tie in the mirror. It's a perfect complement to the photo May sent of her pantsuit. The tie is simple and effective: the exact same shade of red as May's flowers to complement my black button-up. Sav's ever-so-subtly incorporated the lightest of white embroidery, threading vines to match May's. I turn to my sister. She plants her hands on her hips, prepared for a sassy remark.

'Thanks, Sav.'

She raises an eyebrow. 'You feeling okay?'

'I'm just fine. Although I was scared,' I add, 'to ask you for this tie.'

'Serves you right!' Sav elbows me with a huff. 'And?'

'And then I realized I'm probably scared because I didn't treat you as well as I should have. All these years.'

Sav's jaw goes slack. She fully whips her clear, pink-framed glasses off her face so she can squint at me. 'Oh, my god. You're figuring it out.'

'Shut up.' I swat at her glasses, which she tugs away before I can snatch them.

My sister smiles wryly. 'It's your girlfriend, isn't it?'

I feel my ears getting all dumb and warm before she gets the chance to call me out on it. 'Well . . .'

'It *is*.' Sav just chuckles in awe. 'Man. I always knew May had a good head on her shoulders, but I didn't know it was possible for rational thought to rub off on you.'

'Hey!' I whine.

'It's true! In what universe is moving to the East Coast rational?' My sister rolls her eyes so hard I can see the whites.

'Lots of people here don't have options. May definitely didn't. Hell, your own friends on the lax team, you know they didn't, either. But you did, and you took the option we were kind of afraid you'd take. Staying there. It's just . . .' She almost grumbles out her next words. 'I missed having you around.'

'What? What? I didn't hear that the first time,' I tease her, and she just sighs dramatically in that younger-sister way.

'You get it once,' she says with the air of someone's grown mother.

'Alright. Come here.'

For the first time in what's probably years, Savannah lets me give her a hug, and for the first time in what's probably years, she hugs me back.

There are still pencil marks in the wall downstairs at the entrance to the kitchen where Ma and Pop would put a dash for each of our heights every month. Old magnets stuck to the fridge have pictures from when Sav played lacrosse for a year, too, the both of us in uniform, taking a knee side by side. They've hung tons of photos of us all over the house – in the fire truck that came around during block parties, in matching Riders cowboy hats and bib overalls, at OKC games on our parents' shoulders. But all of that is from when we were little enough that the rift between us hadn't formed yet. When that rift shot up, it separated my dreams of getting out of here, and hers of staying and cultivating everything our parents built. We just couldn't find a way around it. Until now.

It's been a while since I felt like we were kids again, and I feel it right now. I'm kind of glad Sav can't see my face, because I wouldn't hear the end of it if she knew I was getting teary-eyed.

## Chapter Twenty-Nine

Roper Rivalry

**May**

The stomping of feet in the stands, and the first few chords of 'Riders in the Sky' by Johnny Cash, the two sounds that any Oklahoma City Riders fan knows like the back of their hand, fill the stadium, audible from half a mile out as we make our way through the gates in full formal. Dressing up on game day is one of those time-worn professional sports traditions, and out here, the rivalry absolutely demands it. Every single one of us has shown up in two-piece pantsuits, detailed in subtle ways that speak to our journeys to collegiate sport.

My pantsuit, not quite a pantsuit, was made by Tía Juana back when I was in high school, and since I stopped growing around junior year, I've never needed a new one. She tailored it off her brother and the youngest of the three siblings, Tío Pablo's, old mariachi outfit, but with the cut of Mumma's favourite Indian outfit from the 1990s. The trousers are wide legged and high waisted, and the top is technically another two pieces. One is the solid black crop-top blouse, matching the plain trousers, and the other is the black duster jacket. Tía and Buela embroidered it themselves, with white vines and gold edging modelled from Tío's mariachi jacket, and red roses on the shoulders. It's what I've worn for years, and I don't plan on switching things up anytime soon.

I'm taken aback when Colt shows up at my side for the walk into the stadium, a pair of Ray-Ban sunglasses resting on his face, sports jacket ironed, matching black to my suit, and most surprising of all, a tie with the exact same embroidery as my duster. I hadn't expected him to actually work up the courage to ask Savannah about it, especially after he went to hide in his mom's garden, but I sent him the photo when he asked, and apparently, here he is. It doesn't spare my attention that this is the first time I'm seeing him in formal wear since as far back as my *quinceañera*, and that he certainly cleans up nicely. Really nicely, honestly. I curse my easily distracted brain.

He tips his head my way with a sheepish smile. 'You look good, Red Card.'

'Not so bad yourself, New Haven.'

Someone's big camera flashes our way, a sobering reminder that this is not only one of the biggest events for Oklahoma sports, but also one of the best-covered. And that means Colt and I can't be lacking at any point this weekend.

We exchange a knowing glance, and he does the corny slide of the glasses down his nose, a nod of his head, a teasing smirk. 'Right on in. They're waiting for you.'

'Oh, Colt, you know well enough that they're waiting for *us*.' I raise an eyebrow. 'Stick to the game plan.'

Side by side, we file inside towards the tunnel, down the halls through to the locker rooms. All the hubbub of the crowd fades out pretty quickly, and the girls trickle steadily into the room, already looking for their bags so they can get to locking in for the game.

Colt and I stop in the hall just before we reach the lockers. Technically he stops first, and then gives me that little glance of his that tells me to hang on. 'I wanna make sure you're okay.'

'Okay?' I feel my hackles rise immediately. 'I thought we had the conversation about—'

'No, I wanna make sure you're *okay*.' He jerks a thumb towards the field, where we can still hear the thrumming of the eager crowd through the walls. 'That's a massive crowd. And if I'm not wrong, there's definitely at least one MLL coach out there somewhere. This is the biggest lacrosse match-up in the South. I'm sure you don't need to be told twice.'

I definitely don't. I've been thinking about it since we came into Chester to help pick up wreckage and fix the stands. The same stands a coach might sit in, this very weekend, to watch us play, hunt for prospects. It's not even just the thought of a coach watching. Colt's a step ahead of me. Obviously having him back home, and at every single lacrosse game front row, has had its perks for our programme, filling our stands for essentially the first time in Oklahoma women's lacrosse history, but the pressure is mounting, too. I had already had to worry about keeping my performance this season consistent, holding onto my tuition, as well as getting us to the championship, and now I still had to decide if I was even going to declare for the draft.

It all floods my brain way too quickly, and Colt must see the terror in my eyes, because he curses under his breath. 'Sorry. Do-over. That wasn't what you needed to hear. May. Look at me.'

He steadies me by the shoulders, and as much as I feel like a confused little kid, I do look at him. His grey eyes bore into mine, and he opens his mouth to say something, closes it, takes a beat. It's a moment before he finally gives me the decisive words. 'Make sure they have hell to pay.'

A tense breath escapes my lungs, and I waggle my head in what I hope is a gesture of 'yes'. What? What is going on?

Coach Dillon yells for him, and he shoots me one last encouraging smile before jogging off to take care of whatever might be going on, still in that damn suit of his, and suddenly, my brain is all thoughts of how well those pants fit him and how his stupid overgrown hair looks extra fun to run your fingers through all swept back like that, and the way 'hell to pay' might have been one of the hottest things a man could say in that situation.

'Hell to pay,' I mouth, even as I tug on my jersey and kilt and tape up my legs. His voice still echoes in my ears when we line up in the tunnel entrance, from where we can see that the stands are completely packed. It's one of the biggest crowds this derelict stadium has ever seen, totally full of fans, the first few rows of the student section crammed with the usual game bib overalls and beers, and yet the only thing I hear, still, is, 'Make sure they have hell to pay.'

The game opens with the hallmark Oklahoma City–San Antonio home game tradition, the Running of the Rider, a local rodeo champ on horseback storming the field with the university flag in hand, and from there, we take command of the grass the second the whistle blows. San Antonio, even one natural disaster less frazzled than us, falls behind at first, and by the end of the half, we're pulling ahead.

It's the third quarter when San Antonio really must have got a verbal thrashing in the locker room, because play starts to pick up. One of their attackers cuts right through our defence for just their second goal of the game. Two turns into three turns into four and, before we know it, the last quarter is on our heels. We run like the Rider is chasing us down the field, and it pays off.

'OPEN!' I yell, as Maddie rushes to the right, dodging a defender and shucking the ball overhead. It lands straight in the head of my stick. One of San Antonio's midfielders tries to rush me, but I toss the ball back to Brianna, who keeps it safe until Jordan is open on attack. Seconds on the board, she swings the ball to Jor, and my best friend whips it straight into the goal so hard that if the goalie blocked it, it'd blow a hole through the head of her crosse. Top cheddar – the ball just slaps the top of the net, and just like that, the whistle blows, and the home fans are chanting, the bass turned up on 'Riders in the Sky' so the entire stadium thrums with roaring and cheering and whipping of orange towels.

Winning a game is a dream. Winning a Roper Rivalry is heaven. The pearly gates are open, and the Oklahoma City Riders are in the playoffs.

The student section is screaming, ecstatic after sitting on their hands all fourth quarter. They'll cost the school a penalty greater than tornado damage if they storm the field, so the best we can do is leap the barriers ourselves, jumping into the student section to celebrate with the sea of orange and white. Beer spills every which way, sticky remains of shooters coating the benches, but the girls couldn't care less.

'MAY!'

'COLT!'

The grin on his face is as broad as his extended arms. 'MAY!'

I don't know how we keep doing it, unchoreographed and unplanned. It's probably adrenaline, I tell myself. All the thoughts fly right out my head, though, when I run straight for Colt, still in his button-down and trousers and that tie of his, and I jump right into his arms. He catches me effortlessly, and I try not to focus on the fact that our bodies are flush against one another right now, or that I'm hanging onto him for dear life, laughing as he spins me around before setting me down gently.

'No kiss this time, New Haven?'

'It's not real, remember?' He smirks, but something in that stupid smirk is absolutely real. Something is certainly simmering, and it's not just the adrenaline.

'As if.' I return his smirk. 'I'm sure you wish it was.'

*MAY! What? May, shut up!*

Colt raises an eyebrow. 'You're the one holding onto me like this.'

No way. He doesn't get to turn it around on me. I move to drop my hands like I just touched a hot pot, but some strange force of nature keeps me from doing so. The CJ Bradley effect. Do I want to punch him? Do I want to kiss him? Why can't I make a decision? 'Don't let it fool you.'

'Hey, there's nothing wrong with going the extra mile to sell it.' Maybe Colt is playing nonchalant, but the flush of his cheeks betrays him. When we put the game plan together those weeks ago, we'd laid the law down. This was all business.

In the pit of my stomach, I know we've been well beyond all business for a while now.

'Oh, I know we need to sell it, trust me.'

'Sure 'bout that?' He gives me that stupid billion-watt smile of his, the one that pulls you straight to him like a magnet. 'We just gonna stand here?'

'Absolutely not.'

I don't know if it's because I want to prove him wrong, or because I'm starting to find myself drawn further into his orbit than I'd like to confess, but this time, when we kiss, it's not like the last. Our bodies melt into one another, my pulse thumping in time with his. His fingers tangle themselves up in the strands of hair sticking out the sides of my ponytail. The smell of his cologne and the taste of coffee on his lips are impossible to ignore, no matter how much I tell myself this is for everyone but us, no matter how much I try to focus on the rising screams of the crowd. I grip him tight like I've got a point to make. And honestly, maybe I do.

'COME ON!' Jordan's full-volume shout saves me from any more rumination about what the hell I'm doing, startling us apart. Colt just shoots me such an easy, sheepish grin. Is he deep in the same thought I am, with all his simple smiles and effortless gestures?

Jordan rushes over and grabs my arm, her ponytail in disarray from a dive into the student section. 'RIVALRY TROPHY!'

We're pulled away from the sidelines in a sea of teammates, and in all the chaos, even as we take the field to raise the rivalry trophy, a tall gold piece of hardware adorned with a statue of a cowboy atop a rearing horse, Colt holds tight to my hand. Maybe this time he's the one holding on, but I can't say I want to let go, either.

## *Chapter Thirty*

Top Ched

**Colt**

Once the team washes up after trophy presentation and photos, it's straight back to formal wear for us as we hit the Riders' victory banquet. Multiple plates of all-you-can-eat buffet later, we head home full, content and exhausted, May and I back to the house together.

I pull the truck onto the driveway, and May stifles a yawn. 'I'm going to go change and get to bed, Colt.'

'Yeah – wait.' I almost forgot. And with the end of the regular season, the Riders off to playoffs, I don't think there's any better time for this. I swallow hard. Nerves? I'm definitely nervous. 'Can you follow me really quickly? There's just something I wanted to show you.'

'Oh?' She moves to grab her duffel, but I hold out a hand

and take it for her. She doesn't look nearly as tired as she did a moment ago.

I lead the way around the side of the house, unlocking the fence to the backyard. We have one of those yards that stretches on and on, until you hit a dip where a little pond sits. Closest to the house is my mom's garden, farther out the stretch that we always used for family Thanksgiving football games. I flick on the floodlights attached to the back patio, and they light up the brand-new lacrosse field.

Lacrosse field is a loose term for it. It's far from perfect, but I tried my best. Mowed it all, bought nets, sprayed the white lines on the grass, midline, face-off circle, the X, all the things.

'Holy . . . shit.' May's jaw goes slightly slack. 'What is this?'

Still in pantsuit and heels, she jogs straight onto the field, right to the circle. 'Did you make this?' she calls, arms raised. 'Colt! This is *beautiful*!'

I've seen May happy before – after games, with a trophy in her arms, when she's with her family or her horses – but this is different. I've never seen her weightless the way she is when she does a full three-sixty, taking in the makeshift field. She looks my way with the broadest smile on her face, her eyes creasing happily, and she gestures dramatically to the nets, the pitch of her voice rising excitedly. 'GOALS! You got goals?'

'Yep.' I grin with a shrug. 'Seeing as the last set got launched into space.'

'Wow.' May grabs the ball I'd left in one of the nets. 'Well, bring the sticks! Come play!'

I grab her sticks from the bag, but those last words – *come play* – are like trying to swallow a big-ass painkiller. The joy

I feel at watching her light up starts to fall away, because I can't. I literally can't play, and I don't know what to do about it, because May Velasco is asking me to join her for a round on the field I've made for us. May, who has practically defined every stage of my life even more than the game has. If I say 'no', it will prove her right. It will prove that I never cared enough.

I kick myself when I watch the smile slowly fall from her face, too. She doesn't deserve that. It's not something she needs to worry about, now or ever.

'Oh, Colt.' Her shoulders slump, and it kills a little part of my heart. 'I'm sorry. I didn't mean to . . .'

'No, um . . .' I shift my grip on the sticks. I know I'm going to be shit, but I don't want to ruin this for her. 'It's okay. Only way out is through, right?'

A crease of worry forms between May's eyebrows, but she nods. 'Just . . . try and clear your head.'

A small, wistful smile tips up one side of my mouth. 'You were better than me at that, you know. Every chance you got. First place you'd go was the field.'

She shakes her head with a tiny scoff. 'I was flighty. The way I'd just disappear to play . . . my parents hated it.'

'Disappear' was about accurate. But May was one of the first people I knew who truly found their place in the game – found solace there. Maybe that was why when I fell for her, I really fell for lacrosse, too.

'It was easier when we were younger, wasn't it?' I pass May her stick before heading to a big backyard bin off to the side to grab mine. 'To just play, clear your head?

May laughs at my quip. 'Everything was easier when we were

younger. Lacrosse was easier. Responsibilities were easier. It was easier to . . .'

She stops herself, a shake of her head.

'Easier to what?'

'Nothing.' May gestures to my stick with hers. 'How's it feel?'

'Foreign,' I say. That's the best word for it. Ever since August, every stick, even my own, has felt like an unfamiliar face.

'That's because – may I?'

I nod. May puts her crosse down and adjusts my grip, her small hands over my bigger ones, and glances up at me with a reassuring smile. 'How about now?'

Now, my eyes can't move from her, and man, something absolutely unreal happens when she gives me that smile of hers. That warm fireplace, blanket in the cold, telling you everything is going to be alright, even when it feels like you have no way out. My hands are warm against the stick, and it moulds to my grip, the same way it has since I was a kid – the way it hasn't felt since my injury.

'Better,' I manage to whisper, and she pats my hand.

'Good. Let's play.'

The ear-to-ear grin May sports as she shucks off her high heels and places the ball in the head of her stick, lined up at the face-off, is contagious. A warmth envelops my chest, and we meet in the middle with our crosses, on eye level.

'Ready?'

'As I'll ever be.'

'Go!' She pushes her stick against mine with a giggle, and suddenly, I push right back. Instinct takes over, and I manoeuvre upwards, getting the ball to shoot up before landing in my net. From the midline, I run, and I swing my stick once I'm within scoring range, whipping the ball right into the goal. The *whack* of the net, the sweetest sound, echoes in the backyard, and for a moment, that's all I can hear. It's silent except for that sound. Triumph.

'DAMN!' whoops May, stick in the air. 'You know what that was?'

She jogs up to me, grinning broadly, and she shakes me by the shoulders, cheeks pink with excitement, mascara-rimmed eyes wide, repeating, 'You know what that was, Colt?'

'Fuckin' top ched.' I laugh as she just shakes her head in disbelief.

'A *goal*. Your goal.'

I'd still be concentrating on the goal if May weren't here with me, but the light giddiness in her voice – decidedly not a part of the anger I've provoked in May for the past weeks – is all I can home in on. Her hair falls across her face in sheets of straightened dark brown so close to black that it reflects the light from the porch. She takes my face in her hands, locks her eyes with mine. 'You are *phenomenal*.'

That's all I want her to know. That she's phenomenal. That every time our paths collide, she changes my life. That when I left, it tore a gash right through my heart, and that the gash is only healed again when I'm with her.

Her nose almost brushes mine, how close we are. Her laughter fades and her smile turns to wide-eyed surprise, mirroring me. My hands rest on her hips, our lacrosse sticks long discarded in the grass. She exhales a shallow breath, her gaze flitting to my lips and back up to my eyes, and damn if that doesn't drive me crazy.

'What are you doing, May?' I whisper, each word a plea against her cheeks. 'What are you doing to me?'

'I don't know,' she murmurs, and her fingers move to lace behind my neck. 'I've had the same question for you.'

So this is definitely not fake. This is definitely not for the crowd of zero people watching us right now. Definitely not like just hours earlier, as unbelievable as that was. What is it, then? Is it real?

We don't get to find out. The patio door slides open with a *squeak* so loud they have to hear it the next neighbourhood over, and Ma's voice yells, 'Who's that in my garden?'

May presses a hand to her mouth, the moment well and truly over, and stifles a laugh that escapes anyway. My mom throws on her glasses, squints, and says, 'Oh! Just the lovebirds. It's one a.m., Colt! Let May get to bed, will you?'

I wince, groaning loudly so I can make sure she hears it. 'MA!'

'CJ BRADLEY! BED!' she shoots right back. Well, apparently my years away from home haven't changed anything for her.

'Bummer.' May extremely casually disentangles her arms from around me, adjusting her duster jacket. 'Guess it's time for bed, CJ Bradley.'

I'll never know how she does it. The simple switch-up, like she didn't just activate every neuron in my brain, and I definitely – *definitely* – saw something light up for her, too. It was clearer than day this time.

She yawns as she walks back across the field, barefoot, snagging her heels and stick on the way, and then, as if it's an afterthought, turns back, shooting me a smirk. 'Night, top ched.'

Man.

## *Chapter Thirty-One*

### Hostile Attribution

### May

The second I get back in the house, over to my temporary room in the fortunately generously finished basement, I think I'm probably going to explode from my repressed feelings. Because what just happened? What just changed? Or did nothing change, and that had been happening all this time?

I stay up all night thinking about it, staring up at the ceiling until I fall asleep because my eyes are literally tired of being open for so long, and the next day, I bring all of it to Jordan.

We start out in the backyard, at the brand-new field, slapping shots into the nets, and eventually, as all things do, it turns into lounging in the folding chairs and drinking sweet tea with just a hint of vodka.

'So, let me get this straight.' She waves an arm at the entire backyard, goals and all. 'He made you all of this. A new field. This was all him?'

'Is it some kind of outrageous, like, unconscious method acting?' I grumble around a sip of tea. 'I mean, we laid the rules for this. We have a game plan. What, is this part of it?'

'Oh, honey.' Jordan sets her Mason jar down and shoots me a matter-of-fact glance that tells me she's seen right through my layers of infinite BS. 'You know this was always a part of it. As much as you love to deny that you're affected by Colt coming back . . . not to mention by having to pretend you're in a relationship with him . . .'

I nearly choke on my drink. 'I'm not – well, I *am* unaffected. I'm not affected!'

'It makes it easier to believe when you say it, right?'

And she's got me there. I plop my jar down next to Jordan's with a thud. 'Jor, but why? Why is the universe trying to bring us together like this, like *whatever* is happening between us right now, if he's just going to leave again? Because we're going to plough towards the end of the season, sooner or later, and poof, CJ Bradley tears right out of town like he was never here.'

'I get the feeling that's what's on his mind, too.' Jordan raises an eyebrow. 'I get that you're worried about him leaving. But May, every second, even when you're not on the field, when he doesn't have to be looking, he's looking. And I'm willin' to bet he's thinking about how he's gonna make this thing work without hurting you again.'

An uncomfortable feeling – that I am heavily wrong and Jordan may just be right – squirms into my chest. I think straight back to the emotional minefield from that night in Albuquerque, and then to the confession in the kitchen after family dinner.

And, of course, everything Rod told me about Colt's time in New Haven, his injury, and the photo. My team picture in his locker.

As if she reads my mind, Jordan adds, 'I'm also putting my money on the fact he's *probably* been brainstorming ways to come back home and *make* it work with you again since the second he got up there, for the record. But it'll take you a few years to wrap your head round that thought, if you ever do.'

She just sits back and stares straight into my soul, the way friends do when they've just read you up and down so hard you want to shrink into your shell out of embarrassment, arms crossed, legs kicked up, everything. As light-hearted as Jordan is, she has that down pat.

'You saw what he did, though.'

My friend shifts in her seat, moving to sit cross-legged in her chair. It's how I know she's getting real. 'I did, babe. I saw every bit of it, trust me.'

'And,' I forge on, 'isn't it right of me to be pissed at him? For making me think there was some hope for us, and then just up and heading out for years? You'd be pissed, wouldn't you?'

'That's the thing, my lovely May.' Jordan smiles wryly. 'I'd definitely be pissed. But eventually, you have to look at it this way. He might not be all that different from you.'

'Different from *me*? I'm not the one who—'

'Who left, I know,' Jordan finishes with a helping of stink eye. 'I've heard it, girl. My point is, yes, he left without saying anything.'

'Just some mom's strawberries bullshit.'

'Yeah. That. Which, I agree, worked against him, in any case.' She rolls her eyes before clasping her hands and placing them in her lap intently. 'But what if Colt was runnin' scared? What if he was scared because he didn't know what the future held, and he thought not saying anything was better than saying something and taking the gamble? And then, what if he's still scared?'

Oh.

'That' – I pick up my jar and take a great big swig of sweet tea – 'sounds delusional.'

It does not, actually, sound delusional. It sounds remarkably similar to some of the things I allowed myself to think for a fleeting second before I pushed them away because, for my own sake, I *had* to move on.

'I'm afraid it's the explanation that makes the most sense to me.'

'It sounds like we're excusing his behaviour.'

'It might.' Jordan fiddles with the straw in her jar, still holding her therapist expression. 'But it also sounds like we're growing up. May, for God's sake, he made you a *lacrosse field*. He's definitely trying to mend something. Not just the relationship between the two of you, but I think he's also trying to mend his sense of self. As an *adult*.'

An adult. In my mind, I've always thought of him as someone who ran away and put more than a couple of kinks in my story. I forget to think of him as *himself*.

'Give yourself space to hate the guy,' Jordan finishes. 'Just don't forget to give him space to grow.'

She leans back in her chair and finishes off her sweet tea, satisfied. I feel like I can barely touch mine any more. Not with the thoughts running around my brain screaming the way they are.

Yes, he's the guy I hated for years. He's the guy who had me staying up all night tossing and turning and thinking the way no other man ever did. He's the guy who annoyed the hell out of me when he shot me that smarmy smile across the field at high school practices and then challenged me to go one-on-one.

But Jordan is right. He's also the guy who always understood how much lacrosse meant to me and made me a new field when the old one got torn up out of the ground. He's also the guy who gushed about my yearly rodeo appearances to anyone who'd listen at dinner. And he's the guy who made sure his tie matched my pantsuit stitch for stitch. No one else has ever put my photo up in his locker, or walked me to class despite not actually having any classes, or honestly, just sat and *listened*.

He has, in his own Colt way, been sealing the cracks he left behind. No blame, no excuses. Just actions.

## Chapter Thirty-Two

Rodeo

**May**

Colt looks absolutely atrocious. In his big cowboy hat and sunglasses, I don't think anyone is going to be fooled by the attempt at a disguise.

My mom pulls out a pair of Pit Viper wraparound shades and holds them out in front of Colt. 'Give these a shot. They'll work even better. They're ridiculous.'

'What? Those aren't ridiculous! They're mine,' Papa whines defensively. Mumma just sighs and taps his shoulder in a gesture of 'shoo'. It's clear where I get it from.

'She's right.' Savannah plucks the other (more normal) pair right from Colt's face and slides on the Pit Vipers. Colt just gives her a pissed little frown. 'There ya go. Now hurry up. We need to find Ma and Pop.'

'Whoa.' Colt holds up a hand. 'The whole thing is that I

*don't* get recognized here, right? So why don't we split up, and I'll—'

'CJ BRADLEY!' a woman's voice yelps. 'Oh, my god!'

He drops his hand immediately, straight-faced. 'Well. We tried.'

The woman, a middle-aged brunette with an OKC orange T-shirt, waves to her friends, pointing Colt's way. It's definitely *so* over for him.

'And with that,' I laugh, 'I'm gonna head out and get ready. Barrel race is in a half-hour. Find a good spot.'

'I'm sure the Bradleys have beaten us to it.' Mumma smiles, and she and Papa give me a shared hug.

'Go get 'em, *mija*.' Papa straightens my collar, ruffling my hair, unfortunately ruining the braids I'd just done about an hour ago.

'Paaaa,' I groan.

'What? It's for *luck*.' My dad presses a kiss to the top of my head. 'Be safe.'

'I will, Papa.'

My parents let me go, and my ever-so-clever father gives me a little nudge Colt's way, who clears his throat and removes his dumb Pit Vipers, cutting his gaze towards the crowd of quickly approaching women. 'You're gonna be great.' He grins, if not slightly bashfully. 'I'm not lying when I say I'm just glad I'll get to see you race again. I've missed that.'

I choke back a *haha, and whose fault was that*, with a keen eye on the aunties drawing near. 'Good. It's a sign you have a heart.'

Colt snorts. 'Okay, Velasco. Knock 'em dead.' He leans down and kisses my cheek, his cowboy hat brushing my forehead. I raise an eyebrow.

He just smirks. 'My version of "good luck".'

\* \* \*

'Rodeo, lacrosse, weather. You balance a heavy plate, May.'

'Don't I know it.' I shoot a wry smile at the girl opposite me. Noemi Montes and I have been barrel racing together since we started riding. Noemi took things to the next level, circuit and all, and she's raced in rodeos as far and wide as the Calgary Stampede by now. I'm pretty sure the only reason my horse still remembers the cloverleaf is because I take him for a slow trot around the barrels every day during chores, and he happily meanders through it, not the fastest, but quite obedient. Rocky has never been anything but reliable.

'Graduatin' this year?' Noemi asks.

I nod. 'Yep. Got some things to work through.'

'I take it you're not going the rodeo route, huh?'

With a glance from her sponsor-laden Western top to my plain blue plaid one, I raise an eyebrow. 'That obvious?'

We share a mutual laugh at that. Barrel racing is basically going to be life and career for Noemi until she decides it's time to step down, after which she'll probably take over her parents' ranch, not too different from what I could see myself doing. 'So what will you do?' says Noemi, spawning my worst fear.

'I don't know,' I admit. It's better I save the energy it takes to lie – especially one this big. And she knows how it is, leaving the ranch. 'The weather's been terrible here lately. I'm not sure if I'll declare for the draft. Every women's MLL team is on the East Coast. I'd have to leave, and who'll look after the ranch after that?' I shrug. 'I wonder if it's better I stay, you know? I can actually make a difference here. Doing research for the early detection programme.'

Noemi looks a little crestfallen at that. Disappointed? She doesn't know me like that, does she? 'Really? I mean, your research is fantastic. Don't get me wrong, it's just . . . we've been at this for years.' She shoots me a wry smile. 'You certainly have competitive fire. You're made for sport, May. The ranch, the research, it won't go anywhere. Your career years will. Trust me.'

The announcer's voice warbles incoherently over the speakers, and I mount Rocky, giving him a pat of encouragement. A sleek brown quarter horse, Rocky's been mine since my first state youth lacrosse match – twelve years ago now. He's sturdy, reliable, and best of all, loving and loved. Rocky only hits the barrels really hard once a year, for the Oklahoma County Rodeo, and he eats up every second of it.

As the crowd roars excitedly outside, I soak in the sound. To be surrounded by cheers, maybe on a lacrosse field, maybe at the very top of the professional league. The high is like nothing else. Isn't it?

Well. Colt's not the only one working on *adulting*.

Noemi gives me a parting wave as she and her horse are called, and they burst right out the gate, speeding around the barrels, making tight turns in the pattern like it's light work, to ear-bursting applause from the crowds when she comes back into the alley – record time.

Rocky and I trot closer to the entrance, and I can hear the announcer's next words. 'And with a special guest in Oklahoma for the season, give a big Okie County welcome to hometown talent and national pro lacrosse player, CJ Bradley!'

Oh. Great.

'Looks like your boy's up front!' Noemi teases as she catches her breath, bringing her horse, Bingo, down the aisle.

'Of course he is,' I hum under my breath. I remember his admitting – at dinner with his family – that he'd watched every rodeo I'd raced in before he left, and how excited he was to be back. I thought it'd be as easy as the girls from the team showing up the way they did every year, my parents, and maybe he'd tag along. Casually. Quietly.

But, as I'd learned the second he stepped foot in Oklahoma, there is nothing casual or quiet about the presence of national pro lacrosse player CJ Bradley.

'C'mon, buddy,' I whisper to Rocky. 'Let's run real fast today.'

The kid helping out with the horses guides us through the alleyway before letting us go, and Rocky and I set off with a start. Dust flies as we hit the first barrel at high speed, a tight turn, and then the next, a beautiful cloverleaf. It's not our fastest, but Rocky is a stunner, and when we head back down the aisle, he whinnies happily, satisfied with the cheering that follows him inside.

'*So* good.' I ruffle his mane, hopping down as the kid holds onto his reins, and taking them once I'm on solid ground. 'You still got it, friend.'

'Y'all were pretty phenomenal.' An unfamiliar voice interrupts my moment with my horse. I look up, and this guy's 100 per cent not someone I recognize. He has the showy yet protective padded vest of one of the bull riders, windswept blond hair, fringed chaps over well-worn jeans, spurred boots. Lots of sponsors on every leather article. Definitely a bull rider. He throws a pearly-white, blue-eyed smile my way. 'Impressive seeing a lacrosse player on a barrel horse.'

I turn back to Rocky, smoothing his coat distractedly. 'I like a little of everything in my life. Do I know you?'

'Not yet.' He sticks out a hand, and I take it. We share a firm shake. 'Jackson O'Hara. I'm just in town for the rodeo. You local?'

I nod. 'Yep. May Velasco. Nice to meet ya. How'd you know I play lax?'

'I'm a friend of Noemi's. She mentioned you were on OKC?'

'Sure.' I eye a patch on his vest. 'And you? National circuit?'

'You got me.' Jackson grins. 'It's how I know her. We run in similar circles.'

'I'd imagine.' I walk Rocky towards his stable, and Jackson falls into step with us.

'So, May. Meant to ask, if you had the chance.' He leans against the stable doors across from Rocky's as I lead my horse inside. 'Would you be down to grab a drink this weekend? Before I head out?'

*Great heavens.* I freeze in my spot. Rocky nuzzles my cheek, like, *Girl? What is this goon doing?*

There was certainly a time where getting asked out by an admittedly fantastic-looking bull rider – at the very pinnacle of rodeo – would have been in my top five. I mean, come on. When *The Longest Ride* came out, I literally prayed for a Scott Eastwood of my own. My twelve-year-old ass had posters all over my walls.

Suddenly, though, I'm taken aback, and honestly, not interested. Colt and I are technically fake. I could carry on a real relationship, right? But it's like the brakes are engaging on auto. Something in me latches right onto the thought of Colt as if we've been together for years. I would *absolutely* be a traitor and a dick if I said yes right now.

Because the way this Jackson guy's looking at me isn't the look you give someone you just want to have a nice friendly chat at the bar with. Which leads me to my next thought: if he knows I play, he *has* to know I'm very publicly 'dating' CJ

Bradley. I don't know where that hasn't been breaking news of late.

'I'm afraid I've got some plans.' I clear my throat awkwardly. Where in the world do I even begin? 'I . . . uh, I have some plans with my boyfriend.'

*Ew.* I wish I could have redone that a tad bit more smoothly. I'm expecting equally awkward disappointment from Jackson, but that isn't what I get. I shouldn't be surprised. This is a bull-riding man we're talking about. The red flag to end all red flags.

'Well, May . . .' He takes a couple of steps forward, steps I'm not too comfortable with when they put us both in Rocky's stable, with Jackson at the door. 'Listen. You're honestly too beautiful a woman to be with some lacrosse guy who's got air for brains. I'm offering you something a little more substantial. Something that's not just a shallow Boston frat boy. Come on, now.' He laughs this fabricated little laugh that screams to me it's time to break a wall and get the heck out of Dodge. 'It'd be a good time, I promise you.'

'Get the fuck away from my girlfriend.'

The breath leaves my lungs in a heavy *whoosh* as Colt's voice cuts the uncomfortable tension. He shoves right past Jackson and straight to me. He doesn't touch me, just shoots Jackson the deadliest glare I've ever seen him muster. My heart's beating a million miles an hour, and it's not the good kind of million miles an hour when I watch the two of them exchange stares. I'm the one who reaches out to Colt first, pulling him close to me with a fistful of his white T-shirt, and he responds immediately, wrapping an arm around me.

'Think on it, May,' Jackson finally quips, raising an eyebrow. I feel Colt's body tense beside me, his muscles going taut, but I tighten my grip, looking up at him with an air of *don't bother*. Jackson's spur-clad boots click off down the alleyway, and Colt, like me, exhales heavily.

'Man. What a prick.' His thumb rubs a circle into my shoulder, his brow knitted as he dips his head to give me a quick once-over. 'You okay? Did he . . .'

'Primary crime was being a creepy jerk.' I shudder a little at the thought of it. God. It'd be one thing if he didn't know I was dating anyone and stepped away peacefully. This was a terrifying other. 'Thank you.' I shake my head, scary images flashing in my brain that I do my level best to push away. 'If you hadn't showed up . . .'

'Don't even make me think about it.' Colt's mouth twitches into a frown. The hand on my shoulder slowly backs off, hovering over me. 'Sorry. It's not my place to, you know.'

'Please don't be sorry.' My tone is nothing like it had been when I gave Colt the same response back at the beginning of the season, a snappy, salty sarcasm that is far from present now. It's pleading, beseeching. 'Really. And, Colt, honestly . . .' The stress I've been holding all through my back and shoulders melts when I finish my sentence. 'I don't mind a little help sometimes. Certainly not with dickheads who try and corner me in stables.'

'Disgusting.' Colt shivers, but his hand falls back onto my shoulder. 'Are you sure you're okay?'

'I will be. Once I get a shit ton of tacos to distract myself from the ick.'

'Done. Tacos on me.'

'Alright, then, hometown talent. Maybe they'll give 'em to you for free,' I prod him in the ribs as we walk on out.

'Oh, no.' He blushes a ditzy pink. Blushing over Tex-Mex and rodeos, this man. 'I couldn't let them do that.'

I roll my eyes, putting on my most exasperated face, and begin preparing some witty jab about how he's always trying to be all dumb and righteous because of his colossal screw-up in leaving the place with the best rodeo on earth.

But the warmth of his presence, the feeling of safety from just being near him, stops me in my tracks.

## Chapter Thirty-Three

Brackets

**Colt**

Screw tacos. I want to deck that guy so hard his veneers fall off.

I was never the one with the kind of fire that started fights on the field. There were guys on the high school team we counted on for that, and when I moved up to the collegiate level, there were guys for that there, too. On the Woodchucks, I'd say it's probably Connor, as temperamental as he can be. But after watching that asshole try to corner May, I'm struggling to grit my teeth and settle for imagining throwing the punches.

She changes out of her Western shirt and into a vintage OKC tee. Her braid mussed, she pops on a baseball hat once we're in the stands, and glances my way for confirmation. 'Does that do it?'

How do I tell her that it *beyond* does it? That she could be in stable-mucking jeans and boots or a pantsuit or the most generic college lacrosse uniform and be the most beautiful woman in the entire world every time?

I swallow hard and nod. 'Looks good to me.'

She returns my nod with one of thanks, coupled with a teasing smirk. 'You still look pissed. You'll scare people with that frown of yours.'

'Sorry.' I try my best to relax my face. The lingering anger won't leave it.

May sighs. She reaches out and presses her hand to my left one where I've been rubbing it nervously against my thigh. 'I am completely fine, Colt. He's just some uppity rodeo dickhead. It's nothing new. My dad told me about some of the guys he rode with when he was younger. I should've known—'

'It's not your responsibility to know *anything* in that situation.' My voice comes out more upset than I'm prepared for. Gruff? Absolutely not. 'It's his responsibility to stop at "no".'

May nods steadily, shifting her brown-eyed gaze towards the ring. 'I appreciate that, Colt.'

She gives my hand a soft squeeze, and I see that her appreciation isn't just words. It's more than that – it's someone who's always thought it was her against the world recognizing that she's not alone. I know it well, because I recently started to realize the same thing.

The rodeo incident sits fresh in my brain for a couple days after the fact. I give May the same space I usually do, let her do her thing, but the 'text me when you get there' messages become more frequent during the rest of the week. Just the way that guy looked at her . . . ugh.

That Wednesday, the National College Lacrosse Association wraps up seeding all the teams, a longer process than usual owing to extremely close scores for the season, and the bracket comes out as we wait on the field, gathered around Coach Dillon's laptop with bated breath. With a stunning record this year, we're hoping for a good spot that will put the Riders straight through to the first round of the playoffs.

'First round,' Maddie hums, eyes squeezed shut and fingers crossed. 'Please. Please. Please—'

'It's here!' Coach announces, and the girls are immediately pushing forward in a bid to get a glance at the screen.

May grabs my arm, eyes wide. 'Oh my god. Okay. We got . . .'

The both of us lean in, and the groan we share is immediate. Great. I thought we'd have been seeded higher, but we fell right in the middle of the pack, second fiddle to the East Coast lacrosse schools. And our first match of the playoffs, first round, will be against . . .

'Alabama?' Brianna presses a hand to her forehead. 'May, look at this bracket! We're against 'Bama!'

'Damn it,' grumbles May. 'Alabama . . .'

'Took you guys out last year,' I finish for her. Yikes. I mean, they could have been a lower seed and really got stuck with a terrific team as their playoff match-up, so this might be the best-case scenario, but the lore goes deep. Playing a team that knocked you out of the national playoffs always holds double weight.

'Yep. And we've *never* beaten them. Our meeting record? Twenty-nine to nothing.' May steps back and plops right down in the grass, blowing a hair out of her face and throwing her crosse in her lap. 'Looks like we're going back for round two.'

'What if' – I pick up her stick and extend a hand – 'I said I'd watched hours of Alabama's film for this exact reason, because I saw you guys lose to them last year?'

May takes my hand reluctantly, narrowing her eyes. 'As long as this doesn't involve setting me up to take a demo shot I'm never going to make in front of the entire team, go on.'

'What if I said I tailored a shot clinic in case you'd have to go up against them again?'

Coach Dillon closes her laptop, smiling. 'Oh, and this is exactly why you are here, Bradley. What if you did indeed tailor this perfect shot clinic?'

'Well, if I did, I'd say we might have a good shot at turning the tide.' I hand May her stick, and she purses her lips.

'You think we can beat the best team in the South in the first round?' Lexi's voice pipes up. She crosses her arms, regarding me with disbelief.

I'm going to be totally honest. Lexi terrifies me. I clear my throat to avoid an unfortunate voice crack. 'I do.'

And holy shit. The girl cracks a smile. 'Then let's get to it, Bradley.'

## *Chapter Thirty-Four*

### Hot Cowboy

**May**

With our day of reckoning against Alabama on our heels, the girls and I are well aware we should probably be living and breathing lacrosse for the next week, but we don't have the luxury of big East Coast lax towns. Tables don't stop filling up in the bar, the festivals don't move themselves a week later, and the cattle don't park themselves in one spot and hibernate till post-season's over. Half the team applies for time off from their jobs and doesn't get it. And those of us working on the farm still end up ankle-deep in muck on the evenings, balancing oncoming finals, lacrosse practice, and chores.

'Bring 'em round, May!' Tía Juana calls out to me from outside the fence, a cold sweet tea – salvation – in her hand.

I turn Rocky in response, and the livestock follow with a resigned lowing. 'C'mon, now. Let's go!'

'¡Vamos, May!' Tía claps a hand against her thigh. She's ten times more efficient at this than I am. My harried pace – and Rocky's leisurely one – aren't quite on par. Now that my horse's annual moment of speed is past, he's got no reason to do anything beyond a casual trot.

'Goin'!' The cattle moo exasperatedly when I herd them into the corral. The enormous pack of gentle giants are a combination of Tía's and ours. While the ranch undergoes major reconstruction, my aunt is letting us keep the animals at her farm in Tulsa where she has a ton of extra barn space. The condition? I have to keep doing my chores – an hour-fifteen drive away. I adjust my hat, swivelling towards Tía and guiding Rocky out of the corral before my aunt comes over to close the gate. I dismount my horse, taking his reins so we can lead him back to the field. 'Where'd you put Colt?'

'Oh, the boyfriend? Got him to work on my four-by-four,' she replies. My aunt's rickety red truck breaks down at least once a week. Poor Colt is probably trying to turn water into wine back at the house.

'You're good at making college kids do the chores,' I tease her, nudging her side so she jumps, nearly losing her sweet tea to gravity.

'My back can't do these things any more!' Tía Juana says in defence. This much is true. Tía, like my Papa, used to be an adrenaline junkie, barrel racing and doing some crazy stunts in show that screwed her back up for good. I'm honestly shocked it's her who walked away with the permanent bodily injury and not my bull-riding father.

Her back issues, coupled with the fact that she lives alone, happily single since she divorced her deadbeat husband at twenty-eight, make for a *ton* of work to be done on her farm, all the time, even with well-qualified ranch hands.

I lean over and take a sip of her tea. The freezing liquid buffered by big ice cubes cools my entire body immediately. We take the short walk to the field where my aunt likes to let her horses run.

A loud sputtering sound emerges from the other side of the stables. 'The truck?' Tía says around her tea.

'Better go make sure Colt didn't blow that thing up,' I reply, and we hustle on over to the back of the barn.

I'm not sure what I expected to see as I idly dust the dirt off my Wranglers and tank top, but it certainly isn't what we encounter.

When the overachiever had offered to help me with my chores in Tulsa for the day, I couldn't say no – I mean, I didn't mind having someone speed up the dreaded process. And deep down, I didn't mind spending the drive with Colt, either. Beside the point. Either way, I couldn't have foreseen him looking this comfortable out on the farm. *Extremely* comfortable. And *extremely* . . . good.

Tía's straw falls out of her mouth as her eyes, like mine, go wider than the tyres on the four-by-four. The hood of the truck is propped up, some Tyler Childers crooning through the speakers, and Colt's deep brown leather boots, no longer as unscuffed as they were when he first arrived here, are screwed in the ground as he leans over the engine, a wrench in his hand, giving something one final twist. He stands briefly, squints at his handiwork, then immediately dips right back down to the engine, and Tía lets out a little squeak.

I think our shock is justified. I could start with the fact that I've never seen jeans fit a man as well as they do Colton James Bradley. For that matter, I've never seen jeans fit a man's spectacular butt as well as they do Colton James Bradley's. Things only get more difficult for us when I drink in his very shirtless torso, the strong muscles of his back and arms moving when he steps back from the truck, rounding it to get to the driver's side. The silver chain of his necklace glitters against his neck, its medallion flat against his chest. I get a full view of his impeccably chiselled abs, at least before he pulls the white tee half-tucked into his back pocket out and over his head, then adjusts the Ariat cap sitting backwards on his head, his wavy dusky brown hair peeking out behind.

Tía and I exchange a knowing look.

Colt plops down in the driver's seat and turns the truck over. It lets out that same putter as before, except this time, the sound persists and the engine roars to life, buffeted by what's now a Chris Stapleton ballad on the radio. He grins at my aunt, and then at me, the corners of his eyes creasing happily. 'All done, ma'am!'

He swings himself out of the truck, as casually as someone who's worked on the ranch their entire life would. I blink furiously. My increasingly complicated and increasingly involved feelings for Colt are one thing. But I cannot have this idiot catch me drooling over the fact that he looks like he was born to rock 'walking womanizer country boy'.

'May,' he says with a cheeky little smirk, dusting his palms off on his jeans.

'Where did you get your buckle?' I blurt.

Colt's eyebrows rise. Oh my god. *May. SHUT UP. Please do not talk more about his belt-buckle, insinuating that you were ogling his belt-buckle. Ogling everything in the vicinity of his belt-buckle. MAY.* 'Your pop, actually.'

My cheeks are reddening faster than I can control them. 'It . . . um . . . you look very—'

'Cowboy,' my aunt finishes unhelpfully. 'My niece means to say you look like a very *hot cowboy*.'

'Huh.' Colt's eyes don't move from mine for a minute. They narrow just slightly in amusement, flecks of brown in his irises glittering in the ruthless sun. 'Hot cowboy. That's a new one.'

My aunt, under the total assumption that this man is certainly my boyfriend, just titters satisfactorily. 'You got yourself a good one, May. Why don't the both of you feel free to get to some more tea in the house? I have a couple of rounds to finish up here.'

Tía Juana struts off, chuckling to herself, leaving me, Colt, and my dumb, big-mouth comment.

'So, May.' Colt leans against the side of the truck, the smirk returning to his face. 'My buckle, huh?'

I could literally hide under the pickup in embarrassment right now. I groan and bury my face in my hands instead: next best thing. 'Let's go home, hot cowboy. Terrorize me later.'

'O-kay,' hums Colt, taking the lead on our walk back to the driveway. My head is still in my hands the entire time. If the way he stood up for me at the rodeo and the moment on the homemade backyard field weren't enough to make me question every limitation I'd set for myself, this might just be my shove over the edge. Granted, CJ Bradley is a handsome angel of a man, but more than that, it's how well he fits right in with this life, *my* life.

He's tempting me in every way. And Jordan's probably right. He's trying, and he's certainly starting to succeed.

## Chapter Thirty-Five

'Bama Rush

### Colt

'I can sing the entire thing.'

'No, you *can't*,' chides Maddie. 'I don't believe it. We learned that in elementary school. Have you been rehearsing?'

Jordan nods vigorously. 'Yes, ma'am. And I know the *whole song*.'

As we walk down the hall of the ridiculously nice hotel, Jordan takes a deep breath, and suddenly, she's belting the entire 'Fifty States' song at opera-singer volume.

'ALABAMA, ALASKA, ARIZONA, ARKANSAS . . .'

'Oh my god.' Coach Dillon looks terrified. 'I had no idea we'd let a ten-year-old on the team.'

'CONNECTICUT! BA-BA-BA,' chants Jordan, with a little wiggle on the last three beats.

'This is why you never challenge her,' May says, her tone that of a tired mom. 'She does this.'

'Has she had multiple coffees on the way out?' I ask her in disbelief.

'Nothing. Just a bottle of water and a grilled cheese sandwich before we got on the plane.' She purses her lips. 'Trust me. This is what I've been dealing with for years.'

'UTAH, VERMONT, VIRGINIA—'

'Okay, okay! OH. KAY.' Maddie extends her arms, fully stopping Jordan on her walk. 'I believe you. I concede. All right?'

Jordan grins proudly. 'Good.'

I find it pretty unserious that this is the same team that will, tomorrow, be required to top the number one in the Southern Conference. I guess it's a good sign they're loosening up, especially after Coach had them watching film all last night before heading out this morning on a seven a.m. flight. Which is why I'm shocked Jordan has the energy of a toddler today.

Loading into rooms is a chaotic process. The girls have to hustle to get their stuff down before grabbing snacks in a big banquet room that's been set up for our team. It's probably the best we've been treated on the road so far.

We are herded towards the press next, where the Riders do their usual rounds at the mic, May and Coach Dillon speaking on the sentiment leading up to the game. Press leads us right up to our time on Alabama University's practice field, for a light run-through of some of our key strategies, and a blow-by-blow of the points I made sure to hit during our shot clinic a week back. Since the match will be played in the evening, something the team's not used to, this is their last chance to get in the most realistic rehearsal possible.

Once we wrap up on the field, we grab a dinner more enormous than we could have imagined in the same banquet hall – they have *steak* – and disperse, everyone trying to settle their minds to get the best sleep possible. I know from experience it rarely works, no matter what you try. I've done melatonin, sprayed lavender on my pillow, turned on every available flavour of white noise to force myself to sleep in the past five-ish years. Something about the impending threat of a game just transcends all remedies.

I end up at the hotel pool, out in the back, with my feet dangling in the water. The heat hangs thick in the Birmingham air. It's going to be a sweaty night game tomorrow, that's for sure.

'You know,' May's voice comes from behind me, 'we've never beaten Alabama. Like, ever.'

'Never?'

'Mm-mm.' She shakes her head, slipping her flip-flops off to my right and taking a seat. She lets her legs hang in the water with a contented sigh. 'Not since the National Championship was organized in '85.'

'So y'all are feeling the nerves.'

'A little bit, yeah.' May chuckles nervously, and her dimples etch their way into her cheeks. A coil of hair falls from her messy bun, and she bats it away so it falls down the back of her neck. I could think of a couple ways to ease her nerves. *Shut up, Colt. God. Not a good time.* 'You know what it's like. Being captain.'

I shrug, nodding matter-of-factly. 'A little bit.'

She lets out a laugh. 'Mister Pro Lacrosse. Woodchucks.'

'Stop it! They're a noble mascot.'

May's snort tells me she's not buying it. I flip her the bird, and she just bursts out laughing even harder.

'You're going to fall in,' I warn her.

'I won't,' she cracks up. 'I swear. Anyway.' With an exhale, the last of her laughter subsides. 'Are you scared?'

'Scared?' The word is a double-edged sword for me. Am I scared? Perpetually. Does she want to hear me be honest, or does she want me to provide respite? I end up choosing honesty. 'I guess . . . you could say so. I'm just scared I won't have done my best in preparing you guys.'

The shadow of a smile quirks the corners of May's mouth up briefly. 'I understand that completely.'

The only sound for a moment is the splashing of water, and then I break the silence. 'When did we become friends?'

May blinks. I think I see a hint of shock in her eyes, just barely. 'When did we become friends?' she repeats dubiously.

'When we met up at Moonie's,' I recall. 'You said something to me. You said we were two steers with our horns locked, all through high school. And that it was a rivalry.' I turn to May. She raises her gaze to meet mine; the only eyes I could stare into from sun-up to sun-down, and then all night long. 'Is this still just a rivalry?'

There's a minute where I fully think she's going to push me into the pool. It's definitely something she'd do. Instead, she replies, 'I think, maybe, that I was wrong back then, Colt. I don't think that it was ever just a rivalry.'

'Really?'

She smiles softly, and it's nice, you know, to not go directly to May Velasco's shit list for once since I met her. But there's still some semblance of restraint in the smile. Something she's holding back. 'Guess it's nice. To, you know, really be friends again.'

*Friends.*

But, for the record, I know I don't just want to be her friend. I want to be the one who puts up her white picket fence and the house for the dog. I want to be the one at the barbecue in her backyard. I want to be at every single match she plays, and I want hers to be the first face I see at every single match I play. I want to tape up her bad wrist and give her a kiss for good luck. I want to wrangle Sav into making me ties to match every outfit she wears. I don't just want to be her friend. I really don't.

Matchday is the definition of fear.

The field is dark in the evening, save for the lights illuminating the grass, and up in the stands, 'Bama fans have shown up in full force. It's an enormous turnout. I try my best to ignore the pointing and questions asking me where May is. We need total focus if we want to nail this one.

I unzip my thin windbreaker and toss it on a sideline bench as the girls jog onto the field. May shoots me a thumbs-up. Her voice echoes through my head – *friends* – but that's not what either of us needs right now. She needs people in her corner, and I'm going to be one of those people, no matter what.

I raise a hand in a gesture of 'wait', and I turn around so May can see the back of my OKC Riders T-shirt. The crossed stick logo is on the front, along with the big cursive 'Oklahoma City', but it's what's on back that I care about.

When I turn around again to face the field, it's hard to make out her expression, what with her goggles and mouthguard, but I can tell exactly what she does next.

She presses her hand to her lips and blows me the biggest kiss.

## *Chapter Thirty-Six*

Pickups and Poor Choices

**May**

It's my name.

He's wearing my jersey.

I'm not completely sure what I'm seeing when he turns around and jabs a thumb at the number on the back of his T-shirt, but it's me. VELASCO, above a big 13.

Honestly? I am in total shock.

I've seen plenty of girls in their football-playing boyfriend's jersey. In high school and then in college, it's not something we're unfamiliar with. As much as I know this is for the plot we've fabricated throughout the season, I can feel that it's so much more than that. I can't help the tears that well up in my eyes.

Colt turns back, beaming proudly, and my feet practically freeze as if the grass has turned to quicksand. Sure, it's about keeping up the narrative for the cameras that click away around us, but when my eyes meet his, all the chaos disappears, leaving just the two of us. Colt and May.

I press my hand to my lips, and I blow him the biggest flying kiss. It's no show. I mean every damn bit of it.

That's the last pleasant lull I get before the match hits us head-on.

During last week's practice, Colt took us through manoeuvres used by the men's MLL players to get the ball through a particularly keen defence – a level up from what we're used to. After watching footage from the last match, it's clear there's no way to beat a team this solid by dancing around them. The only way out, he said, would be through. And it wouldn't be pretty.

We take it literally. Evading penalty carefully, we plough through the defence to get our balls through, playing more aggressively than we've ever played before. At one point, Jordan swings her stick so fiercely I think she could probably cut wood with it if she tried. And at the end of the game, tight on numbers, Maddie makes one last Mad Dog goal: our now signature no-look twizzler, smacking the back of 'Bama's net like we have rent to pay.

The first time in *history*.

'OH MY GOD,' screams Jordan when the horn blows and the scoreboard blinks. By two goals, we've beaten them, and earned a spot in the second round.

All of us, even the girls on the bench, storm the field, jumping all over each other at the midline, yelling and wailing and crying. Somewhere between Jordan's arm and Lexi's ass, I manage a mangled sob of, 'I'M SO PROUD OF YOU GUYS,' and the girls sob in return. This isn't the end of our season – by no means the end of my journey. If I decide to leave lacrosse after this senior season, I don't intend on leaving quietly.

\* \* \*

Come Sunday, back from game-day chaos, Colt and I swing by the drive-through diner to grab burgers, against all potential dietary regimen costs. We dig into greasy heaven in the back of his truck, sitting on a pile of ridiculous chevron-striped blankets as we share a basket of fries and a pack of my favorite Busch Light Peach. We're parked up in the middle of the field a good mile outside of the new and improved Eagle Rock sign. It's so clear out here I can trace each and every constellation my parents taught me. I start with Orion, dragging an imaginary line across the three stars in his belt.

'Now,' I ask Colt around a fry, 'where in the hell did you get that shirt? They don't make May Velasco merch, I'll have you know.'

'I, uh . . .' He laughs nervously, putting down his burger to regard me with complete attention. 'I know that. I, um, I stole my sister's Cricut machine.'

'Huh. You did all of that for . . .'

'Well, uh, for you. Obviously.'

*For me.* Damn it. No one but CJ Bradley could say something so cheesy and yet send a shiver from my head to my toes.

'We still have such different destinations in life, Colt.' I pick up another fry, and a dull wind comes through, tousling Colt's wavy brown hair – that stupid (splendid, but stupid) 'flow' of his – as I glance up at the sky of perfectly clear stars. 'You, professional lacrosse, far from home.'

'And you?' he says quietly.

'I guess I seem like a square.' I shoot him a smirk. 'You think I'm a square.'

'I never said that.' Colt shakes his head, but the slightest smile sneaks out.

'I have things I wanna do, but my best option is staying home. Holding it down. You have choices. We have different destinations,' I repeat.

'Hmm.' He chews in thought before swallowing, swirling the beer in his can around a few times before he speaks. 'May, I think . . . we don't get assigned a direction in life. I get that I probably don't understand what it's like to become an adult here, where everything is so uncertain. But I think you choose your destination. And I think there comes a time when someone with the sort of talent you have has to make a choice as to who they wanna be.'

Colt's dusky eyes glitter, magnetic, drawing me closer. I raise an eyebrow, setting down my beer and planting my chin on my hands. 'A choice?'

'Yep.' His breath fans my cheeks. My eyes flit to his lips. On a normal day, I'd stop myself there. But something about the stars, and the truck, and the low rasp of Colt's voice . . . all inhibitions leave my body. I'm doing exactly what I told myself I wouldn't. Over, and over, and over, and apparently, it didn't work. 'Are you gonna be ordinary, or extraordinary?'

My breath catches as his fingers brush my temple, tucking an errant curl behind my ear. 'You still got time, you know, before you make that choice. May.' The soft, sweet whisper of Colt's voice caresses my skin, a teasing smile entering his eyes before it traces its way across his lips. 'But if you care, I think you're pretty fucking extraordinary.'

The bass drum in my heart starts thudding on cue. Suddenly, my stomach is a flurry of something I've not felt since high school, not since I thought Colt was going to kiss me after the championship game sophomore year, and then stupendously didn't, probably because the guys swept him away for a victory lap of the field. Every so often, I wonder if he would have kissed me. Now, I think to myself, I might be getting my answer.

'No one's watching, New Haven.' My voice is a quavering sound that floats on the air and dissolves a moment later, threatening to cave to the hand that cups my cheek. 'You don't have to pretend here.'

'I'm not pretending.' Our knees are touching, a strangely intimate feeling, and he pulls me closer by warm hands at my waist. 'Are you?'

I don't expect a bit of what I do next.

All at once, my lips crash against Colt's, the taste of celebratory peach beer on both our parts invading my senses. It's not at all like the tame, orchestrated kisses we've shared in the public eye. It's unbridled, raw, and much needier. His hands travel down my body, marvelling at every curve in a way no man's hands have marvelled before. I wrap my legs around his torso, pulling our bodies closer to one another. His fingers tangle in my hair, his eyelashes fluttering against mine. I move a hand to his chest and give him a little nudge in the right direction.

'May,' Colt laughs as he falls back against the floor of the truck's bed with a grin that possibly, maybe, couldn't be any *hotter*.

I lean down and kiss him again, and his grip on my hips tightens, fervent and searching. His fingers just brush the hem of my shirt. *Keep going*, I want to beg him.

'What if someone sees us?' he murmurs, his index fingers hooked through my belt loops as I lean back and do a quick three-sixty scan for the both of us.

I make my decision pretty quickly. 'Then,' I lean right back down and whisper my next words at his ear. 'To hell with 'em.'

With a grin, Colt pulls me back down to him, and he presses his lips to mine. My senses are overwhelmed in the most blissful way – the taste of the beer, the feeling of his skin against mine as he tosses my tank top aside. My hands roam until they find their way beneath his shirt, and I pull it right off him as quickly as I can. I relish every beautiful part of him. There is a shit ton I hate about lacrosse guys, but I will never complain about the wonderfully defined muscles and the abs. The perfectly toned six-pack on CJ Bradley. I have no comments or suggestions. I hum happily as my fingers trace their way down the sharp V just below those abs, and Colt gives my ass a squeeze, pushing our bodies close enough together that I can clearly feel the evidence of just how extraordinary he thinks I am. My eyes widen. Oh. My. God.

'This okay?' he murmurs into my hair. His hands are in my back pockets. *Back pockets*. We're in the bed of his stunning truck. This is, as much as I hate to admit it, actually a dream come true. Yes, it's absolutely okay. It's beyond okay.

'Yes,' I try to say, except it turns into more of a needy keening when Colt kisses his way down the side of my neck. Any language in my brain turns into incoherent mush. Tomorrow, maybe I'll look back on this and have to do damage control, but right now, I have nothing to lose. And frankly, I have so many things I've yet to feel.

I'm beyond thankful when Colt finally finds the button of my jeans. I wiggle out of them as quickly and effectively and eagerly as I possibly can.

'May, if you'll let me, I wanna apologize again to you.' Colt's chest heaves against mine, and in one swift move, his hand protecting the back of my head from the floor of the truck, he rolls us over, tugging a fold of the blanket with us. I'm still holding onto him like my life depends on it, my thighs at his hips, legs pulling him close to me, but cohesive thoughts become a thing of the past when I hear the rasp in his voice. The small silver medallion around his neck swings above me as he brings his lips to mine, his hair tickling my forehead, and then, one sweet, husky word out of that beautiful mouth: 'Properly.'

Immediately, I'm nodding vigorously. 'Please,' I try my best to say. He's literally killing my brain cells. How is that possible? How is a man so gorgeous?

Colt cracks a mischievous little smile before his hands take over, dragging a honeyed path down my body until his eyes meet mine, crinkled in the corners with full knowledge of the state I'm about to be in.

I might be tripping, but at this point, I'm pretty positive a string of 'pleasepleaseplease' is about all I can muster.

'Spread those beautiful legs for me, May,' Colt says, every vibration of his voice in his chest travelling right to mine, and let me tell you, I am happy to oblige. He lets out a satisfied hum. 'You good?' he murmurs, thumb stroking my cheek.

'Yeah. Yeah, yeah.' This time, my response is clear as day. I'm so good, actually. And I'll be even better in about five minutes, which Colt knows, because with a kiss to my abdomen and a squeeze of my hand, he says, 'Brace yourself.'

Whatever bracing I do isn't enough for the feeling when he slides a finger inside me. I dig my heels into Colt's back, a grateful moan emerging from my body, one that's amplified when he adds a second finger – *oh my*. 'Shh,' he whispers with a teasing grin. 'The fireflies are gonna hear you.'

I'd laugh if he doesn't adjust his touch in some magical way that feels *just right*, so right that I have to tug him down to me. He finds a rhythm that my body responds to without even trying. If this is the apology, I'm more than willing to accept. I'll take further reparations, too. Actually, I'll probably take whatever he has.

Various combinations of 'Colt, please,' tumble straight from my lips. Our eyes meet dead-on. I plead he's read my mind, and I'm proven just right when he lays a kiss on my collarbone, and then at my sternum, and then lower, until I'm practically biting down to keep from howling hard enough to scare away every firefly in Eagle Rock. My fingers are lost in Colt's hair, and my soul feels like it finally – finally – leaves my body when relief crashes over me, the sort of fireworks I've never, ever felt before. My chest rises and falls with heavy breaths that only a good match can usually get out of me. *Oh, May, just imagine what else this man has up his sleeve.*

'You're so perfect,' he mouths, lips moving against the side of my neck. 'So perfect.'

Well. CJ Bradley *definitely* just apologized to me. And I'm eating up every crumb of it.

My hands creep down to the button of Colt's jeans, and I press a kiss to his cheek. I whisper, 'I accept your apology. I'm gonna thank you for it.'

## Chapter Thirty-Seven

Reckoning

**Colt**

About an hour in the back of the truck, and one gas-station stop later, we casually wind up back at my house as if nothing at all had just happened. 'HOME!' May calls out upon our arrival, and then the screen door slams behind us, protesting noisily as always. So many familiar things, but so much change.

Wordless, save for a parting smile, we head in our separate directions. Once I'm all ready for bed, I head to climb under my covers, but my bedroom door creaks slightly ajar.

For the first time since the Velascos have temporarily moved in, May stands there, hair piled on top of her head, yawning hard, her pillow in her arms, and I don't have to say anything. We run through the motions like we've been doing it for ever. She curls up beside me, her head to my chest, wearing shorts and a huge T-shirt with a map of the historic OKC Diamond

Quad on it, and I drape my arm over her, her leg laid across mine. No pillow wall. No distance between us. She smells like roses and Busch Light Peach.

I've known it for a good part of my life. That's the first time, though, that I really, really think about it. I think about the fact that I am in love with Manmayi Velasco, and I choose to forget about the logistics. In that moment, it doesn't matter that I might leave and she might put her guard back up. All that matters is that I am unconditionally and unabashedly in love with her.

I wake to the sound of the shower running, and I run a hand over the space next to me – empty, save for a lingering warmth from the heat of May's body and the indentation she left in the sheets. I check my phone. *Fuck.* It's seven-thirty a.m. on a Tuesday. She has class, and I have a ton of my MBA stuff to work on.

I find a shirt somewhere on my desk chair and pull it on, stumbling bleary-eyed towards the stairs and down to the kitchen. Sav has a seven-thirty class that she's probably already at. Pop's shift at the hospital started at six-thirty. The Velascos head out early every morning to tend their remaining cattle and oversee construction of their new ranch. And Ma's likely just left to teach her eight a.m. lecture, leaving no one but the two of us in the house. Sure enough, my mom's signature sticky note is slapped on the side of the fridge: *Pancakes and berries inside. EAT THE BERRIES, COLT. Feed May.*

Great. It'd be nice to have a distraction or two running around the house right about now.

'Colt!' her voice comes from upstairs.

*Nonchalant*, I recite my mantra for the day. I can't risk scaring her away. Unfortunately, that lasts about two seconds. I run right up the steps like my life depends on it. 'Yeeeaahhh!'

'Colt!' May's still yelling from the bathroom. 'I can't find my hair towel!'

I mentally curse my sister. Always moving shit around in there so she can get dressed up for all of three lectures. May's towel turban, purple with white and yellow daisies, is definitely not outside on the towel rack. 'Savannah!' I hiss, rifling through the linen closet in desperate pursuit of the offender.

'Is it out there?' May calls, as exasperated as I am right now. I'm basically throwing half the closet over my shoulder looking for this thing. If it doesn't show up . . .

The bathroom door creaks open behind me. I whip around, and I am decidedly unprepared for the sight that greets me.

So maybe I'm going to go ballistic. Or feral. Or both. I remember picturing May in my house, in my room, fitting right in like our lives were made for one another. I think the sight of her, cheeks flushed, water dripping down her temple and jaw, her curly hair soaked, and nothing at all on her person except for her matching lavender bath towel, might do me in.

I blink a couple times. Remind myself this situation is not about May's long, tanned legs, still glistening with water. Or the gentle curves that the towel does a poor job of concealing. It's not an easy reminder to give myself. My rational mind is checked out. I'm definitely not thinking with my brain when I rewind back to last night, to the way May's skin felt flush against mine, her nails digging into my back . . .

'My hair towel,' May says, a slightly concerned look on her stunning face.

'Huh?'

'Did you find it?'

'Um – let me see.' Towel. You're on a mission, damn it, Colt. I turn myself cleverly towards the linen closet so she can't see the evidence of her immediate effect on me. At this point, I'm practically begging my dick to leave this conversation as soon as possible so I can save some semblance of face. I shove yet another stack of washcloths to the side, and fortunately, there it is. The towel turban.

She sticks out a hand, and I cough, looking away as I push the thing in her general direction.

'Thank you,' she grumbles. She promptly disappears into the bathroom and slams the door closed.

Way to make things harder, May.

I hit the bathroom the moment it's free, brush my teeth, and take what might be the most thorough shower I have in a while. Suddenly I'm self-conscious. Do I smell like lax bro? Does May think I smell like lax bro? I'm not sure, but all the Dove soap I'm using had better do the trick.

Tugging on my jeans and T-shirt for the day, I thunder back downstairs. May's backpack is slumped against the leg of the dining-table chair she sits at, half-eaten pancakes in front of her as she chews, humming a happy little moan, closing her eyes for just a moment to savour it. 'Colt, what did your mom put in these?' She waves her fork my way.

I'm a bit busy trying to distract myself from May's happy little moan as it strikes me that it's pretty similar to some of the blissful sounds I had the pleasure of hearing back in the bed of my truck, but the mention of my mom snaps me out of it a little too well. 'Oh. Uh, it's her signature biscuit mix pancakes. She uses Bisquick. Nothin' to it.'

'No way.'

'Yes, way.'

I grab myself a plate and heap on the pancakes, pop them in the microwave, and then add berries. I sit down across from May and grab the syrup. 'So.'

'So.' She smiles wryly, swallowing a bite of pancake. 'You sleep well?'

*Haha. As well as a man could when he's hyper-aware of his every-stage-of-life crush asleep next to him.* 'Sure. You?'

She shrugs. 'Sure. Thanks, by the way. For letting me sleep in there last night.'

'You don't have to thank me,' I say way too quickly. 'Considering—'

'Considering,' echoes May. I watch as she chases a strawberry around her plate, pushing a loose wave of semi-wet hair from her face. She's traded her jeans for sweatshorts today, paired with a UOKC Meteorology T-shirt. 'We don't need to . . . make it a big deal. Do we?'

I blink. And then I blink again. Don't need to make it a big deal? Call me a dud, but that was kind of the biggest deal of my life in a really long time. I'd hoped it was at least top ten for her. Maybe.

'May . . .'

'Colt.' She finally stabs the strawberry with terrifying conviction, locking her eyes on mine. 'Remember when I mentioned we have different destinations?'

I nod warily. This doesn't sound great.

'Well . . . I think I have an idea of mine. And I think I'm going to be extraordinary. At meteorology.' Her eyebrows furrow nervously. 'I'll stay in Oklahoma for the foreseeable future. And you'll head right on back to New Haven.'

I feel like I've just been kicked in the chest by that temperamental horse Rocky. She's not declaring? May Velasco, the best the entire *South* has had in lacrosse in years and years, isn't going to declare for the MLL draft? It's a let-down for the sport. It's a let-down for our game plan, considering what we've accomplished – bringing attention to women's lax at OKC. Getting May on MLL radar will have been in vain. And honestly, it's a let-down for me, because I'm selfish and I saw a chance, a glimmer of red-card May, the May who'd break any rule to get her way. But above all of it, it's a let-down for May. May, who will work a nine to five until she retires, and then, who knows, maybe she'll have all these what-ifs to live with. I see them in her eyes already.

'We've just started repairing this bridge,' she goes on. 'I don't want to sink it before it's even built. We'll be miles and miles away. You'll be on contract . . .'

She stands up and walks her plate to the sink, rinsing it before racking it in the dishwasher. Maybe nonchalant was my mantra, but she's the epitome right now. And it's kind of terrifying.

'So you're saying . . .'

'Heat of the moment.' She shoots me a forced smile. 'We'd just won a huge match. Spirits were high. It happens.'

May grabs her backpack and darts out of the door, but her words stay behind. My heart thunders like an oncoming storm. Am I pissed? Sad? Confused? I'm not totally sure any more.

# *Chapter Thirty-Eight*

Strawberries

**May**

I zone in and out endlessly during my Instrumentation lecture. God, what a snooze fest. I fight sleep every time I have this lecture. This time, I'm fighting off thoughts, too. Thoughts about the enormous pile of horseshit I just dropped on Colt.

By the time Dr Stearns utters the golden words, 'And that'll be all for today,' I'm straight out of my seat and outside to the Diamond Quad. The fresh air, humid as it is, is sobering.

It's one thing to touch another human being. It's one thing to hook up and move on.

'In fact, I don't actually have to do any moving on,' I ramble to Jordan as soon as I get to practice that afternoon, extra early. I texted her an SOS: *pulling my hair out rn. i have updates.* 'Right? Because it doesn't actually mean anything. It's just the physical. And it shouldn't mean anything. I can't be distracted during post-season, right. But with him . . . it wasn't. It *so* wasn't. Jordan, I don't know what came over me, but it didn't feel casual. At all.'

'And that's a bad thing?' my best friend muses as she sticks out a leg in a runner's stretch.

'Terrible. I know you said I should understand that he's scared, that he's trying, but I . . .' I shake my head, tucking a knee to my chest to stretch it. 'That doesn't change the fact that he'll leave in less than a month, you know. And after everything that happened between us, that kinda shit tends to come to the forefront of your attention.'

'Well, what'd you say to him about it? This morning?'

I wince. The shame is a sack-full of massive rocks that presses straight down on my chest. 'I said . . . that. I said he'd leave, anyway. And that it was all in the heat of the moment. Which it was.'

For the first time, I think, since I've known her, Jordan is just silent for a minute. As she clambers to her feet, she finally speaks. 'May . . . you guys are the definition of right person, wrong time, do you know that?'

'Way to encourage a girl.'

Jordan rolls her eyes, chuckling. 'It's not discouraging. If I were you, here's what I'd do.' She cocks an eyebrow. 'I'd start by acknowledging the fact that maybe, there will never be a right time. And that if he's truly the right person, that time is something you have to make for one another. He's working on being real with you. Sharing his fears. Insecurities. Now, I think it's time you do the same with him.'

'Do you . . . do you remember when he left the first time? Like, the last time you saw him?'

'Kind of.' Jordan shrugs. 'Here and there. Why?'

'I replay it. All the time.' I swallow hard. 'How the hell do I tell him that I think about how he left all the time? And that it's made me terrified that this will be just like before?'

'Bye, Colt! See ya soon!'

The idiot was probably one of the most popular kids in school at that point. Objective term. He pranced through the halls like he was overjoyed he'd never have to see a shred of Prosperity High School ever again. He doled out parting waves, and a couple of hugs, easily, so I assumed either he'd said his hardest goodbyes earlier in the day, or that no goodbye was hard for him. I wasn't sure which it was. I hadn't got a goodbye yet.

The night before, we'd hit the ranch field together – one-on-one, as always. I'd said something along the lines of 'Who'll you scrimmage with in the back of a farm in Boston?'

He'd just laughed and replied, 'Guess I could try and find someone. Won't be the same, though.'

And that was it. I look back and think that maybe that was his version of 'see you', though. That maybe any other variation on parting ways would have caused the both of us a hell of a lot more pain.

It didn't dull the hurt I felt when I stood by my locker, waiting, watching him with pleading eyes, watching him for the last time. He bumped knuckles with one of the guys on the team not far away. I steeled myself for one of the roughest goodbyes, and the most complex one, I'd ever have to give.

Colt was so close to me I could smell his cologne when he drew right past me. He turned on his heel, walking backwards as he grinned and said to so-and-so that he'd miss them or told so-and-so that he'd be back soon. But I didn't care about that garbage. I cared about the fact that he had just passed me right over. Like my face wasn't even vaguely familiar.

I blinked quickly to hold back the tears that were rapidly welling up in my eyes, blurring my vision. It would only be a year, I reminded myself, and then he'd be back. That was probably why he hadn't bothered saying bye. It wouldn't even be that long. None of those excuses did their job, for the record, and when we found out that a year would turn into four would turn into a career, the sparks of anger in my chest fanned into a blazing fire.

Three hours after the end of the school day, my phone pinged with a text message.

*Hey May! Hope your senior year's amazing. Been great playing with you all these years. Take care. Sending you strawberries from Mom's garden. Keep in touch.*

Strawberries.

I saw those damn strawberries on my front porch non-stop for the next week every time I closed my eyes.

And then, as the weeks went on, and the taste of the strawberries finally left my mouth, a new feeling wiggled its way into my body. It was a feeling I hadn't ever anticipated having.

It was envy.

I was jealous of CJ Bradley.

He got to take off. He had options. He could leave.

Sure, we could talk about it all we wanted. Maybe we made the sorts of promises teenagers did when they were young and naïve and didn't know that this world was a cruel one, that this was the kind of place that was out to wrench people apart instead of bring them together. We promised that one day, we'd go pro, side by side, and that in this world that tore dreams to shreds, we wouldn't let ours die.

But all of it was doomed to fail, anyway. Because Colt didn't realize the luxury he had. The luxury I longed for.

As our teammates trickle into practice, and I head towards my bag to lace up my cleats, that old wound Colt left me with opens up again. Every stitch is plucked out until all I feel is an emptiness in the centre of my body. Just like before.

He's going to leave again. That much is certain. But if I don't get myself in order, he's going to leave without knowing why I did what I did this morning. And if I let him go like that, I'm no better than he was five years ago.

# Chapter Thirty-Nine

### Hell or High Water

**Colt**

*S wish!*
The ball impacts the back of the net effortlessly, from just about halfway up our scaled-down backward field. The field I'd made for her. What a shit turn of events. She got me back out of my head, back on the path to playing again, only for all of this to happen.

*Swish!*

With a swing bordering on sending my stick flying out of my hands, I chuck the ball straight into the net, the shot clipping the top of the goal before slapping the back of it so hard it sends the frame shaking. For a minute, the faint vibrating of the metal is all I can hear.

'Top ched,' says May from behind me.

On a normal day, I'd probably turn so fast I'd risk dislocating my neck. Today, I find any excuse for why I don't look back at her. I hum in agreement instead.

'So. Charleston next Saturday.'

May laughs nervously. 'Right. Our first East Coast team of the season.'

The nerves aren't a sound I'm used to hearing from her, but it makes sense. Two of her three past years on OKC, the Riders have fallen to an East Coast team in the quarter-finals of the playoffs. The girls have never made it farther than this.

'Do you think we have a chance, this time?'

'Don't really feel like it matters what I think.' I pick up another ball with my stick, tossing it and catching it back in the head. 'You're the captain.'

May says, 'Sure. But we're a team. And on teams . . .' She walks right up in front of me, impossible to ignore, and sits down, cross-legged, in the grass. 'We talk. Which I owe to you.'

'What is there to talk about?' I throw my stick aside, but I reluctantly sit down, too, running a hand through my hair. 'You made it pretty clear how this is gonna go.'

'Doesn't feel nice, does it?' The corners of her mouth tip up in a smile, but it's one of sadness. One that weighs in her eyes and pulverizes my resolve to look at. 'To be left alone with nothing but a shitty goodbye?'

*She's not wrong.*

Well. That's not really something I can say anything to. I blink, gulp. 'May—'

'As terrible as it is . . . I'm sorry.' She clears her throat. 'I shouldn't have said the things I did without an explanation.'

'You don't have to explain anything,' I stop her. 'I've put you through enough. You have a right to take things easy.'

'Maybe. But I also have a right to tell you that this fake thing we have going on . . .' She gestures between the two of us. 'This thing is not fake, Colt. It never was.'

Twin flames of relief and nerves fill my chest. I shake my head.

'You know, I probably would have picked everything up and moved to Boston with you for college if you'd actually asked me what I wanted,' May blurts.

It feels like someone's stick just checked me square in the head.

She would have *moved* with me? To Boston? My parents would probably have rather trodden on hot coals for the rest of their lives than stay in New England. May Velasco would have moved?

'But you didn't,' she continues. 'You didn't ask me. You didn't say goodbye to me, either. Why didn't you say goodbye, Colt? Huh?'

I remember it as clearly as day. The hallway, the glimpse of May out of the corner of my vision. Of the tears in her eyes, of the pleading. Just like that, fear had taken me over. 'If I had said goodbye to you,' I tell her, 'come hell or high water, I probably would have picked everything up and put it right back in my parents' house and refused to move to Boston. Just so I could stay with you.'

'Oh, Colt.' May's voice is barely a whisper. 'Why on God's green *earth* did you never, ever tell me any of that?'

'Is it a good enough answer to say 'cause Dylan Wright was your *chambelan*?'

'Oh my . . .' May reaches out and smacks my arm. 'Shut up. Will you go on and tell me?'

'Because . . .' *No time like the present, Colt. Come on.*

This is only the bit I've waited years to tell her. The tiny little crumb of information that has pretty much defined my life ever since May set foot in my world in that ridiculous pink equestrian jacket. I've guarded it with my life, for what feels like for ever.

'Do you – do you remember when I was stuck on that goal for days? Sophomore year? Close to sectionals?'

May's eyes narrow in thought, but she nods tentatively. 'Yeah . . . How could I forget? You were insufferable. You kept goin' back there every night. I was about sick of it.'

That last part almost makes me chuckle. I'd spend the evenings after school on the Prosperity soccer field, stuck in a rut, just me and the goal I'd set up on the grass. I couldn't get that shot, no matter how hard I tried: it was the no-look twizzler.

'And you remember when you finally got *totally* sick of it?' I continue. I'm practically sitting on my hands to combat the nerves.

Thankfully, her face lights up in recognition. 'I went with you sometime round ten days after you started that desperate quest of yours.'

'And you got pissed 'cause I'd just stand there,' I recall with a laugh.

She rolls her eyes, but a wistful smile tugs at the corner of her mouth. 'Thought you'd be able to make that goal score itself.'

'Except you said something.' I swallow hard. 'About how I wouldn't know if I'd be able to make it or not if I didn't try. You said, "Just take the fucking shot, Colt."'

May hums in acknowledgement. 'That was one of my finer moments. It was . . .' Her voice trails off as her eyes meet mine. I kind of hope she reads me, right then and there. Saves me the nerves that threaten to pull me under when I think about what I'm a sentence from telling her. But I have to do it now. I've already put it off five years longer than I should've.

'May, I-I guess I didn't take your advice.' I let out a bitter laugh, one that's more upset at myself than anyone else. 'I got scared instead of taking the shot. You were my closest friend, man. I didn't know if you would look at me like I was an idiot when I told you I couldn't even bring myself to say bye to you because that's how terrified I was of screwing up our friendship. Because May, I kinda didn't realize just how much I needed you until that damn plane took off. And when the stupid wheels left the ground . . .' My throat stings, my vision going blurry. It's as unfamiliar to me as timidity is to May. 'That's when I realized I'd fallen for you. Now, granted, I've clearly taken a couple hard falls in my life, some more kneecap-ending than others . . .'

Now it's May's turn to stifle a laugh, but her eyes look a lot like mine feel. Full of tears.

'. . . but I've never fallen as hard as I did when I sat on that plane and looked out of the window. Out at where I was leavin' you behind.'

'Just take the shot,' May echoes her own words quietly, and we share a tentative smile. 'God. You must be great at giving those pep talks to the Woodchucks before games. Have you ever moved your team to bawling before?'

'Once or twice.'

She chuckles, shaking her head, and bats a tear from her cheek. 'You're a *character*, do you know that? With this – this dialogue about wheels? Colt, wheels? Where do you get this?' May looks up, a hand to her forehead, and then back to me. 'Do you know how long I've waited for this?'

'For what?'

'*All* of this.' May does some wildly vague waving of hands. 'So everything that we did this season, to . . . to pretend—'

'Maybe we were supposed to be pretending,' I put in. Another tear trickles down May's cheek, and I reach over, thumb it away. She doesn't stop me. 'But damn if I wasn't faking a thing.'

She grips my hand, gives it a squeeze. 'Can I tell you something *insane?*'

I nod.

'I think I've stopped hating you. But I'm still jealous.'

Wait. *Jealous?*

I probably have the blankest look on my face as I regard May, and things begin to come together. Starting with that sting of envy in her voice when we'd sat and talked out on the porch after the tornado. 'You were jealous?'

She nods. 'You moved so easily. Went pro so easily. Left it all behind so easily. So yeah. I guess you could say I was jealous. You still move so easily, you know. I'm still jealous.'

'You're . . .' I trail off as the pieces start to float together. I'm positive May can probably see a lightbulb going off over my head. 'So you *do* have lacrosse dreams.'

'I guess. You remember all the stuff we used to shoot shit and talk about. I guess at some point I really wanted to play box, you know, for Team USA or in the Olympics or something. But that was before the weather. And before the ranch. That,' she says, the word a punctuation mark that abruptly ends a moment of hope, 'is for the ones like you. The ones who have the courage to do whatever it takes to chase their dreams.' She shrugs, and that little shrug, the gesture of giving in, breaks my heart. 'I appreciate everything you did, you know, Colt. To keep this narrative up all season. But I suppose, at the end of the day, declaring won't be on the cards for me.'

May Velasco is supposed to be nothing short of a quickly burning fuse. Always running hot. Refusing to back down from a fight. That's May.

'Don't get me wrong,' she puts in with a raised finger, scattering my thoughts. 'I'm never *not* going to be upset about it all. At least to an extent. But . . . I recently had someone tell me that as much as I need to give myself space to hate you, I need to give you space to make amends.' May props her chin up on her hands, and she gives me this smile that's distilled with regret. 'All those years, I was so caught up in *resenting* you that I forgot to stop and look at you. Really look at you. At how well you've done for yourself, Colt.' When she leans back, the smile on her face this time is no longer just sad. It's still melancholy, but it's layered with something new – pride. She's *proud* of me. 'I used to play in makeshift fields behind farms with you, CJ Bradley, and you're a Major League Lacrosse captain now.'

My heart swells with the look in her eyes, that of admiration, but it falls when I grasp the implication of her words. That she'll live out her days watching. That *she'll* never become a Major League Lacrosse captain.

'I'll make sure you enter that draft,' I try, my voice weak. 'Know that I'll do that shit for you.'

'How will you make sure I enter it?' Her smile falters slightly, and when it returns, it's forced, her eyebrows drawn upward. She looks tired. Resigned. 'You won't be here.'

She's not wrong.

'You'll leave again.'

Yeah, I'm leaving again. I don't know when I'll be back. *If* I'll be back. I've already overstayed my time off.

I scratch the back of my neck awkwardly. 'Training camp starts—'

'In two weeks. I know. We watch the MLL.' Maybe it's supposed to be teasing coming from May, but it comes out dejected. 'If we win the quarter-finals, if we move on to the semis . . . you won't be there.'

'May—'

'Colt. You won't be there if somehow, some way, we *win* the damn thing.' She uses her palms to wipe the last of the tears from her cheeks. Erasing the evidence. 'And you won't be there when I make the decision. So . . .' She sniffs, pushing herself to her feet. 'Maybe the way I left things earlier in the week was for the best. You know?'

'May – no. There's no way.' My words come out running together, feverish and desperate. I take her hands in mine when I stand up with her. 'Please, May. We can't just be right person, wrong time for the rest of our lives, can we? How do we live with that?'

May pushes herself up to her tiptoes and presses a kiss to my cheek. 'Still such different destinations,' she whispers, her hair brushing my skin. 'You'll have to live with your destination. And I with mine.'

She picks up her stick from beside us. I watch her retreating as she heads back up to the house through the sliding patio door.

## *Chapter Forty*

Painless Pain

**May**

Orchestrating the fine details of a fake breakup is much harder when it feels awfully real.

'You ought to make sure you shed a few tears. Make sure that after the match, even if we lose—'

'By God, that won't happen,' I cut into Jordan's musing.

'Yes,' she agrees. 'Make sure that you do a dramatic little pull-him-into-the-tunnel with you for a very important conversation. And then after, sprinkle some tears. I guess. I'm not sure how movie stars do it. But seeing as you're making the objectively wrong decision . . . it shouldn't be hard.'

My best friend's usually light voice has a new kind of bite to it. It's that kind of upset someone gets when they spend hours giving you handcrafted advice, and then you go and flip them the bird by ignoring it.

'Forget the guy.' The corner of Jordan's mouth twitches angrily. 'I can't believe that after all these years, you're letting me declare for the draft alone.'

'Jordan . . .' I start softly, placing a hand on her arm, but she shrugs me away. She's *definitely* pissed, not to mention very disappointed.

'We had plans, May. Lots of them. And you have so much potential. I'm just struggling to understand . . .' She shakes her head with a sad scoff. 'It's whatever. We've got a game to win right now.'

Jordan trains her sights on the roaring crowd all around us in the bleachers. Bigger than the first rounds, and more riled up, the crowd is primarily Charleston. It makes sense. They're a fantastic team. They were seeded much higher than us. Their fans are terrifyingly loud when their team is announced, rushing the field with the spirit squad shaking pom-poms nearby.

Owing to Chester being under capacity – not big enough for an East Coast school, believe it or not – the match is being played at Charleston's Slader Stadium, which is about double the size of what we thought was a lavish home field. Charleston's green and gold covers the bleachers about as far as the eye can see. Not a soul from as far as Oklahoma should be out here given how expensive tickets are, but there are clutches of orange and white in the forest of Charleston's fans that make me feel just a little bit more confident.

'The away team, the University of Oklahoma City Riders Lacrosse!'

I've never stepped out to the sounds of booing till this moment. It's easy to forget that in the South, lacrosse is nowhere near as cutthroat as it is out here. Nevertheless, I remember someone mentioned a stat that had hung in my brain: winning would make us the first Southern Conference school to make it to the semi-finals of the National College Lacrosse Championship. The men haven't even managed it. We'd be the first.

'HOLD IT TOGETHER, GIRLS!' I yell, hoping my resolve falls over the girls as they take their positions.

For a brief moment that I immediately regret, my eyes catch sight of Colt on the sideline with Coach Dillon. If we win, we get a first. But right now, seeing him with our coach, as he's been all season, is a last. I shake it off, blinking and turning my attention to the circle, where I step up to take the draw.

'All the best,' the captain from Charleston chirps.

I muster a smile. 'Thanks. You too.'

It's a nice sentiment, but I can tell we're going to be in for a tough game from her hair. Today, Brianna, shaking from nerves, did her best to get us all right for the match, so I still ended up with a nice ponytail braided into two, but the girl across from me is sporting complicated Dutch braids woven with ribbons, hair up with bows and all. We're so screwed.

And so goes the first half. Charleston is on top form, bolstered by their home field, not to mention the cameras. Usually, the crowd are the only ones who get to watch it all go down. This time, the entire game is being broadcast live. Every failed pass, every time Charleston's attackers break our line: all of it is being preserved for all eternity.

After a badly needed half-time reset, our run back onto the field is met with, predictably, jeers from the Charleston fans, but by the exit to the tunnel, Colt stands, hands on knees, practically screaming encouragement over the sound of the crowd to make sure we hear him.

My heart wrenches when I reach him, because I know the last thing I should be thinking about right now is the impending end to the months I've had with him. But he takes all that away when he stops me, taking my hand and pulling me to him. Wide-eyed, I don't protest.

He takes my face in his hands, moves his hands to the back of my neck when he presses his forehead to mine. 'Make sure they've got hell to pay, May,' he says, every word clear as day.

A surge of strength floods my limbs when he lets me go. I run all the way out onto the field, to the beat of thundering marching band drums and opposing team chants.

I can feel it coming from our team before the whistle even blows. The same energy we had in Alabama. The onset of aggression, the sort that's about to dominate the second half.

With moments remaining in the fourth quarter, when I take the draw, I snatch the ball. I don't pass, this time. I choose the riskier route, but the one where I see payoff. I run it through the defence, chancing a couple of yellow cards the way I nearly smack a girl out of my way, but once I'm out, I connect with Jordan on attack, and the goal is immediate.

As soon as the ball hits the back of the net, we run to each other, and Jordan leaps on me like a kid trying to get a good view at Disney World, all her anger from the beginning of the game totally dissipated. I laugh and hold her up as she lifts her stick, roaring, 'LET'S GO! LET'S GO, SOUTH CAROLINA!'

With just one point over Charleston, the final buzzer blows, and it's insanity.

'RIDERS ON ME!' I scream over the unhappy Charleston fans, practically fighting back tears when my girls run over, covering their faces, their mouths, choking back sobs of joy. 'RIDERS ON THREE!'

Instead of hands in, we link arms, our heads bumping one another, our cries blending together in symphony as we crash to our knees.

'May,' Lexi, the ever-stoic, frightening goalie sniffs, slugging my shoulder. 'Couldn't have done it without you, squid.'

'I . . .' I don't make it to words, just start bawling like a complete baby, and I like to think the girls know exactly how I feel without the specifics, because they all sit down in the grass with me and just cry. Even Coach and Colt come over, and Coach, absolutely overcome by emotions for the first time since I've known her, is a blubbering mess, immediately absorbed by our circle. Colt stands with a proud smile on his face as the cameras circle us, and I reach out to him, let him take me into his strong arms, wrapping them around me, holding me up after the kind of match that feels as if it's melted my limbs.

He presses his hands to my cheeks, his steel-grey eyes glimmering with pride. 'I know you said you think I've done well for myself, May, but I got no need to put Prosperity on the map.' He smooths my frizzy baby hairs back with a deep breath. 'You already have.'

If my legs hadn't already been Jell-O, that would have done the job.

I tug Colt to me and mesh my lips against his, leaving no questions unanswered, no lies, no pretending. I don't do it for any media or any press or stories or anything. I do it because he's given me so much this season, and I'm really, really going to miss him.

After we all wrap it up and head to the locker room to debrief, I follow Jordan's instructions, extra dramatic, making sure the watching camera doesn't catch the calculation on my face when I take Colt's hand with a nod towards the inside of the tunnel. 'Can we talk?' I whisper.

'Yeah. Yeah.' His Adam's apple bobs as he gulps. *Fake breakup.* It's anything but.

We find a quiet spot in the adjoining hallway, down at the end of it, where there's a door ajar, and I slip through. It's just an empty auxiliary closet, but I figure it'll do. I'm ready for this to be swift and painless.

'So. This is it,' he says. The banality of it is almost disturbing. This is how our fake relationship comes to an end. In some closet in Charleston.

'That, out there, felt like goodbye, didn't it?'

'Little bit.' Colt smiles half-heartedly. 'Couldn't ask for a better one, though. I got to watch you guys absolutely destroy an East Coast team. Got to see you come into your own these past couple months. You lead those girls into war every single game, May. Don't forget how powerful you are.'

*Swift and painless.* It's turning into the exact opposite. Damn it, Colt. My lower lip starts to quiver. No *fucking* way. 'It takes a team to be that powerful, you know. And you're a part of mine.'

*Don't go*, I suddenly want to cry. *Please, please don't go. Do anything but go.*

'You're not making it easy.' He chuckles, but he's biting back tears, too. The typical storminess in his eyes is glassy now, his strong, barely stubbled jaw ticking as he tries to hold it in. 'Can you tell why I avoided you when I left in high school?'

'Oh.' The sound is one I didn't know myself to be capable of. Helpless, broken, guilty. 'I'm not makin' it easy. Am I?'

He shakes his head, the idiot, using a palm to push a tear away, and that does me in. 'Come here. Come here, Colt.'

And in that dingy Charleston closet, tears rolling down our faces, we just hold each other like we are one another's life preservers. I clutch Colt so tightly that my hands fist the fabric of his shirt. I hug that man as if he's the sole island in the middle of a deserted ocean.

For real this time.

## Chapter Forty-One

Wheels Up

**Colt**

'And I talked to my parents. You're welcome to stay until the house is—'

'I know, Colt.'

May, clearly pushing away her emotions, stands with fists planted on her hips, in her trusty denim shorts and Riders T-shirt combo, the shirt with a jagged hem that curls up, product of a DIY crop-top job. Her hair, thrown into two low space buns at the back of her head, reflects the setting Oklahoma sun, glowing a brown-red as she steps forward, pointing to the truck. 'Go on.'

I cough awkwardly. She's seen me in pretty much every form of broken at this point: physical, mental, emotional.

'May—'

'Do you *want* me to call your parents up so I can tell them their son's stalling?' She raises an eyebrow, deadpan.

'Please don't,' I say way too quickly.

'That's what I thought.' She crosses one leg over the other, leaning against my truck. 'Gonna get a move on, then?'

'I guess I have to.' I drag a hand through my hair, glancing up at the clear blue sky. God. Clear blue sky. Huge family dinners. May and I walking to class together. Constellations like you never see in New England that are perfectly visible at night.

I *have* missed home.

She opens the door to the driver's side of the cab. 'I've put a can of Red Bull in your bag. Drink it before you get to TSA. But wait a minute, actually.'

May turns back to the house, and she bolts so fast I think she's going to lose a sandal. She's back within the minute, with a big gift bag. 'May, I can't take this.'

'You can. Here.' She shoves the bag into my arms. 'If you're going to take for ever to leave like this, you might as well open it now.'

I sigh, but I remove the tissue paper from the top. I pull out the gift. A custom, genuine straw cowboy hat, with a brown leather band etched with flowers. Roses.

'May.' I take a sharp breath in through my nose as my fingers run over the roses. Just like the ones on her Roper Rivalry suit. 'This is . . .'

'It's just a little something we wanted to leave you with.' She looks away, clearing her throat. 'All right. Get in the truck.'

I oblige and step up into the truck, one foot at a time. But I don't want to. I want to share a million more moments with May.

I want to go for a ride with her down the Prosperity trail. I want to crack open seltzers and play a round of lacrosse under the dim lights of our backyard. I want to take her out to dinner and then laugh so hard at something she says that my drink almost snorts out my nose. I want to walk around town with her, wearing her jersey, so everyone knows I'm hers. I want to hear my name leave her lips like it did that night in the back of the truck, over and over and over. I want to see her smile when she makes a perfect goal, and the dry Oklahoma wind blows just right, and she looks like an angel, beaming as the sun beats down and the breeze tussles with her ponytail. I want to ask her if she's ready for bed, and I want her to tell me she has to finish the chapter first. I want her in her glasses. In nothing but her giant Diamond Quad map shirt. I want her in pantsuits, in lacrosse uniforms, in Wranglers, in boots with butterflies on them. I want her in the first house we buy. I want her in my heart. I want her in my life.

'Thanks,' I say as I start the car.

Her brow furrows, her full lips turning downward. 'Well, yeah, of course. We couldn't send you back without a proper hat.'

I shake my head. 'Not just for the hat, May. For everything else. For finding the room in your heart to forgive me.'

She laughs, one that dissolves quickly. Sweeping a hair from her forehead, she looks down at her sandals. 'There was always room for you there. Always will be. If you ever feel like comin' back.'

*God.* It's been five years, and I'd still drop everything, cancel my flight, fuck my contract over, just so I could stay here with her.

I do the next best thing. I swing myself down from the truck, and I let the space in my heart I've always saved for her do the talking. I take her face in my hands, and I press my lips to hers. I move my hands to her waist, and hers loop behind my neck, tangling themselves in my hair. We kiss like we're in a bid for oxygen, and the only place we can get it is from each other. Her cropped shirt comes up, the both of us so close together that my belt buckle presses right against her body. My grip on her creeps up to her ribs, just skimming the bottom of her bra. When I pull away, I feel like she takes a part of me with her.

'I'm always gonna feel like coming back,' I whisper, my lips brushing her ear. 'Save a room for me in the new house.'

'I will.' Her chest rises and falls against mine, and she steps back so I can climb into the truck once more, driver's seat, click on my seat belt. The engine thrums. I grip the handle of the door.

'Win that championship.'

She bites her lip, but she nods. 'We'll try.'

'Try?'

'We will,' she corrects herself with a chuckle, wrapping her arms around herself. 'Don't forget to clear your head, Colt.'

'I won't,' I assure her.

'Bye.'

'See ya.'

I finally close the door and, with it, I get that dumb stinging feeling in my throat. Maybe I'm allergic to goodbyes.

May waves as I pull out of the driveway, and I wave back. I do my damnedest to save the image of her in front of my house, with those messy space buns and that chopped-up shirt of hers; to save every detail I can remember of her face, down to the way her eyes, shaped like almonds, tip up just slightly, and her eyebrows talk before she does, every trace of her on my skin, every feeling, every note of her perfume. Every piece of her.

I get to the airport right on time. I down the Red Bull that May gave me in under five minutes before I hustle through security, whipping my carry-on and my lacrosse bag around behind me until I reach my gate just as boarding starts. I wait for them to call business class, and once I'm on the plane, I finally relax, collapsing in the leather seat.

I'm all good until a heavy wave of guilt hits me as the plane taxis down the runway, picking up speed.

The wheels of the plane go up when it takes off. Just like the first time I left this place, I think to myself – as I leave Oklahoma, as I leave May – that I've fallen that much harder, all over again. I think about the fact that I'm never going to be able to clear my head completely when I play. I can't. There's still one thing I *have* to think about when I pick up my stick, always.

Her.

## Chapter Forty-Two

Where You're Meant to Be

### May

'Tell me the story, Mumma.'
My mother laughs, leaning back against the couch and tipping her head over against mine, where it sits on her shoulder. 'Which one?'

'The only one.'

'My dear May. You are *all* grown up now. You don't need me to tell you stories.'

'This one, I do.'

'Sure.' Mumma pretends to roll her eyes. My mom is a sweet woman at her core: forgiving, kind, but fierce when it comes to her family, and determined to make sure I stand on my own two feet sooner rather than later. Nevertheless, she won't ever pass up an opportunity for me to be her little girl again, even for a moment, and I can tell from the quiet smile on her face that she's glad I'm still asking her to tell me this story. *Her* story.

I'm glad she's glad. Selfishly, I just need someone to assure me that somehow, it all works out. Always. No matter how.

'Once upon a time, a young woman came to America for university from Canada, when she was just four years younger than you are now.'

'And?'

'And she met a young man in Oklahoma, where she was going to school. She asked him where she could get a really good double-double around here. He looked at her, laughed, and took her out for coffee. It was not a double-double. And as you know, nothing can top Timmie's. But it was really delicious. So they got more coffee together. Again, and again, and again, and they fell in love.'

'Did she fall in love with the coffee, too?'

'Not as much as she did with the double-double. But she adapted,' quips Mumma.

'Good stuff.'

'Of course. The two of them dated for four years. They had all their best-laid plans straight. A house on his family ranch in Eagle Rock, which he would inherit, their agriculture management degrees in hand, ready to take the family business to the next level. They would have a couple of chickens, some cattle, horses and, best of all, just one child, hopefully a daughter so she could teach her dance . . .'

'My deepest apologies, Mumma.'

My mother just shoots me a look before she continues. 'Accepted. They wanted to get married. Except there were quite a few issues, but the greatest was that her family had no idea, and she insisted they must not come to find out. She was a Punjabi Sikh, he a Catholic. In neither of their religions would the two of them be permitted to have a faith-based wedding ceremony. And both their families . . . if they knew, they would certainly object.

'So, against all odds, she got married to him in a tiny, tiny ceremony in Oklahoma City. His friends, and her friends. It wasn't that they hated their families, they each loved them very much. But both of them knew they would not allow this. And each of them couldn't live with the idea of, well, *living*, without the other.'

I squeeze my mom's hand as a vice grips my chest. 'And then?'

Mumma points to the photo on the mantel. Mumma, in a red and gold salwar-kameez, small gold umbrella-shaped kaleere dangling from her bangles, stands arm in arm with my papa, who wears a simple suit and a red tie to match her – along with, of course, his cowboy hat. They have the broadest grins of all time across both their faces, and if you look closely in the background, you can see just how small that ceremony was: maybe twenty chairs total. 'That was that. He came clean to his family first, and they weren't happy, but that was before they met her. Certainly, she was so charming and lovable and beautiful—'

'Oh, *certainly*.'

Mumma grins. 'So beautiful that she won them over immediately. The two of them moved onto the ranch, and they adjusted to life out there on the farm. She struggled, though. No neighbours. No one but themselves for miles. At first, she felt so isolated, so . . . displaced. But she learned to love the farm, the same way her parents—'

'Nanaji and Naniji.' My maternal grandparents.

'Exactly. The same way they had learned to love it when they first married and moved onto Nanaji's family farm in Gurdaspur. And maybe that was the reason that Nanaji and Naniji, when this young woman told them about her husband, were so gentle, and willing to accept this new development – not without some drama, of course, but eventually willing. Because they saw a part of themselves in their daughter and son-in-law.

'And eventually, the woman began to feel less and less lonely. She went into town, found friends in the other women, many of whom had started out feeling just as isolated as her. She fell for the ranch the way she'd fallen for her husband. She started teaching dance out of a barn studio he built for her, and slowly but surely, her side hustle blossomed. A few years later, the two of them had their daughter. Their one and only.' Mumma lays a kiss on the top of my head, poking my ribs with every word. 'Manmayi. Corina. Velasco.'

'Mom,' I laugh, batting her hand away.

'May,' she shoots back. 'They taught their daughter to love the farm, too. They taught her the importance of hard work, of passion, and of chasing your dreams. Most importantly . . . they taught her to never, ever let the odds keep her from believing that somehow, some way, everything will end up right where it's supposed to.' Mumma's warm smile is a salve, taking away everything that stings and replacing it with hope. 'Just like us.'

'Will it?' I whisper, curling up so my head is in my mom's lap. 'Even if it seems like we made the wrong decision? Like I made the wrong decision?'

'Oh, *puttar*.' Mumma strokes my hair, her rings clicking together in synchrony. 'It may feel wrong in the moment. It often does, for that matter. But every decision you make brings you closer to where you're meant to be.'

*Where I'm meant to be.*

What if I'm meant to be in the MLL? What if I'm meant to be in Colt's arms, in Colt's truck, in Colt's life? What if my mom is wrong, and I never end up there? Because it really seems like I won't. Ever again.

## Chapter Forty-Three

Missed Me

**Colt**

The instantaneous media campaign that follows me to New Haven is gutsy. Photos of May and me from earlier in the season are all over Twitter, labelled, 'I think CJ Bradley and May Velasco broke up???' and, 'THE lacrosse couple apparently didn't last.' I do one of those dumb obligatory Instagram story posts at the insistence of the Riders PR team: *May and I have peacefully parted ways. We decided this was in our mutual interests, and we have no hard feelings* . . . yada, yada. The fake statements are easier to write than any real words I ever had to muster to talk to May.

'Getting back to a hundred per cent isn't linear.'

Dr Mendoza leans back in her chair, crossing one leg over another. 'I want to make sure you feel that you're fully prepared – that you have all the tools you need to navigate this season.

And part of those tools include the ability to accept what is not in your control.'

'Accept what is not in your control' is Dr Mendoza's favourite sentence. I mean, I get it – what happened to me wasn't something I could stop or start at will. She loves to tell me it's not a disease that she can 'cure'; that it's a state I need to learn to live with. And sure, it makes sense in theory. It's a lot harder in practice.

*Don't forget to clear your head, Colt.*

All the tools. I think Dr Mendoza might be a little concerned if I tell her my primary tool is wistful memories of my grade-school lacrosse rival-slash-love of my life. I try a less jarring approach.

'I played back in Oklahoma,' I tell her. As much as she scared me in our first few sessions together, I came to respect her pretty quickly. She's pretty much the only person I can talk to and know, for sure, that whatever I tell her won't go anywhere. Patient–provider confidentiality is great.

'And how did that happen?'

'The thing is – I don't know. I don't know how it happened. The first few times, I froze up, and then one night, it just . . . happened.'

'Well, that's amazing news, CJ!' Dr Mendoza sets her little pink notebook to the side and clasps her hands. 'You don't sound excited enough about this.'

I'm not, considering I'll have to repeat the feat without the one variable that I'm pretty sure made it possible. 'What if I can't do it again?' I finally ask.

'Oh, but CJ.' She smiles encouragingly. 'You did it once. So we want to rewire those thoughts, and we want to ask – what if you *can*?'

\* \* \*

The first day of training camp dawns on us, sunny but temperate weather with a morning brisk enough to warrant a hoodie and shorts combo from most of the Woodchucks. We pull up bleary-eyed, nursing energy drinks, with royal blue merch and screaming woodchuck silhouettes as far as the eye can see. Training camp is essentially an intensive two-week session of practice, overseen by sharp-eyed coaches, which determines what position you end up playing for the season. If you want your favourite spot, you'd better get ready to go to bed totally immobile each night after practice.

'Hey.' JJ prods my side gently before we hit the field. His eyebrows are wrinkled slightly as he clears his throat. He's walking on eggshells. Yikes. 'I've . . . seen some things. What happened with May?'

Further out, Rod coughs all dramatically loud, doubling over and smacking his chest for effect. *Snitch.*

'Nothing, really.' I smile tightly. 'She and I, we rekindled something we didn't really think about, long-term. I guess . . .' May's words come to mind. 'We just have different destinations in life.'

'Seemed like you had the same destination.' Even Connor, normally raring to go and start smacking some cannons into the net, looks crestfallen. 'Just different ways of getting there.'

I try not to let that bit screw its way into my head when we start warming up, stretches first, then laps around the massive practice field. It's humongous, well-furnished, state-of-the-art, all the other jargon you could use to describe it. But it doesn't have the same charm of that hack-job backyard field. A pang of something I initially don't recognize cuts into my chest. *Homesickness.*

Coach puts us through the usual drills, passing, running, and then the one I've been dreading: taking shots. Rather than one of May's sticks, this time it's my own in my hands. Not the same one I went down with during last year's crash-out, but it feels like it as the team lines up in single file for the fast-paced shot drill.

'You miss it?' Rod huffs as he runs from the goal, post-successful shot, to end up behind me, pulling the thoughts right from my brain.

I just nod through breaths that are quickly picking up at the mere thought of facing the net.

'You miss her?'

The homesickness trickles back. Oklahoma will always be home. This trip back helped me realize that. The sort of homesick I feel, though, isn't because of Oklahoma. It's because of May.

I nod again.

'Can't believe you,' grumbles Rod. Ahead of us, JJ calls out, 'TOP RIGHT!' and subsequently whips one right into the promised corner to cheers from the guys up front. Rod whoops before looking back at me. He rolls his eyes. 'Neither you nor her.'

Now the only one in front of me, Drew, sprints, kicking up grass in his wake, before chucking his ball into the dead centre of the goal. I take a deep breath, putting Rod's words aside, focusing on the task at hand.

Unfortunately, this time, as much as I force myself to forget what he's said and lock in, I can agree with him. He's right. We both messed up.

'COLT!' Coach calls, throwing the ball my way.

*Clear your head. Just take the shot.*

My stick goes up on instinct, the ball hitting perfectly in the head. I speed right towards the goal, no hesitation, no questions. Just feeling it. The pressure of the ball shifting when I cradle it and wind back for the shot just before my cleats hit the X on the ground. The shift of momentum when I bring the stick forward, and . . .

*WHOOSH.*

The shot soars into the upper left corner so hard that the frame of the goal vibrates, just like it had out in the backyard in Oklahoma.

I jog around the waiting line of guys as they slap my shoulder with shouts of congratulations, to the back of the line. Cheers go up in front when Rod makes his second shot, and it isn't long before he joins me, all smirky and satisfied.

'Looks like she brought you back from the dead,' he says with a jesting punch to the arm.

I manage a smile. 'Only she could have.'

'Someone told me you missed me.'

May smirks, her dark hair flying out behind her as she slows her horse down to a casual trot to match mine. She holds the reins with two fingers, and she brushes a stray lock of hair from her shoulder, revealing the strap of her tight black tank top. Her gold heart necklace from her *quinceañera* makes little clicking sounds when the pendant hits the others around her neck: a horseshoe, a locket. The thick buckle of her belt glimmers in the totally unconcealed sunlight, cinching perfectly fitting Wranglers around her waist. Her butterfly boots squeak in the stirrups.

From slightly behind her, I can see every detail of the tattoo of a flower bouquet just above her elbow, on the back of her arm. Even slowing down, she's still faster than me.

'Hold up,' I call.

She laughs, the richest sound I've ever known, and turns to look back at me. Her hair skims my cheek, and when she reaches out with a daring arm, her fingers brush my jaw, her rings kissing my skin. 'Keep up, Colt.'

With a whoop, she speeds up again, that finicky horse of hers galloping faster and faster, his hooves beating the ground.

'Come on!' I pat the side of my horse's head, but he's not having it. We don't move any faster. 'Hey, May!'

She's well ahead of us now. I watch as her horse traces the corner of a pond, water and dirt flying up around them. I can't see anything – I can't see her – in all the dust. 'MAY!' I yell. 'MAY . . .'

I shoot up in bed. My chest is pounding, and honestly, my head too.

Great. It's not enough that everyone around me won't shut up about her. She's swinging by my dreams now, too.

*Damn it, May.*

## Chapter Forty-Four

On to the Next

**May**

The Oklahoma half of the crowd joins us in a screamed rendition of the school's 'Orange and White' chant. Maddie whoops, raising an arm to signal *louder*, and they obey, every word of the song echoing through McNeill Athletic Complex Field in Washington, DC.

On neutral ground, we stepped onto the field for semi-finals, poised to go up against number three ranked Galena Christian University from Vermont. I'm not the proudest of how I entered the game – definitely not at 100 per cent – but the atmosphere of this stadium, brand-new at least to us, started to work its magic in the second quarter. A strong finish, coupled with a second-half slump from GCU, was our propeller to the end of the match.

Maybe Colt isn't here, but his absence didn't make any difference in the crowd we brought in tonight: an Okie cheering section as large as five student sections, all waving their orange towels, this time emblazoned with the semi-final match logo, so hard and long their arms had to be on the verge of falling off. We built this, all season, and the payoff is finally here. Proof that our absolutely ridiculous plan somehow worked wonders for our lacrosse programme.

'TO THE SHIP! WE'RE GOIN', TO THE SHIP! WE'RE GOIN', TO THE SHIP!' the chant morphs, Jordan and I linking arms, bouncing up and down with the team as they jump all over us, screaming joyfully. The two of us grip one another tight as we share in the happy tears. One game left, just the one, until our college careers end forever, and we get to play in the College National Championship.

The final destination of the season will all come to a triumphant end in none other than Boston, Massachusetts, where we'll play the championship match in a larger-than-usual field to accommodate for the excessive crowds this season. In past years the matches have been held at the University of Boston – Colt's alma mater – soccer-field complex. Initially, that was the plan. But just weeks before the championship, the National College Lacrosse Association shifted the venue. This year, we will play the National Championship, or more fondly, the 'Natty', in the New England Bobcats' CashMatch Stadium, home to the region's professional football team. As in, Super Bowls, celebrity status, most-watched-sport-in-America professional football team. I'm still in shock when they put us up in the beautiful Hyatt in the centre of the city, just a ten-minute drive from the stadium. It's like nothing we've ever experienced before.

'And *here*,' proclaims Jordan as we all raise our mandated

mocktails to the centre of the table at dinner in the hotel's bougie restaurant later that night, 'is to the *very* first Lady Riders team – no, the first *Riders* team, to *ever* play in a championship!'

I don't know what our opponents for the big match – three-years-in-a-row champs, Augusta Tech University's Clippers, from Maine – are doing right about now, but we don't look anything like we're gearing up for the biggest game any of us will ever play tomorrow.

We clink glasses with whoops all around, and a 'Yes, ma'am!' from Brianna that prompts us to turn her way.

'So . . .' Maddie begins diplomatically. 'Bri, our hair game's gonna be untouchable, tomorrow, I hope?'

Bri's face breaks into a huge grin. 'Just wait till you see the Pinterest board.'

About halfway through the dinner, the thus-far-banned topic of conversation crops up. 'You know,' mentions Paige around a bite of the delicious wings we ordered, 'we're only about two and a half hours from New Haven.'

All eyes around the table swivel towards me expectantly.

I did a pretty great job of deflecting about the entire thing, initially. If there's one thing I'm good at, it's keeping my personal life locked down, even in a tiny-ass town like Prosperity, where everyone's noses are constantly in your business. But once the stuff started to flood social media, and Colt had to post that PR-mandated mess explaining our 'peaceful parting of ways', I kind of couldn't keep the act up any longer. I mumbled some hasty shit about overwhelming differences and hoped that would satisfy the girls.

'Guys, he's at training camp,' I tell them exasperatedly. 'I am *not* going to New Haven. And he is *not* coming to Boston.'

'Why not?' Brianna asks, fiddling with her dark brown curls. 'You clearly had it bad for one another.'

'Ooooh,' the team croons shamelessly. God. Can't these girls let a breakup be a breakup?

'Do any of y'all who went to Prosperity *remember*,' yapper Jordan starts as she leans forward dramatically, 'when May had her *quinceañera*, and she chose that Dylan Wright to be her main *chambelan*?'

I feel my cheeks heat up at the mere mention of the event. Okay, so I'd chosen Dylan. But I'd only chosen him because Colt, the dumbass, had his head so far up his butt he couldn't tell he was giving me the most mixed signals in *history* around the time of my quince, and so all I could think about was how embarrassing it'd be if I asked him and he said no. Or worse – that he'd do it *as a friend*.

'How could we forget?' croons Maddie. 'He wasn't hotheaded, Colt, but when it came to May . . . he pulled out every stop.'

'He looked like a cat straight out of the bathtub during May's dance with Dylan.' Jordan cackles, smacking my back so hard my soul almost jumps out of my body. 'Sittin' there all grouchy with his feathers ruffled while y'all *promenaded*.'

'Put a lid on it, Jordan,' I grumble and smack her right back. She just giggles uncontrollably. This girl hasn't had a drop of alcohol all night, and she's giggling. But this entire Colt/Dylan thing is news to me. Maybe it's that the night of my quince was a whirlwind, and I probably blacked out on account of stress through most of it. Maybe I just didn't pay attention. Either way, I'm rifling through my vague memories of the party all of a sudden, desperate for evidence. It takes too long for me to catch myself and realize that if I were truly over CJ Bradley, I wouldn't be doing these mental gymnastics in search of signs from *middle school*.

I'm truly *not* over him.

'I had y'all's first-dance song picked out,' Lexi raises her hand.

*Lexi? LEXI?* My jaw is literally slack. 'Girl – you had *what* picked out, now?'

'Oh, *Lexi*!' Maddie claps her hands gleefully. 'This is gonna be good.'

'"Lady May",' says Lexi proudly. 'Tyler Childers.'

*Awwws* ring out around the entire table, all corny smiles and goo-goo eyes and clasped hands.

'But seriously, May.' Jordan holds a hand out, and the girls gradually quiet down. 'Are you . . . okay?' The knowing in her eyes is a different kind from what the rest of the team has shown me over the past week, and they are truly sweet, each and every one of them, but only Jordan is aware what really went down between us. And only Jordan watched me go through what I did when he left the first time. 'Not gonna run away to New Haven in the middle of the night?' she teases gently. 'Leave us high and dry for the natty?'

'Nah.' I manage to push a smile across my face. 'I won't.'

'But *are* you doing alright?'

The smile wavers. Am I doing alright? I'm a little bit angry at everyone, including myself. I'm a little confused, and I'm a *lot* conflicted.

'I'll be okay,' I tell her.

I need to be okay. I have a team to lead into battle in less than twenty-four hours.

## *Chapter Forty-Five*

Natty Day

**May**

Hours after the sun rises in Boston, Massachusetts, the entire team, all thirty-six of us, and Coach, are awake, although we also already know that not one of the thirty-seven of us slept peacefully, and that we have all been up since before sunrise. This has only been years in the making. A couple of hours of sleep are nothing to lose.

We warm up in a separate area of the athletic complex designated for our team, spending the morning in rich silence, until it's time for us to make our way to the lockers. The away locker room is set up for us in a nicer way than any of us have ever seen anywhere. Every locker is labelled with a name and number for the day, the corresponding uniform ironed and hung up inside, along with our national logo-embroidered duffel bags, which, depending on the outcome of this game, could become either a happy souvenir or buckshot to the chest.

We listen to Maddie do her pre-game affirmations, the same ones she does before every match, as we get into our kilts and jerseys. They're brand-new, with the same logo on the left shoulder. *WCL Championship 2025*. The material is white, with printed orange letters and numbers crisper than our own university-made uniforms.

'I am resilient. I am strong. I am passionate,' chants Maddie, like she's trying to summon the ghost of self-esteem. At the other end of the locker room, Brianna is lining the girls up so she can get going on hair. I pull my kinesiology tape from my bag and start taping up my shins, then switch to medical tape for my bad wrist.

As I press the pink tape to my skin to make sure it sticks, Colt's voice whispers in my ear.

*That good?*

*Sure*, I reply.

*Get out there. Get a red card or two, while you're at it.*

'Not today,' I mouth with a little laugh. As much as both of us know the rules of the sport well, that idiot always wants me to get a penalty. Some guys like getting heartfelt handwritten cards from their girlfriends. My dumb fake boyfriend would probably ask for a red card.

*You look awfully pretty when you get pissed. Even prettier when you start to blow your top when the ref goes for the card.*

I tear the tape with my mouth and toss the roll back into my bag. With a sigh, I look up at the ceiling, decorated with the dramatically lit outline of the New England Bobcat itself.

*Colton James Bradley, where are you when I need you most?*

* * *

We don't need to enter the field properly to hear how amped up the crowd is – and how many of them are out there. The roaring is almost quadruple what we heard back in DC. You can barely hear the throb of the music when the Clippers rush out of the tunnel, pumping the crowd up so they move from ridiculously loud to borderline deafening. It's not really that many people in the grand scheme of things: professional football matches fill the entire place up, and this is maybe a small fraction of capacity. But for us, in a sport that's been in the back corner our whole lives, this is everything.

Before the game gets into full swing, we meet our parents in the tunnel for wishes of good luck and encouragement, at least for the next couple hours. We keep it short and sweet as we always do. Papa and Mumma know the drill. We exchange hugs, and my parents give me their last few bits of advice, as always.

From Mumma: 'Play it smart, May.'

From Papa: 'Wreck 'em.'

'All right, ladies. All right. All right.' Coach makes her way down the line of us once we're in the tunnel, giving each of our shoulders a firm pat. 'I want you girls to know that it means so much to me – *so* much, that we are here right now. That each of you have put in the hours on the field, and off it. Many of you, I've watched you go home and work two, three jobs to keep yourself here. I've watched you wait tables and kiss frogs and literally muck *shit*—'

Maddie bursts out laughing, triggering the rest of us on impact. Coach rolls her eyes, but she bats away a tear. Coach Dillon, the stoic queen of OKC lacrosse, and tears? I don't believe it.

'And every little thing you've done, I want you to know that it has a permanent place in my heart. That this *team* has a permanent place in my heart. Always. Whether we win this, or we don't.' Coach sniffs, and we immediately surround her in a big Riders hug. 'Oh, you girls,' she laughs from inside our circle. 'Come on. Get ready to go out there. May, darlin', take it away.' Coach gives my hand a squeeze, and I nod, signalling to the girls to back up.

'Let's do this. Riders on three, Riders on me, y'all hear?' I grin, adjusting my goggles from where they sit on top of my head. 'One, two, three—'

'RIDERS!' we scream at the top of our lungs, the loudest we ever have, just as the announcer's voice comes on over the stadium.

'For the very first time in *history*, making their Division One College Lacrosse National Championship Debut, the University of Oklahoma City Riders.'

The girls burst out the tunnel with their sticks in the air, howling to the sky as the walkout song of our choice, Luke Combs's 'Ain't No Love in Oklahoma' blares in the stadium, the enormous chunk of OKC fans packing the stands on their feet, towels already in the air. I run out last with the UOKC spirit stick, a crosse that's been in the school for generations, with a dozen ribbons in a dozen shades of orange and white tied around it, one for each past captain. I jog under the tunnel of crosses the girls make for me, coming out on the other end to raise the spirit stick at the fans, who roar in reply. The energy is palpable. In just about two hours, we could be standing here as champions.

We stand for the anthem first, and at the end, post-applause, break to the bench to strategize. Coach, binder in hand, is already prepared.

'Okay, girls,' she says, head down. We all crowd around tight. 'I'm gonna put May at the draw. I want my starters on. Cover May's right. No matter how the ref puts that ball, the girl that takes draws for AT is going to try and force May to the right – always does. I've instructed May to use that momentum to carry the ball back, hopin' that puts us in possession for the first play. Sound good?'

Nods and affirmatives all around. This is it. First play of the championship.

We jog back on and into positions. Lights flash and massive cameras follow the game as I line up at the midline, opposite the girl from Augusta Tech. I look up for a brief moment, and my heart thunders in my chest when I let myself take it all in. If I give it my all tonight, push it as hard as I can . . . we could walk home with the biggest piece of hardware we've ever had. And I could open major doors for my career. For the MLL.

But only if I decide I *want* to open those doors. Isn't this beautiful? This crowd? This sport? Isn't this what I want to do for as long as it'll have me?

I shake away the thoughts. I can't do that right now. I can't think about what I have to gain and lose weeks from now when there's so much on the line right here.

The ref lines me up with the AT girl, the heads of our sticks against one another, ball in between, our feet on the midline. I meet her eyes through the grilles of our goggles. She has the same look of fiery intent as I do. I know Coach mentioned she'd go right earlier, but I don't know. Something in my chest, something in the way the ref's placed the ball, tells me she's going to push to the left this time – where she thinks I won't go.

The whistle blows and, putting my legs into the push upward,

I forgo the intended right and flick my wrist to the left, letting her help me win control of the ball. I bring my stick upward, my eyes on the ball, and sure enough, the pressure from her end only helps the ball to careen upwards and down onto the grass. One correct decision. So many to go.

As I scoop up the ball, looking for an opening, I hear Brianna's trusty, 'HERE!', and I send it right to her. It's a clean pass, and then Brianna runs it before connecting with Jordan, out into the clear. My best friend has to do some darting to evade defence, and in the end, AT is too unpredictable. Jordan makes for a shot, and in a flash, the ball's with the goalie – deflected. Just like that, AT's already in possession, and we're in the hole.

The end of the half sees us down 2–7.

'We won't make it to the end at this rate,' groans Maddie as we peel ourselves from the locker room after a pep talk from Coach Dillon. It was rousing – one of her best – but it does nothing to help the despondency we feel when we think about getting back out there.

'We have to.' My own voice sounds exhausted. 'Think of how far we've come. And Mads – you're the future of this team. Jordan and I, our chapter comes to a close this season.'

Maddie swallows hard, nodding. A junior, she will be the one who stays on after us and – more likely than not – will take up the mantle of captain.

'Guys,' Brianna pipes up, 'there are thirty minutes left in this game. *Thirty*. Our story's not over just yet.'

Jordan, still on the bench, stick discarded in front of her, taping up a stubborn ankle, looks up, and she finds me among the girls, locking eyes with me. It's all about this moment for us. We've played side by side since our very first match. This is full circle. We have thirty minutes to keep that alive.

'We,' I start, 'are the only Southern Conference team to ever play a championship. The *only team*. If we take this game, we'll be the *only* Southern Conference team to touch a championship trophy, men or women. The *only* ones to ever hold that title.'

'And the *only* team led by a woman of colour to win a championship,' Jordan adds, nodding my way. 'We're here because we have a point to make.'

I purse my lips. In all the chaos, I forget what it means for me to be here – what it means for so many women in this sport. 'Exactly. And I don't give a shit if we lose, we're not leaving until we make that point.'

A silence fills the locker room as each and every one of us, including me, sit with those words.

'Riders on me,' Jordan sticks a hand out, moving to the middle of the room. 'Riders on three. Come on, y'all. Come on.'

Every girl puts her hand in, and I count us down once we're all shoulder to shoulder.

'One, two, three, RIDERS!'

We storm back out double time, taking position up and down the field. I prepare for another draw against the same girl. Do I go risky, or play it safe and stick to her right-side tactic this time? The position of the ball gives me no cues.

I blow a hair from my face, letting the blood rushing behind my ears be the only sound guiding my hand.

When the whistle goes off, I choose primal. I choose to let nothing but instinct tell me what to do, and suddenly, the ball's arcing over my head one moment, and in the net of my crosse the next. I cradle it back to a safe space on the field, from where I can plot my next move.

'Move right!' I call out to Jordan. I chew on the inside of my cheek as I jog towards the right of the field. Playing it down the right is my best shot at an opening. AT's been weak that side all game. Right?

'PLAY LEFT, MAY!'

*There's no way.*

I can't be distracted now. I can't falter when the ball's in my hands. This is all in my head. I'm under duress, the game approaching its end; I'm hearing things.

I spare the briefest glance at the sideline.

Beside Coach Dillon stands CJ Bradley, a hand on Coach's shoulder, on the verge of crouching, leaning forward with a muscular arm pointing at the opposite side of the field. Those stormy eyes are wide, his hair pushed back under a backward cap. He fully turns to gesture to the left, and I catch a glimpse of the back of his T-shirt. VELASCO #13. My jersey.

'LEFT!' he repeats, waving towards their side. 'PLAY LEFT!'

My body doesn't have time to question what my brain wants to overthink. I dart left all at once, practically screaming to Maddie, 'LEFT, MADS! LEFT, LEFT!'

Maddie recovers quickly, and when I chuck the ball over to her, she cradles it immediately, and on foot, sprints behind the goal. She shoots around the back – and she *scores*.

We all screech in unison as Maddie throws her stick down, pumping her fists. We surround her in celebration. Three–seven. This story *isn't* over yet.

My eyes immediately move to Colt when I run back to my position. He nods encouragingly, pacing the sideline the same way Coach does. Initially, I wonder just *how* dehydrated and stressed I must be for hallucinations to have come into play, but then I hear his voice again.

'Don't back down, May! Don't fuckin' back down!'

I don't know if he's here for an hour, for a day, for a week, or if he'll disappear from my life again after this game. I don't know if he's feeding me lies coated in sugar to hide the truth. But I do know that I've always trusted his match judgement, sometimes more than my own. I'm not ready to stop now.

The fourth approaches faster than I can keep track. The crowd is fired up, every single person on their feet. The stadium is deafening as the clock ticks down. We are 13–13 after an action-packed second half. Tied. AT's seen everything from us. Just one thing we haven't pulled out yet.

Cornered, Jordan yelps, and I call out ball so she can pass back out to me to regroup. *Shit.* They're covering all my attackers. I sure as hell don't think I could suffer through overtime. So what the hell can I do now to take this game?

'TWIZZLER!' Colt shouts from the sideline.

No way. No way I'll make it up to the crease in time for that. Twenty seconds. Nineteen. Eighteen.

With no other option, no other ideas, I raise a hand so Jordan can see, swirling it in a loop. *Twizzler.*

If the defence is going to cover all my attackers, I'll have to use the defence to launch my goal.

I break straight through the midline, running as fast as my legs will carry me. Defenders charge my way, but I careen left and right. A pass to Maddie, and a pass back to me. I send it to Jordan. I can practically feel the Oklahoma crowd biting their nails as the seconds pass. Five. Four.

'HIT ME!'

I slip around a defender, and as she reaches out for the pass that Jordan has made my way, I line myself up, back to the defender, and force a spin, turning her away from the ball, and turning myself right towards it. The ball hits the head of my stick. I don't have the time to look. I whip it straight at the net, praying the goalie's caught unawares. Praying the goal is good when the final whistle blows.

And then the horn.

'THAT'S FOURTEEN–THIRTEEN, RIDERS . . .'

A strangled cry leaves my throat as I toss my stick, clapping my hands over my mouth. I hit the ground immediately, the turf scraping my knees, but I don't register the feeling. All I can register is endless, boundless euphoria.

*The* only *Southern Conference team to touch a natty trophy.*

*The* only *team led by a woman of colour to win a championship.*

'HOLY SHIT!' Jordan screams, crashing to the ground right beside me, wrapping her arms around me as we both shake with sobs of respite. The girls on the bench storm the field, our entire team forming a bubble by the goal. I hear Coach's shrieks as she joins us, all of us one great, crying mass as confetti rains down around us, tangling itself in hair and sticking to sweaty uniforms. Orange and white confetti.

The cameras hover over us as we finally stand. I find my way to my feet shakily, in shock.

'May,' Jordan squeezes my shoulder with a laugh, tipping her head back towards the outside of our circle. 'Someone's here to see you.'

I turn around with a jolt. Colt, arms crossed, smiles proudly from a few paces away. His presence is quiet, but his eyes speak volumes.

'Hey!' I call, pushing my goggles as they slip down my forehead as I fight back a smile awash in tears. 'Couldn't clear your head?'

He lets out a laugh and shakes his head. 'Not a chance.'

## Chapter Forty-Six

### The Right Time

**Colt**

May whips around, her ponytail flying about in the breeze, the orange and white ribbons tied around it fluttering recklessly. Her thick lashes flutter, her lips parting slightly. Her cheeks are stained with tears, flushed red from exhaustion, and her brow, glistening with a sheen of sweat, creases when she jogs away from the circle of her teammates, stopping a couple feet from me. Grass covers her cleats, more dirt caking the bottom as she screws one foot into the ground idly.

'Hey!' She shoves her goggles up over her hair like a headband. 'Couldn't clear your head?'

'Not a chance.'

She cracks a smile that disappears as quickly as it manifests, replaced by an unconvinced expression. She draws closer to me, a tentative step here, another one there, and I mirror her. She moves her hands from her goggles, crossing her arms the same way mine are.

'You made it.' Her eyes skate across my bright orange Riders T-shirt-jersey. 'And this particular choice from your wardrobe?'

'OKC colours are mandatory,' I reply matter-of-factly. The little roll of her eyes that she responds with sends my stomach into hysterical somersaults.

May uncrosses her arms and drapes them over my shoulders, cocking her head. 'Still wearing my jersey. My number. Am I supposed to read between some dumbass lines?'

Clever. I can't help the smirk that crosses my face. 'What, can a guy wearing his girlfriend's jersey not make it known that he's hers?'

'Oh, girlfriend? Mine?' She widens her eyes, leaning back in faux surprise. 'Suddenly you're mine? I should do this "different destinations" bullshit more often.' She moves her gaze to our feet, sweeping a curl from her face with a sigh.

'Clearly, it did its thing.'

May scoffs, but she's smiling now. 'And so you came all the way here?'

'Well, don't give me too much credit. It's just under a three-hour drive.'

'Your coach?'

'We sort of gaslit him into letting us go for the sake of equal and accessible opportunities in lacrosse. JJ's very into that sort of thing, actually.'

I recall his address fondly. He's really quite the eloquent speaker. Came prepared with notecards and everything.

'JJ,' laughs May. 'I knew it. Then again, I shouldn't be surprised y'all are such enormous fans of the Lady Riders, should I?' She reaches out and pats my cheek gently, her fingers lingering there with her next words. 'Putting up my poster in your locker is a real creep move, champ.'

'Wait – how . . .' I sputter excuses for words. How on earth would she know what's in my New Haven locker? That shit is top secret. I swallow so hard I think I might gag on air. 'It's not – I'm not—'

'You're funny.' She tilts her head with a smirk. 'I'm flattered, really.'

The last of the confetti falls around us, and the chaos of the fans disappears, fading into the background, as I drink her in. Every detail I'd memorized so meticulously, right here in front of me.

'I guess there's one thing I have to ask you, if you could spare me a minute. Probably busy now that you're a National Champion, but . . .'

May beams up at me, her thumb tickling the side of my neck. 'And what might that be?'

'I'm done running and hiding.' I take her face in my hands, lock my eyes with hers, and this time, I refuse to let an ounce of fear control me. 'I know I fucked up. Irreversibly. This second chance to do things right has been one of the greatest blessings of my life. I'm ready to shoot first and ask questions later, if you are. I'm over the whole right person . . .'

'. . . wrong time.' May clicks her tongue, nodding matter-of-factly. The tingle of anxiety swirls in my chest as I watch her calculate her next words. 'I mean, I *have* been told there's no such thing as the right time, you know.'

Oh, God. That doesn't sound good. 'No right time?' I choke out. This is it. I'm so screwed.

Her stern expression breaks into an enormous, beautiful grin, her eyes tracing the planes of my face. 'And if there's no such thing as a right time . . . what in the hell are we waiting for?'

I thank every force of nature at work out there when our lips collide.

The rush when I feel her touch again is unparalleled. Maybe it's only been weeks, but it's as if I've waited ages for this. I can still feel her smile against mine, her warm hands pulling me to her through my shirt. Just over ten years in the making, everything that brings us together in that moment, and now, all finally worth it.

She pulls away with a giggle, and she says, 'Are you over your beef with Dylan Wright yet?'

I almost burst out laughing. That dumb main *chambelan* battle feels like a thing of the distant, distant past now. 'I'll bury the hatchet,' I give in. 'But only' – I press my forehead to hers with a smirk – 'because *he's* not the luckiest guy in the world.'

May blushes the slightest shade of pink, and I only feel luckier when I cover her burgeoning laugh in another kiss. Curls escape her braid and thread themselves between my fingers. Her eyelashes brush my skin with every flutter.

I, for the millionth time, get to fall in love with Manmayi Velasco all over again. Except this time, I'm not going to walk away and run circles around my feelings. This time, I'm not afraid to love her so hard that I'll need another lifetime to make sure she knows just how much she means to me.

## *Chapter Forty-Seven*

From Home

**May**

*One Month Later*

'The Wi-Fi out here is horrendous. I swear, I'm about to move us to New Haven so we can get a decent—'

'JJ, if you don't shut up for *once* in your life, the Wi-Fi will be the *least* horrendous thing in this room.'

I bite down on my tongue to keep from laughing as JJ crosses his arms and pouts like a toddler when Colt shoots a glare his way. Inviting the guys to watch this was a fantastic idea. It provides me with free entertainment to calm my currently haywire nerves.

The Women's MLL logo pops up with a chime, taking over the enormous projector screen in the Riders' boardroom with fancy animations and theme music, buffered with the slight glitch that has got JJ so miffed. 'It's starting!' announces Rod.

'It's starting!' his daughter, Talise, echoes him, clapping her hands happily.

Our parents laugh as we all settle in, pretending we aren't wound up as tensely as a taut fire hose. Colt's arm is around me on one side; Jordan, who's also up for draft tonight, is on the other; and from behind me, Mumma and Papa clutch my shoulders, while in the seating behind us, Coach Dillon, along with our entire Riders team – including the men's lacrosse guys – waits nervously, making for a very, very full boardroom.

With the women's season beginning in a month, a staggered start from the men's season, modelled after American soccer schedules, it feels like I've barely had a minute to breathe since the big game, and then since walking at the UOKC's College of Liberal Arts and Sciences graduation. That was my biggest hurdle for such a long time, and I finally did it as a College Lacrosse champion.

Up on that stage, posing for my photo, I had my degree in hand, but if I'm being honest, the championship game was still fresh in my mind. The second I touched that enormous trophy, holding it up over our heads as the team wept for joy, all the alternate options I'd dug up lost meaning. To physically *touch* victory like that is a rush like nothing else. It's a rush like barrel racing and storm tracking all rolled into one couldn't even give me. And that was when I realized I had to declare. There were no two ways about it.

Jordan taps at the laptop that sits in front of us, making sure we're hooked up to Zoom in case we have to come on. The camera feed will run continuously, and if one of us is selected as a pick, we'll be displayed on the live programme. With the aforementioned 'horrendous Wi-Fi', we're not extremely confident this system will work.

'With the first pick in the 2025 Women's MLL Draft, the Philadelphia Liberty select McKayla Evers, Northern Virginia University.'

'That's okay. No worries,' Coach chants from above us, as our parents pat our shoulders assuredly. There will be six rounds of picks. No worries. We'll be okay.

The second pick, and then the third, fly past. Jordan and I clutch each other's hands so tightly I'm pretty sure we're cutting off one another's circulation.

'With the fourth pick, the Rhode Island Reapers select Jordan Gutierrez-Hawkins, the University of Oklahoma City.'

Jordan is on her feet in a split second, shrieking the loudest I've ever heard her and bringing me along. We're jumping up and down so hard I think I'm going to break an ankle.

'YOU DID IT!'

It's so surreal to watch your best friend, the person who's had your back since the day you picked up sticks, to move up like that. The video call pops up onscreen, and Jordan speaks on receiving the opportunity to do right by the sport of lacrosse, and finding the passion to proceed forward. If anyone deserves it, it's definitely her.

The first round flies by, and before we know it, we're on the eighth pick, last of the round. Every limb in my body feels like it's full of lead.

'On the clock now are the New Haven Woodchucks.'

'Holy shit.' Colt's flipping out next to me, basically hyperventilating. 'The Chucks are picking. Okay, May. No pressure. No pressure.'

'You look like *you're* the one waiting on the draft, not me.' I slug him in the arm, but he's the outward manifestation of all the anxiety zooming around inside my body right now. The next four minutes are agony as we wait for the announcer to declare the Woodchucks' pick.

My eyes are squeezed shut. I decide I'm going to rely on my sense of sound. I can't look. Mumma's hands knead the tension in my shoulders as the announcer clears his throat.

'With the eighth and final first-round pick in the 2025 Women's MLL Draft, the New Haven Woodchucks select Manmayi Velasco, the University of Oklahoma City—'

'OH MY GOD!'

I don't register that the scream bouncing off the walls of the boardroom is mine at first, at least until people are jumping up out of their seats all around us, my parents and Coach in hysterics behind me, Jordan shaking me by the shoulder from the right. The presiding members of the Woodchucks are absolutely ecstatic; Rod is holding Talise and dancing her around the room. Colt practically keels over dramatically before standing again, looking at the ceiling in disbelief, hands on his head like someone's shocked uncle.

'MAY!' he howls, cupping my face in his hands. 'MAY, YOU'RE A WOODCHUCK!'

I don't even care how weird that sentence sounds. I leap right out of my chair and into Colt's arms, hanging onto him for dear life as he spins me around, and I plant an adrenaline-fuelled kiss smack on his lips, one that he returns readily.

'Start picking colours for our picket fence,' he teases as the announcers, in the background, crack a joke about how our boardroom looks like it's about to lose its roof.

'Our picket fence?' I grin, my fingers tickling the back of his neck, finding the cold metal of his necklace among the stupid little waves of hair that peek out past his ears. 'Are you sure about that? Are you ready for my mess, CJ Bradley?'

'I'm so ready for the mess. As long as it's yours.' His hands on my waist, his thumbs rest on top of the thick leather of my belt. 'Love you, Red Card.'

'Love you, New Haven.' I scrunch my nose. He mimics me before brushing his lips across my forehead.

*Woodchucks.* What a thing to call your lacrosse team. Too bad I'm going to have to get used to it.

# *Epilogue*

### Colt

*Prosperity, Oklahoma, Three Years Later*

'I hope you know that tomorrow will be an even longer, more hellish day.'

'I'm sadly well aware.' I stifle a yawn, lying back in the slightly overgrown grass beside May. Her curled hair still holds, half of it pinned up by red roses that are now more or less flattened. She rolls over to her side, resting her head on her right hand, her left on my chest. Her fingers trace the knot in my matching crimson tie. 'Planning all this shit was a lot easier than doing it,' I add.

'Wasn't it just.' May cracks a mischievous grin. Oh, no. She scans my backyard, checking the somewhat faded white lines drawn across the grass, and nods with satisfaction when she confirms it's still up to her standards. 'What do you say?'

'May, I think I'm about to fall asleep right now.'

She drops a kiss on my cheek before she lugs herself to her feet, dusting off the grass clinging to her black salwar-kameez outfit. She tosses the white stole embroidered with red roses and green vines matching those on her mariachi-inspired pantsuit over her shoulder. Big gold hoop earrings inlaid with diamonds sway back and forth as she rushes over to the backyard gardening bin. On her feet – she has on a pair of close-toed slippers, matching black velvet with roses. There's no way at all she can be doing this in those damn shoes of hers.

'Got it!' She emerges victorious with two practice lacrosse sticks, one in each hand. Her long braid whips around when she turns, so the chunky gold tassels at the end almost whack her in the face.

For a moment, I just stand there and stare at the woman in disbelief. But when you're getting married to May Velasco, you kind of have to suspend that disbelief for the rest of your life.

'Well. We already escaped our own pre-wedding event.' I smirk, slinging my suit jacket over my shoulder and standing up. 'Why not push it?'

'That's the spirit, New Haven.' May tosses a stick to me, and just like every other time we've done this, I catch it, checking the stringing of the head. Perfect.

She grabs a ball, throws and grabs it out of the air a few times. The thick white and red bangles on her wrists shake so hard with every movement that they create a deafening cacophony. 'Let's take a draw?'

My eyes travel back to her shoes.

She just raises an expectant eyebrow, her false-lashed eyes fluttering.

'Why *don't* we at this point?'

May is getting a kick out of my sarcasm. She sets us up at the half-size face-off circle in my backyard, ball between both of us, and we get our sticks parallel to the ground, crouching down in front of one another. I think my dress slacks might rip. I've played lacrosse in a lot of situations, but never in a button-down and silk tie. Oxford wingtips? That, I've unfortunately done once before.

A lock of hair falls into my face, out of its mandated gel-back, and I blow it aside. May's eyes fall on mine like a predator on prey, the corners creasing with a sure smile.

'I got you this time, Bradley.'

'Don't be so sure.' I wink. 'Bradley.'

'We aren't married yet, cowboy.' She clicks her tongue. 'You gotta prove yourself first. If you lose the draw, I might have to leave you at the altar. You'll have to take that dance to "Lady May" solo. And May-less.'

'And if I win it?' Fat chance. The smell of May's perfume, peony and sandalwood, drifts my way. The fitted top to her outfit highlights her curves a little too well for any of this to be considered a fair game. Under the light of the moon, the highlighted planes of her face take on a regal glow.

'Whatever. You. Want,' she mouths, drawing my eyes to her full, maroon-stained lips. Damn it. Distraction and motivation are warring right now, as they tend to with May.

Gazes locked, she says, 'On three.'

'One.' I grin. 'Three.'

The ball shoots up into the air almost immediately, and I'm not sure on whose account, but motivation wins out. I run after that thing like my life depends on it, May not far behind, swinging her stick out ahead of mine, her extra couple pounds of jewellery clinking loudly.

Somehow, even in those ridiculously tight shoes, she manages to reach her stick out and snag the ball. I try to block her, but she darts around me, nearly taking my eye out with her braid, and slaps one straight into the net.

'Aw, best of three! Come on, May!' I beg, throwing my stick to the side and my hands in the air. She shakes her head, chin high with pride. This is what I get for marrying a professional lacrosse player.

She sets her stick down with mine, crosses her arms with a sly smile. 'That puts you at the altar all on your own, CJ Bradley. Don't perceive my presence tomorrow. Any last attempts to win your wife back?'

'Maybe just the one.'

I walk right up to May, reach around her, and sweep her into my arms, one supporting her back and the other under her knees. She lets out a little squeal, but she doesn't fight me (a relief, given her history with starting battles on the lacrosse field), just laces her fingers behind my neck, eyes wide.

'Don't you *dare* let me go,' she scolds me, a bashful smile sneaking out as she bites her bottom lip before tucking her head in the crook of my neck and shoulder.

I carry her towards the sliding patio door as she rests her head against my shoulder with an expression of contented bliss on her face. I've waited years to see that look from her, that look where there's nothing to be upset about, nothing to worry about, and now that it's finally there, I know I've done my job right.

'I won't ever, Mrs Bradley.'

# Author's Note

While it is not yet a reality, *Cross My Heart* manifests the world of lacrosse as one that is on a par with the 'hype' surrounding leagues today such as the NFL, NHL, and more. The fictional Major Lacrosse League is, in the novel, described as a rather large-scale, fan-heavy base. In the real world, the sport is just making its resurgence. Leagues like the PLL are young, and their players balance day jobs with lacrosse 'side hustles'. The very first women's league, the WLL, played their very first match just a week ago, from the writing of this note.

*Cross My Heart*, though fiction, sees lacrosse as many players hope to one day see it: a hotbed of opportunities for players of all genders, including sponsorships and camps, as well as a truly major league entailing a full-time career.

With the burgeoning popularity of the sport of lacrosse in the United States and Canada, I would like to note that its roots are not as 'Ivy League' as the sport has become. Lacrosse originates in Indigenous tribes of North America as a deeply ingrained cultural tradition that was not adopted by the Europeans till much later. Originally, lacrosse was known as stickball, and this iteration is still played by many Indigenous peoples today, as is referenced in *Cross My Heart*.

Ultimately, the European adaptation of lacrosse led to many of the leagues and teams we see today. However, teams like the Haudenosaunee Nationals – stemming from the Haudenosaunee Confederacy (Iroquois to the French) – aim to continue incorporating the proud tradition of lacrosse into their culture on a larger scale. While they are the sole Indigenous lacrosse team in the world at the moment, the Haudenosaunee are also globally ranked third at the sport. Currently, the team is fighting for a place in the Olympics under their own flag and name. I was grateful to be introduced to this team and their history by a close friend, and am equally grateful to pass on the knowledge of their mission to reclaim lacrosse.

In another vein worth mentioning, I want to address the friction between men's and women's sports at the college level – and the fact that it is, slowly and steadily, changing for the better. In fact, and in spite of the existing funding gaps I address in *Cross My Heart*, many schools' women's teams outperform men's teams at that particular sport, in their respective leagues (I've had the privilege of watching the Caitlin Clark era at the University of Iowa unfold first-hand!). As such, rather than focusing on the divide between the genders in this novel, I found it interesting to concentrate on the *rise* of the women's team, a phenomenon we've had no shortage of in the past couple of years. At Iowa, women's basketball shot to popularity to such an extent that ticket prices went from initially free for students, to over $400 (exceeding even student football ticket prices) to watch the game at which Clark's jersey will be retired and hung in Carver. In lacrosse, particularly, teams like Northwestern University have laid a precedent for struggle that produces incredible success stories, and the door, I'm excited to say, is ultimately wide open for more such stories.

I hope you've enjoyed this novel, and I hope you are able to appreciate the beautiful sport of lacrosse for all its nuances and rich history in the real world as well!

## *Acknowledgements*

For this one, I'd like to start on a special note. Thank you to the three out of the Core Four, my sanity and the inspiration behind May's OKC Riders: Ilaria, Isabelle, Ria. Could you tell?

As usual, I'm so grateful to my family for always encouraging me to make time to write, and for always being the first ones to send photos of books out in the wild. To my mom for being my sounding board, and my dad for being my cheerleader. To Aashna, for laughing with me when it's time to get over it, and to Aakash, for the underpinnings of NFL knowledge that played deeply into this book. To my beautiful grandparents.

We went through a *ton* of versions when we were coming up with this book. You wouldn't believe some of the sports we had May and Colt playing before lax. So it's all thanks to the people who got us here: my amazing editor Amy, for giving me a mission and helping me run with it. To everyone in cover design and marketing, and the amazing Mallory, the force behind the art. To the entire tireless team at Avon Books UK!

And to Ilaria for the lacrosse idea that we initially laughed about until we realized it was serious, and suddenly we were at the kitchen table with chips, salsa, and a Goodnotes diagram of a lacrosse field, plus some high school lax lore.

I also have an extremely special thank-you to my incredible dear friend (and technical advisor) Shawna, the real-life #13, for literally spelling out women's lax for me!

In the words of Emma Gaughan when I first told her about CJ Bradley: 'I love him bad.' This is about all you need to know to recognize how thankful I am for her. And to Jahanvi, Addy, and Chandana, who heard it first around the coffee table. To Sophie, Ana, Maria, and Madeline (who did Albuquerque recon for me) in all their radiant capacities. To Alicia, and for Alicia. To Hiruni. To lovely Lina.

I'd be remiss not to thank the best creative writing teacher a girl could've asked for. Thank you to Batz for cultivating my love for words, and for letting me keep showing up, and to Liebs, to whom I continue to present new books at least annually.

And to the beloved Booksta friends without whom this section would be incomplete: Teigan, Ams, Chloe, Caylynn, Apoorva, Bekah, Danielle, I hope I've got you all! To the phenomenal authors I have had the pleasure of getting to know: Bridget, you are an absolute light and talent! Megan, Maggie, Avon sisters. Riya, Parveen, Vai, and the original Desi Girls: Ruby, NM, Bal, all hugs all around.

I also want to thank everyone I had the pleasure of speaking to (and withholding information about this book to!): Riley and Carson, TG1F (Nicole and Kate), and Driveé.

To Iowa for teaching me about what it means to love a team so much you'd literally sit through storms for them. GO HAWKS!

To the junior year emotional maturity curve. A book like this doesn't come without a cost, and I feel I paid mine. I'm working on it. I'm not perfect. But it's true: fiction is never totally fiction. It's those not-so-easy experiences we weather that bring that fiction to life.

Last but most certainly not least: to the readers. You show up time and time again, and I am so grateful and in awe of you. This one's for you. Never forget to let the good in.

**Formula One meets *The Hating Game* in this rivals-to-lovers romance between a legacy driver and F1's first woman driver, perfect for fans of Hannah Grace and Lauren Asher.**

**Racing starts. Rapid hearts. Revved engines . . .
The brand new, grumpy x sunshine, sports romance you need.**

*She sends his heart into...*

## Overdrive

ESHA PATEL